detention

emilia rose

trigger warning

This book is considered a dark romance and includes murder, decapitation, sex trafficking, and more. If any of these things make you uncomfortable, I suggest not reading.

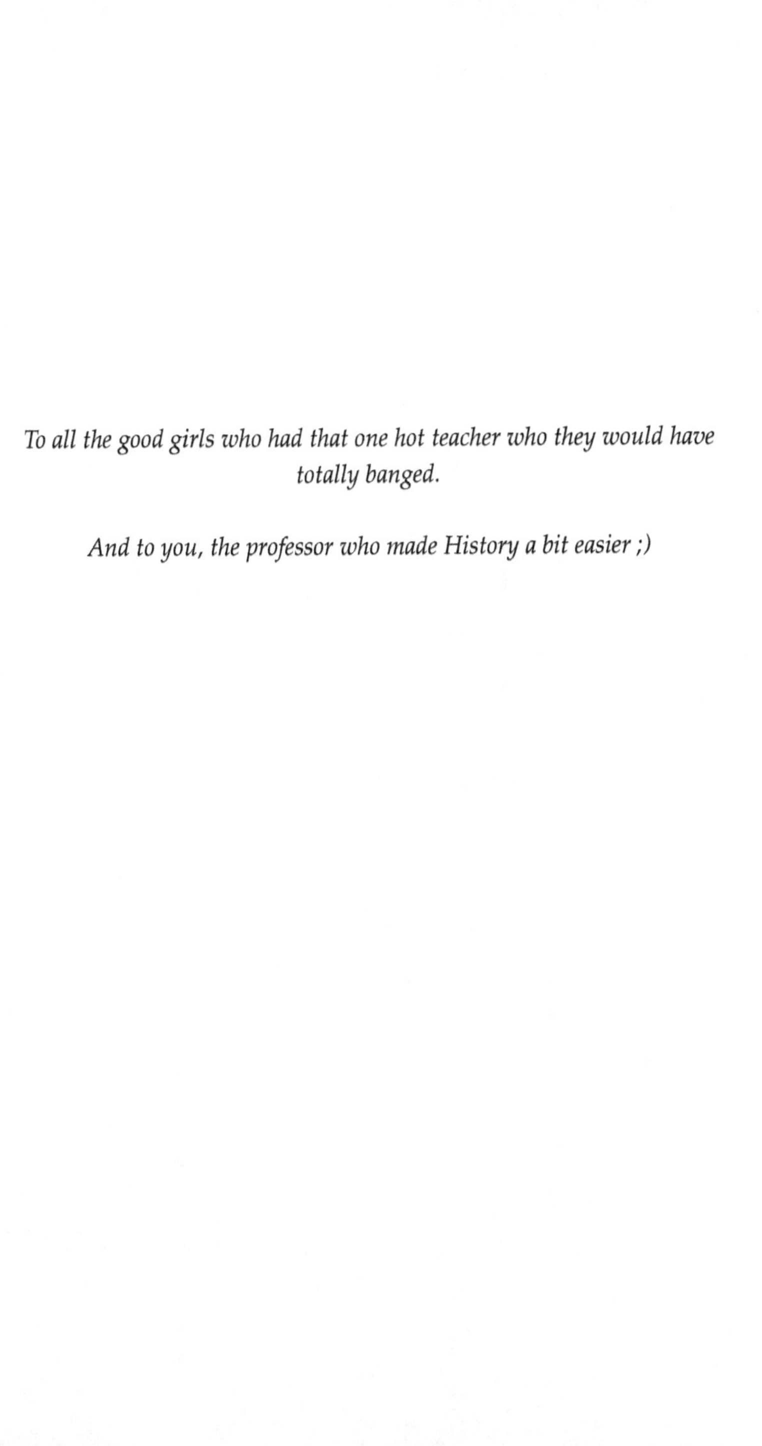

To all the good girls who had that one hot teacher who they would have totally banged.

And to you, the professor who made History a bit easier ;)

1

callan

FOR THE PAST FIFTEEN YEARS, I had hated September 21 with a fucking passion.

I stared emptily into the bathroom mirror and glided my razor across my jaw, careful not to nick myself with the blade. Sunlight flooded into the bathroom through the large window that over-looked our pool.

Bottles of champagne littered the backyard, probably from Georgina, who had been out back until four in the morning last night, doing God knew what. She had been on the phone, giggling with her girlfriends, the shrill sound waking me from my sleep multiple times.

Growling to myself, I pressed the razor harder against my skin and gritted my teeth. A decade and a half of pure fucking torture with that bitch—my waking up in the middle of the night to her crying or screaming or cackling, listening to her complain about how we needed a fucking private jet because she hated flying first class, having sex maybe once this past year. And that was after she had come home with another man's cologne on her neck.

But I didn't give a fuck about that anymore. I had stopped caring about her years ago.

Our bedroom door opened, and Georgina waltzed into the room with glazed-over green eyes and drenched in ten-thousand-dollar perfume. Without saying a word to me, she snatched her shampoo, conditioner, and toothbrush and thrust them into her travel bag.

After deciding that it wasn't worth the time to ask where she was off to on our anniversary, I averted my gaze and continued shaving until my facial hair was trimmed and evened out. I wiped off the excess shaving cream with a towel and turned.

"Where are you off to like that?" she asked, rummaging through the bathroom closet.

"To work."

"You should quit."

"And do what? Stay home with you all day?"

No fucking thank you.

"You would rather teach some kids about geography?"

"I teach Literature."

She waved dismissively. "Same thing."

Of course it was the same thing to her. She hadn't even had to study in high school because her daddy had all the money in the world to pay off teachers and principals and even me at that time.

"You complain about me not asking you to go out with me, but you always blow me off. There's no point in asking. You'd much rather spend your time with a bunch of kids who don't know left from right than sip on drinks in Paris with me. It's like you don't love me anymore, Callan."

I suppressed an eye roll and stepped into my walk-in closet to dress for the day. If I didn't want to get away from that bitch, I would gladly quit working at Redwood Academy and travel to Paris with her to sip drinks.

But I'd rather not watch her get drunk and flirt with every French man in sight.

"Why don't you love me?" she asked.

Did I ever love her?

Ignoring her, I fastened my tie around my neck and adjusted it in the mirror. She always had to pick a fight, but especially on our anniversary. She knew I hadn't loved her for years now, but she couldn't do anything about it. She fucked with me every chance she got.

Once I finished dressing, I stepped out of the closet to see the bedroom and attached bathroom now empty. *Good.*

I grabbed my wallet from the nightstand and hiked my bag over my shoulder, walking out of the bedroom and through the mansion —which Georgina's father had gifted us years ago—to the garage.

After I deposited my bag onto the passenger seat, I drove to Redwood Academy—the only place in this fucked up world where I had some peace and quiet. Ironic, wasn't it? Being around seniors and those asshole teachers every day was easier for me than being around her, which was precisely why I hadn't quit.

We had the money. I just couldn't handle that bitch.

Fifteen long minutes later, I parked my car in the staff lot and dragged a hand over my face. Students strolled from the senior parking lot to the buildings, some gathered out front. I scanned the crowd, searching and searching and searching for … *her.*

Sakura Sato—soon-to-be valedictorian and literature lover— walked from the student parking lot to the front entrance of Redwood Academy with her hands fastened around her backpack straps, her straight hair pulled into two braids, and her wire-framed glasses sitting high on her nose.

I followed her with my gaze, spotting Gunther Zurn and some of his friends in her path to the doors. He said a couple of words to her, to which she smiled softly and nodded, weaving her way through the group and into the building.

Before I could stop myself, I leaped out of the car and grabbed my shit. My hand tightened around my leather messenger bag strap as I quickened my pace to the front entrance. Gunther Zurn had sat next to Sakura in my class since the beginning of the year, but they had never once spoken to each other.

When I walked past Gunther and his goons, I gripped my

leather bag even tighter, desperate to hear what he had to say about Sakura, aching to know what he had said to her after years of not even looking in her direction.

"She's fucking sexy with those braids." Gunther whistled to his friends, leaning against the front stair rail and shaking his head. He kicked his skateboard up and held it by his side, leaping down the steps to head to a secondary building. "Catch you guys later."

Forcefully, I yanked the door open and stepped into Redwood Academy.

I didn't like him talking to her. I didn't even like him *looking* at her.

Sakura Sato was the only student at Redwood who gave me her full attention while in my class, the only student who actually fully read the material that I assigned for homework, the only student who ever asked me for extra credit when she already had an A-plus.

And, fuck, had I wanted to give her some extra credit for a long time now. But she was my student, so those fantasies were off-limits. Against my morals. Shamefully wrong. Yet so fucking sweet.

Those corrupt thoughts fed the attention-starved man my wife had carefully constructed for the past decade and a half, the monster she had watered with manipulative lies and cruel judgment, the villain who would one day have Sakura Sato.

2

WALKING DOWN THE HALLWAYS ALONE, I headed toward Literature—my favorite class—with Mr. Avery. Dad might want me to become an engineer, and Mom might want me to become a doctor, both wanting me to dive headfirst into the science and tech field once I went off to college. And while I knew I'd be able to succeed in those paths, I didn't love those subjects.

I wanted to read more literature, study famous poets and writers through the centuries, and understand the meaning behind the stories and words they had written. Sure, science and tech were the future, but art was everything and more.

The past. The present. The future.

Without art and beauty, there was no point in life. I truly believed that.

Sighing softly to myself, I climbed the stairs to the second floor. It had been three periods into the school day already, and nobody had once wished me a happy birthday. I shouldn't have minded because I hadn't expected anything, but I wanted my senior year to be different.

That's what I get for having no friends and being antisocial.

Holding my books to my chest, I followed a couple of students down the hallway to Mr. Avery's class. Gunther Zurn—a druggie who had skateboarded off the principal's desk last month—pulled open the door in front of me, spotted me behind him, and held the door wide open for me to enter before heading in behind me.

"Thanks," I said, walking to my desk in the front of the class.

Mr. Avery glanced up from his large desk, one brow arched at Gunther and his straight teeth gritted together. Gunther and Mr. Avery had never gotten along, mainly because Gunther was a straight-up junkie with a foul mouth who liked to interrupt lessons.

After a couple of moments, Mr. Avery stood, grabbed a whiteboard marker from the front, and turned to me. "Miss Sato, happy birthday."

My eyes widened slightly, and I sat up in my chair, unable to suppress the grin that stretched across my face. Warmth spread through my chest, heating every bit of me.

Someone actually remembered.

"Um"—I giggled nervously to myself—"thank you, Mr. Avery."

Giving me a small smile, he turned around to write today's lesson on the board. I pulled out my notebook for today, crossed my legs, and gulped, glancing up at his muscles flexing through the back of his baby-blue dress shirt. Mr. Avery was my favorite teacher for more than one reason.

When Mr. Avery placed down his whiteboard marker, glanced back at the class, and caught me staring at him, I quickly averted my gaze and smoothed out the fabric of my skirt, hoping that he didn't think much of it.

He was my professor. It was wrong.

But he was the only person who seemed to care in Redwood, the only genuine professor who loved teaching his subject to the class and enjoyed time with his students.

I scrunched my nose and shook my head, pushing the thought away. My hormones were just messing with me. That was what happened to everyone when they turned eighteen, right? They couldn't control their filthy thoughts anymore. Maybe even before then too?

Because these thoughts had been happening *a lot* around Mr. Avery. More than often.

These past few weeks, I hadn't been able to stop thinking about him calling me after class, about him telling me that he had extra credit he could give me—and definitely not the textbook kind.

While I didn't know the first thing about sex and foreplay and guys, that didn't stop my hormone-driven mind from thinking about everything a man like him could do to me. His mouth on my skin. His hands on my body. Him inside me.

My cheeks flushed.

Him inside me?

Breath catching in my throat, I pressed my knees together and suppressed a whimper. At least, I hoped nobody heard it. Warmth exploded through my pussy at the thought of Mr. Avery being inside me, pumping into me on his desk, whispering filthy things in my ear.

Things that nobody ever had said or done to me before.

I pressed my hand against my thigh and dug my nails into my flesh, wishing the ache between my legs would disappear. My pussy was gushing with wetness, my gaze focused on the bulge in Mr. Avery's pants.

"Sakura," Mr. Avery said, "why don't you take this one?"

I gulped, my gaze flickering from his face to his pants. "S-sorry, which one?"

Mr. Avery clenched his sharp jaw and leaned on the podium, his gaze lingering on me for much longer than I'd have liked. I nervously swallowed again and scrambled through the assigned reading from last night as my cheeks flamed.

God, this is so embarrassing.

"Page sixty-nine."

Fuck.

Some people in the back of the class snickered at the number Mr. Avery had said out loud, but I just found myself growing warmer all over. I flipped through the book to the designated page and desperately tried to push the thought of Mr. Avery and me doing ... *that.*

What the hell is wrong with me?

"Miss Sato, would you like me to repeat the question?"

After swallowing all my pride, I glanced up at him and nodded. "Please, sir."

At my words, Mr. Avery seemed to tighten his jaw even more. He stared down at the book in his hands and blinked a few times, letting out an unsteady breath through his nose.

Did I anger him?

A few moments passed, and then he shut his book. "Why don't you guys read the next two chapters during class? No homework for tonight, hmm?" he asked, not sparing a single look at me, which meant that I'd messed up.

Big time.

I didn't want him to be angry with me. His class was the only one I actually had fun in.

Gunther Zurn raised his hand. "You want us to read by ourselves?"

"You can do whatever," Mr. Avery said, busying himself with papers on his desk.

The class erupted into chatter, but I didn't have any friends, especially in this class, so I opened to the next chapter and peered up at Mr. Avery again. I really hoped that he wasn't angry that I hadn't been paying attention.

I loved his class, but he was too distracting sometimes.

He sighed deeply and ran a hand across his forehead, glancing down at his lap, then back up at me.

Fuck, he was angry—or at least upset. And I didn't blame him. I was the only student who usually even paid attention in his class, and I had been straight-up *preoccupied.*

So, I scrambled to my feet, smoothed out my skirt, and hurried to his desk. The ache lingered between my legs, but I forced myself to stand like a normal human being for once, to control my damn body.

"Mr. Avery?" I asked, gnawing on the inside of my cheek. "Can I, um, talk to you for a moment?"

3

callan

FUCK.

I looked down at the bulge in my pants, hoping to hide it underneath the desk, then up at Sakura, who bounced on her toes in front of me. She played with the hem of her skirt and teetered back and forth.

"I, um, wanted to apologize," she whispered, gnawing on the inside of her cheek. "I should've been paying attention, and I wasn't. I was just, um"—her gaze fell to my hand on the desk, eyes averted—"just a bit distracted—that's all."

The way she fucking stood in front of me, playing with her short skirt and glancing at me through her lashes ...

I closed my eyes and inconspicuously pressed my hand to the front of my pants underneath the desk, desperate to stroke one out.

"And what were you distracted by?"

Sakura snapped her eyes up to me, cheeks burning even redder. "Wh-what?"

"What were you distracted by?"

She pulled her knees together and swallowed hard. "Um ... just some things."

"At home?"

"N-no, s-sir."

"Sakura," I said, breathing unsteadily through my nose, trying to control myself but slowly losing. "Don't call me that."

"S-sorry, Mr. Avery," she said quickly, fiddling with her fingers. "I was just distracted by …" She glanced around the room, her eyes on everything but me, and then she furrowed her brow. "By Gunther."

Gunther?

Gunther?!

Why the fuck is she distracted by him? What did he say to her? What did he do? Is it blackmail? Is he fucking her? Fingering her? Touching her in my classroom, outside the classroom?

I needed to find the fuck out.

"Sorry," she said, turning around to head back to her seat. "It won't happen again."

No shit, it wouldn't happen again. I'd make sure of it.

When she returned to her seat, Sakura ran her slim fingers over one of her braids and silently read a couple of pages of the chapters I'd assigned for today's class. Under the table, she kicked her legs back and forth, her skirt riding another inch up her pale thighs.

I didn't know whether to stare at her bare legs or glare at the fuckup sitting next to her.

Fuck September 21. I hated today.

Fifteen minutes later, after I forced myself to keep busy with grading papers, I looked up from my desk and caught her staring at me again. Cheeks growing red, she glanced back down at her book and gently rubbed her thighs together, like she had been doing all throughout class.

I turned back to the papers scattered across my desk, my dick twitching inside my suit pants and growing harder by the second. She had been giving me that look all week, then grinding her legs together like I didn't notice.

She was driving me fucking insane.

And I tried. I tried to keep myself together, tried to push the thoughts of her away.

But I hadn't been able to stop thinking about her. I hadn't been able to get those big brown eyes out of my fucking head. They had haunted me every night this week while I tried to relax, to sleep in bed, when my hand was wrapped around my cock.

When the bell rang through the class, students jumped up from their seats and hurriedly packed up their belongings. I leaned back in my chair and snapped my computer closed, ready to get out of this stuffy classroom for a few moments to breathe.

Or maybe to the restroom first to take care of the problem in my pants.

After grabbing my phone, I stood and glanced over at Sakura, still in her seat and packing her books into her backpack. Gunther Zurn lingered behind the other students, his gaze fastened on Sakura's braids and his skateboard hanging by his side.

"I didn't know it was your birthday," Gunther said to her.

Sakura blushed. "Oh, um, yeah …"

"Happy birthday."

She gulped and tucked some loose hair behind her ear. "Uh, thank you."

I clenched my jaw and drew my tongue across the back of my teeth. Gunther was fucking talking to her again, tearing her attention away from me. Gunther was distracting her, in my classroom, in front of *me*.

He didn't know that Sakura Sato was mine. All mine.

My phone buzzed in my pocket, and I pulled it out to take my mind off them both.

Georgina: Room 457.

Georgina: I'll be waiting. ;)

Fury boiled inside me. I gritted my teeth and snatched a pink slip of paper from inside my desk drawer, unable to think of anything else. My life was shit. My wife was cheating on me. I wanted Sakura Sato all to myself.

Georgina had made me into a monster that I never wanted to

become, a monster who'd give his best student detention and violate all his principles as a teacher at Redwood just so he could have more of her attention.

As the rest of the her classmates hurried out of class, Sakura stood by her desk and deposited her books into her backpack. I stared at her profile, at the hair that had fallen out of her braid and into her face, at those full lips I had imagined fastened around my cock so many times.

"Sakura."

She glanced over at me, her cheeks rounding. "Mr. Avery, I wanted to—"

Before she could say another word and make me regret this, I shoved the detention slip into her hand and drew my tongue across my teeth. "I will see you after school today for detention, Miss Sato."

A plethora of emotions crossed her face until she furrowed her brow. "Wh-what?"

I picked up my messenger bag and walked out of my classroom toward the teachers' room before I could stop myself. I didn't care what it took or how much money I'd have to spend to keep teachers and students quiet. Today, Sakura Sato would be mine.

4

sakura

WITH TEARS IN MY EYES, I stared at the word *DETENTION*, written in large red capital letters, on the slip of paper in my trembling hand. In all my years of schooling, I had never once gotten detention, been written up, or even scolded by a teacher.

But today, on my eighteenth birthday, my favorite teacher had given me detention.

For nothing. I had done nothing!

Maybe he had caught me rubbing my legs together during class and wanted to punish me for it. Maybe I had angered him by not paying attention, but people didn't pay attention in class all the time.

Why had he singled me out?

I walked down Redwood's hallway toward the detention classroom, unsure if I wanted to demand why he had forced me to come here tonight or bawl my damn eyes out. I tried so hard to be a good girl, someone who colleges competed for, a student who excelled not just in the classroom, but in volunteering and athletics as well.

Stupid Mr. Avery.

Deciding to push away the tears because I didn't want

Redwood's worst students to see me cry, I grabbed the door handle and prayed that this was all some sort of mistake. Hell, I didn't even believe in a god, but I needed one right now.

"Sakura has detention?" someone asked from behind me.

My heart leaped in my chest, and I jumped away from the door, glancing over my shoulder at Gunther Zurn. He shook his head playfully and snickered, walking into the classroom and throwing his backpack onto a random desk.

After swallowing my pride, I stepped into the room and let the door click shut behind me. I glanced around nervously at the students in the room, students that I would never get caught dead with. They either did drugs, hung around Poison—Redwood's gang —or vandalized school grounds for fun.

Mr. Avery sat at the front desk and arched a dark brow when I walked into the classroom, his full lips pulled into a smirk. I hurried up to him and placed the detention slip on his desk, shaking my head.

"Please, Mr. Avery," I pleaded. "This has to be a mistake. I can't have detention."

"Miss Sato, I thought I made myself very clear in class," Mr. Avery said, crossing his arms over his chest, his muscles flexing through his light-blue shirt. "You have detention tonight, and there's nothing you can do to get out of it."

"But I ..." I glanced down at the desk and pushed away more hot tears. "I didn't do anything. It's my birthday. I have a perfect record and even perfect attendance. Whatever you think I did, I promise I didn't do it. Please, you have to believe me."

"Ahh, that's right; you turned eighteen today, didn't you?" he asked.

"Yes," I said, nodding like a madwoman and hoping he'd show sympathy. "I did."

"Well then ..." He paused and leaned forward toward the desk, placing his elbows on the top and glancing at the students behind me. Then, he lowered his voice. "There is something you can do."

My eyes widened. "What? Please, I can't have this on my record."

After clearing his throat, he gestured to the other students. "You're dismissed from detention for today. I need to deal with Miss Sato for now. Make sure you're back tomorrow. Some of you are facing suspension."

Most of the students behind me shot up from their desks and hurried out of the room before Mr. Avery could change his mind. Most, except Gunther and his three partners in crime—Frazer, Conway, and Torrence. For some reason, they lingered behind.

But all I wanted was for them to leave, so I could do whatever I needed to get out of this detention. I would grade all his papers, wash his classroom floor by hand, even buy him groceries, if that was what he asked for. Anything.

"What're you holding Sakura back for?" Gunther asked, like he gave a fuck about me.

"That's none of your business, Mr. Zurn." Mr. Avery leaned back in his chair, flipping one ankle onto his opposite knee, his suit pants tightening around his crotch. "You're welcome to stay if you and your hooligan friends have nothing better to do."

I nervously glanced over my shoulder at Gunther, Frazer, Conway, and Torrence, who looked at each other and then ... took a seat in the front of the classroom, taking up the desks and watching Mr. Avery intently.

After a couple of moments, Mr. Avery narrowed his intense hazel eyes at them, almost as if daring them to stay. The four guys looked at each other, and then Gunther glanced over at me. Then, they all stood up and hurried out of the classroom.

When they were gone, Mr. Avery turned his dark eyes on me. I sucked in a breath and swallowed nervously, shifting from foot to foot. Whenever I had seen him before, his eyes always looked so welcoming, so soft.

Nothing like this.

And for some awful reason, it was making me hot in all sorts of places.

"Please, what can I do?"

Mr. Avery pushed back his seat and placed both his feet on the bright white tiled floor, his legs spread in the way all guys at Redwood did to take up the most fucking space possible. And all I could seem to stare at was how tight they were around … *that* area.

"Miss Sato, eyes up here," he said.

Cheeks flushing, I looked back up at him and pressed my lips together.

"You want to know what you can do to make this detention go away for good?"

"Yes, sir," I said.

He patted his knee. "Come here."

My eyes widened, and I sucked in a sharp breath. Mr. Avery patted his knee again, his large hand sliding up his long leg.

"It's your eighteenth birthday today, right, Sakura?" he asked, grabbing his throbbing cock through his suit pants and stroking it down his thigh to the head. "I have something for you to suck on to get out of this."

"Mr. Avery," I whispered breathlessly, my nipples hardening in my bra. "Isn't this …"

"Isn't this what?" he asked, tilting his head at me, almost in a condescending manner. "You think if anyone finds out, they'll say something to the principal? The school board? This is Redwood, Miss Sato. They don't give a fuck if I bend my best student over my desk and fuck her senseless."

5

sakura

HEART RACING, I crossed my arms over my chest and stared at him. "You can't be serious. This isn't right. This …"

Warmth pooled between my thighs, and I pressed my legs together. Fuck, this wasn't what I had expected. I'd thought maybe he wanted me to clean his whiteboards or help him with something on the computer. Not this.

"If you want to get out of detention, you'll come here," Mr. Avery said, his voice hard.

After deciding that college was worth more than a fucking blow job, I scurried over to his side and stared down at him while he leaned back in his chair and eyed me with that smirk on his lips and all that audacity.

"Knees."

"My … my knees?" I asked, glancing down at my bare legs that would surely bruise.

"On your knees, like a good girl."

Swallowing hard, I knelt between his legs, my fingers shaking and my panties sopping fucking wet. I didn't know why this was making me feel this way. I should feel so disgusted—so fucking disgusted.

But Mr. Avery had been my favorite teacher for the past four years. A handsome man in his early forties with streaks of gray in his dark black hair, the smartest damn teacher here at Redwood, and … a man who wanted me to suck him off on my birthday.

"Do you know what to do? Or do you want help, Sakura?"

I wrapped my shaky hand around his waistband, never having been this close to him and knowing that this was forbidden territory, and pulled his zipper down with my other hand, my heart pounding hard against my rib cage.

"I've never done this before," I whispered, seeing his hard-on through his briefs.

It was so much fucking bigger than I'd imagined any dick being, so thick and hard too.

Mr. Avery chuckled darkly. "Don't tell me a good girl like you hasn't had a dick in her mouth before. Have you not been fucked before either? Do I get to take your precious little virginity today too, Miss Sato?"

Staring up at him through my lashes, I nodded and tried desperately to cool my flushed cheeks. I was a virgin, plain and simple. I didn't hang around guys, not because I didn't get horny and want one, but because my studies and volunteering came first.

"You should feel honored to get my cum buried deep inside you today as a birthday gift." He pulled on my braided pigtails and tugged my face closer to his throbbing cock in his briefs. "Because you're the only girl good enough to earn something like that."

He pulled me down so forcefully that my mouth wrapped around the front of his hard dick through his underwear, the cloth becoming wet almost immediately from my saliva. Heat gathered in my core, and I whimpered softly.

With the wetness between my legs, I wrapped my fingers around his waistband and pulled down slowly, his cock appearing from inside of them. Inch by inch, I kept pulling until his entire dick sprang out of his pants and smacked me in the face.

My heart raced. I had never seen one up close before, only in pictures.

After taking a quick peek up at Mr. Avery, I gnawed on the inside of my cheek and wrapped my hand around the base of it, barely able to touch my fingers. It felt so hard and … God, I didn't even know how to explain it.

"This is wrong," I muttered to myself.

But the ache in my core wasn't helping to convince me of that.

"Open your mouth, Sakura," Mr. Avery said.

Staring up at him through wide eyes, I parted my lips slightly. Nerves rushed through my body, hot adrenaline making me squirm. Mr. Avery pressed the head of his cock against my bottom lip, and I wrapped my lips around it, tasting his salty pre-cum.

"Good girl, Miss Sato," he said, grunting softly and leaning back in his swivel chair. He took my braided pigtails in his hands and pulled them lower so I'd take more of him in my mouth. "Just like that."

I got three inches deep and gagged, my eyes burning already, but I didn't pull back. Instead, I pushed the feeling away, pressed my thighs together, and took more of him in my mouth.

When he hit the back of my throat, I opened my mouth to get air and gagged again, spit and drool rolling down my bottom lip. Mr. Avery stared down at me with those dark and devilish eyes, a smirk fixed on his lips.

"Take more of my cock into that tight throat of yours, and I'll write this detention off."

Determined and now horny, I sucked more of him into my mouth, barely able to fit it all. He was deep down my throat, choking me with his dick and stroking himself around the front of my neck.

As he took his hands away, I pulled back and gasped for breath, desperate for him to touch me. I needed something, anything. My body was aching in places that it never had before.

"More," I breathed. "Please, touch me."

He took my chin in his hand and ran his thumb across my lower lip. "Look at you. You're just another one of Redwood's cum-hungry sluts."

My pussy tightened, and I whimpered, "No, I'm not."

I was just horny as fuck now.

He chuckled darkly and grasped my jaw. "No? You're on your knees, begging for me to touch you, begging for me to fill your tight little schoolgirl mouth with my cum, hmm? Only cum-hungry sluts do shit like that."

"I'm not," I said.

He dropped his hand from my chin to my throat and pulled me off my knees, then laid me across his lap, my breasts pressed against his bare thighs and my ass nearly hanging out of my skirt. With one hand, he pulled up my skirt and caressed my ass.

"No?" he asked.

I pressed my thighs together, the wetness pooling between them. "No."

He spanked me right across the ass—hard.

I crossed my legs and pushed my ass up toward him, hoping his next smack was a bit lower, against my panties. I needed some friction.

Again, he spanked me, his bottom fingers brushing against my soaked panties. I whimpered and squeezed my eyes closed. He was so close, and I was so damn wet.

"More," I whispered. "Please."

He smacked me across the ass cheeks again, even harder this time, his bottom fingers hitting my clit. I threw my head back and moaned, a wave of pleasure shooting through my body and making me feel oh-so good.

Instead of spanking me again, he sank his hand between my thighs and rubbed my aching clit, grabbing my hair with his other hand and tugging up on it. "Your pussy is soaked for me, Miss Sato. Is this what you've been wanting every time you stay late?"

When I didn't answer him—because I was too embarrassed—he slipped his thumb into my mouth.

"Hmm? Is this what all those early morning and after-school study sessions you've begged from me were for?"

Before I could answer, he pulled me off his lap and forced me to stand, and then he patted his knees. "Come here. Sit on my cock. I want to finally put it inside your tight little aching hole. It's so wet for me already, and I've barely touched you."

After crawling up onto him, I hovered over his cock. He pulled my panties to the side and positioned himself underneath me, the head of his cock rubbing against my wet entrance. I sucked in a breath, nerves shooting through me.

This is happening. This is really happening.

He grasped my hips and sank me down on him, filling me inch by inch. I had only put my fingers inside me before, and his cock was much thicker than my slender fingers. At first, he hurt, sliding into me, but when he stilled deep inside me, pleasure consumed me.

With his hands all over my body, I threw my head back and moaned softly.

He wrapped a hand into my hair and pulled it back slightly, his mouth leaving hot kisses all over my neck. "You don't know how long I've been waiting for you to turn eighteen."

I rested my hands on his shoulders and slightly moved my hips up, pulling him out.

"And the way your pussy keeps fucking clenching on my cock, I bet you couldn't wait either." He gently bit down on my soft spot, his scruff tickling my skin. "How many times have you thought about me?"

Desperate, I moved faster, up and down on his dick.

"Too many to count," I whispered.

He slipped his fingers underneath my top and bra, his hands groping my small breasts and moving over my hard nipples. I clenched at the feel of a man's hands all over my body for the first time ever and moaned into his ear, the sensation making me so warm.

When he pulled my top over my head, I gasped softly at the sudden chill that ran through me. Mr. Avery dipped his face between my breasts, his lips running across the end of my bra and his hot tongue between my cleavage.

I slipped a hand into his hair and tugged softly, moving my hips faster on his cock, loving the feeling of being filled. Euphoria rushed through my body, making me tingle everywhere. As I continued to bounce up and down on him, he undid my bra and pulled it off my shoulders. My breasts spilled out of it, exposing me to him.

It was hard to imagine that someone like *me*—Redwood's good girl and straight-A student, who was always brushed over by people—had made a teacher so horny that he had to give me detention on my eighteenth birthday.

Mr. Avery sucked one of my nipples between his lips, his teeth grazing against it, and then tugged on it. I screamed out, unable to hold it back, and arched my back, bouncing up and down on him faster and faster.

"More," I begged, pussy tightening. "Please, more."

He sucked on my nipple harder, his hands groping and kneading my ass. I dug my fingers into his shoulders and stopped moving, the pressure too intense in my core. I might've touched myself before, but I'd never felt like … felt like this.

It was too much. Too …

Mr. Avery slammed my hips back down on his cock, and I screamed out again in pleasure. Wave after wave rushed through my entire body, the ecstasy shooting through me and making my legs tremble uncontrollably.

"Oh my God," I whispered, the orgasm continuing to hit me hard.

"Fuck, Sakura," he grunted against me, pounding into me for a couple more moments.

Then, he stilled.

My eyes widened, and I tried desperately to scurry away from him. If he stilled, then he was coming deep inside my pussy—his student's virgin cunt—filling me up to the brim with his hot cum. And I wasn't on birth control.

"Mr. Avery, please," I whispered, trying to scramble. "I'm not on birth control."

Instead of pulling away like I'd thought he would, he tightened his hold on me and slammed his cock even further up into me, so his cock was as deep as it could go. "Fuck, Miss Sato … that only makes me want to keep filling your tight little virgin cunt."

Somehow, in some fucked up way, his words made me clench on him harder.

When he finally pulled out of me, he set me on the desk and spread my legs, holding them in the air to force me to watch all the cum spilling out of me. My eyes widened slightly, my pussy pulsing and pushing more out of it.

And it just kept coming out, more and more.

There was so damn much of it.

Mr. Avery scooped his cum onto two fingers and stuffed it back inside me, glancing up at me. "Do you see me stuffing my cum back into you, Sakura?" he murmured, his eyes dark. "And you not pushing me away? Your pussy is hungry to swallow my cum, as *you* should be too."

"Mr. Avery," I whispered, watching him push more and more inside me.

"From now on, I will use your pussy whenever I want."

"Wh-whenever you want?" I repeated, eyes growing wide.

"And you'll do as I say," he continued. "If I want you to rub your clit for me during class, you're going to spread your legs enough for me to watch as I teach, and you're going to get yourself off until you're coming in front of everyone."

"B-but—"

"No more rubbing those legs together unless I say so."

My cheeks flamed. Oh God, he had definitely seen me.

"Do you understand?"

"Y-yes, sir."

6

callan

SITTING BACK, I watched Sakura crouch down to pick up her clothes that were littered around the floor. Her straight black hair that had slipped out of her braided pigtails fell into her face, covering her huge doe eyes that had been glazed over with lust for the past thirty minutes.

After blowing out a deep breath and cursing myself for what I had done, I tucked my bloody cock back into my suit pants and vowed to clean it up later in the shower. I would be home alone for the next week at least. It wouldn't *just* be a shower.

Once Sakura smoothed out her skirt, she swung her backpack over her shoulders and glanced down at the ground. "I, um ..." She looked back up at me and tucked some hair behind her ear. "Does this mean that my detention is off my record?"

I drew my tongue across my teeth, hungry to have another taste of her. Never once in my life had I believed I'd write a student up just to get what I wanted, but here we were, with her juices all over my cock.

"Do you want it to be, Miss Sato?" I asked, strumming my fingers across my thigh.

She sucked in a sharp breath, cheeks flushing. "What if … what if I say no?"

A low chuckle escaped my throat, and I stood. "I'd expect you to be here tomorrow too."

Like I had already told her not to, Sakura pressed her thighs together and then chewed on the inside of her cheek. "Please make the detention go away," she whispered. "I don't want it on my transcript, but I want …"

She fastened her hands around her book bag straps and held them tightly, staring at the ground again and sucking in a breath so sharp that it sounded more like a squeak. I raised my brow at her and stepped closer, looking down at her.

"You want what?" I asked.

"Nothing." She shook her head and hurried to the door. "Nothing. I just, uh …" Instead of slamming the door open and hurrying out of the classroom, Sakura stood at the door with her back turned to me. "You made me feel so good, Mr. Avery."

And then, without another word, she raced out of the classroom and down the hall.

"Fuck," I grunted, shaking my head and briefly shutting my eyes.

What I had done was beyond wrong. What I had done could get me banned from teaching forever. What I had done went against every single one of my standards, of my principles, of my values.

But fuck morals.

One day, I would leave that bitch of a wife and finally be fucking happy.

With someone who actually gave a fuck about my job; about the books that I had this class read, learn, and understand; about me. Whether they cared for the right reasons or the wrong ones—like Sakura—they *would* care.

I grabbed my messenger bag, swept through the classroom to ensure all evidence of what had happened vanished, and then locked up my classroom for the night. The janitor wheeled his trash can through the halls, nodding at me once I passed.

As I exited the building, Sakura sped down the road, away from the school and toward the commercial section of Redwood. From behind me, someone snatched my shoulder and yanked me backward.

I ripped myself away, twirled around, and grabbed him by the front of the shirt, shoving him against the brick building. Gunther stood there, plastered to the fucking wall with his teeth gritted together.

When I realized that it was him, I growled and released him. I didn't have fucking time for an annoying shithead like him. It was bad enough I had him in my class, flirting with Sakura while all I could do was watch.

He wouldn't bother me during off hours.

"What the fuck did you do to Sakura?" he asked.

"I released you from detention," I said, turning around. "You should have left."

"She just ran out of the building. What did you do to her?"

With fury licking at every last one of my nerves, I spun back around and clenched my jaw. "Why the fuck do you care, Gunther?" I gritted out, pissed off at this man who interrupted every one of my classes.

Gunther scoffed, stepped past me, and shoved his shoulder against mine.

I seized his shoulder and slammed him back against the building. "You're not going fucking anywhere until you understand two things. Don't touch me again, and don't you dare try to weasel your way into my business. You know what I do outside of school, the people I'm connected to."

Jaw tight, he glared at me. "No, I don't."

Back-talking me like a fucking prick.

He knew who I worked for outside of Redwood, the shit I had done with the mob. And this fucking kid wanted to test me.

"Do you want to find out?" I growled.

After glaring at me for another moment, he ripped himself away and leaped down the stairs with that stupid-as-fuck skateboard.

When he landed on the sidewalk, he threw it down and skated off Redwood property.

I grumbled to myself and walked toward the staff parking lot, pulling my jacket together to shield myself from the crisp fall wind. Most cars had vanished from the teacher and student lots.

A blue Ferrari F8 sat alone in the student lot with none other than Blaise Harleen—Georgina's brother's kid and my idiot nephew —sitting in the passenger seat with Vera Rodriguez, a straight-A student, in his lap.

Opening my car door, I tossed my messenger bag inside it and slid into the car, knowing that I could use whatever *that* was against Blaise if I needed to blackmail him into doing something for me.

And that *something* would be getting rid of Gunther.

7

sakura

AFTER SKIRTING into the CVS parking lot, I pulled on an oversize sweatshirt and pulled the hood up. I didn't want anyone to see me here, especially buying the morning-after pill. I refused to be caught dead here by someone from Redwood. That'd be the end of my life. Literally.

I scurried past the automatic doors and into the pharmacy, glancing up at the signs above each aisle. Not aisle one. Nor two. Nor three. Four maybe? My hands were sweating now.

Where the hell is—

"Can I help you with something?"

I jumped back in surprise and placed a hand over my pounding heart. A kid, who looked to be only a couple of years older than me, stood next to me with a huge smile on his face. My gaze dropped to his name tag—Jim.

"Oh! Um …" I swallowed nervously and bounced on my toes. "Feminine products?"

"Aisle nine."

Cheeks flaming hot, I hurried to aisle nine and thanked the Redwood gods that I didn't know him from school. I was a loner, a nobody. But while not everyone from Redwood knew me, I knew them. And that didn't make it any better.

I would forever fear that they'd recognize and expose me.

Rushing down the aisle, I quickly searched for the pill. Pads. Tampons. More tampons. Panty liners. Adult briefs.

Gosh, they have Plan B stuff with feminine products, right? Maybe? Where the heck is it?

Once I reached the end of the aisle, condoms *finally* appeared on the shelves. I eyed the boxes, wondering if I should get any. Responsible adults like Mr. Avery *should* be the one buying them, but …

If he had wanted to use them with me, he would've.

Warmth rushed through my core, and I bit back a whimper. He should've wanted to use one, but he hadn't. And when I'd told him that I wasn't on birth control, he had come inside me anyway, as if he loved the thought of getting his most innocent student pregnant.

Pressing my thighs together, I cursed to myself for reacting this way. I should be freaking out. My teacher had just stepped over all the boundaries, giving me detention for his own personal gain and stealing my virginity.

He stole my virginity.

More like I had given it up willingly to him because I was a horny woman who had been aching for a man's touch for far too long. His fingers, his hands, his mouth … had all felt so good. I didn't want to tell him, but I wanted more.

So much more.

"Feminine products are up here, miss," Jim called from the counter.

My entire face burned with embarrassment. I forced myself to smile at him, then nodded and tossed the idea of buying condoms aside. Mr. Avery wouldn't use them anyway. He'd rather slip into me raw.

Once I grabbed, like, three different boxes of Plan B, I hurried to the counter and hoped that there was a self-checkout available. While I didn't know this Jim guy, I didn't want him to catch me buying this.

Hell, I didn't want *anyone* to catch me with these pills.

Closed. See next available cashier.

After reading the sign on the machine, I pursed my lips and scurried to the counter where Jim stood. He eyed the boxes of Plan B and raised an eyebrow.

"Are you sure you need all three?" he asked, like it was his business.

"Please, just scan them," I whispered, looking around nervously.

The automatic doors opened, and I spotted a Redwood Academy sweatshirt from the corner of my eye.

Fuck.

Vera Rodriguez hurried into the store with her long chocolate-colored hair all disheveled and her soft pink lips swollen. Like me, Vera was at the top of the class, a studious nerd with straight *As*. Not only that, but she was, like, the prettiest girl at Redwood.

At least she hadn't looked over here yet.

Jim lifted his gaze and grinned at her. "Let me know if you need help with anything!"

Vera glanced over in a daze, her gaze landing on me. My eyes widened, and I turned back to the counter and pulled up my hood even further. I didn't know if that made it ten times more obvious that I was *trying* to hide something, but I didn't care.

Maybe she didn't recognize me.

Hopefully.

After pressing a couple of buttons on the register, Jim asked, "Did you find everything you were looking for today?" in a monotone, almost-mechanical voice, as if he had asked the same question fifty times already today.

"Yes."

"Do you have a CVS card?" he asked.

Annoyed that he didn't just let me pay, I pulled the CVS card out of my wallet and let him scan it so I got my reward points.

He pressed another button on his screen and hummed. "Would you like to donate to children in need?"

I gritted my teeth and nodded. "Sure. Sure. Just hurry up."

"How much?"

I nearly slapped myself in the face. If this man didn't stop asking so many questions, then Vera would surely be up here in a couple of moments with her items and would spot not one, but *three* boxes of Plan B.

She'd think I was a whore or something.

"You can round up, if you'd like," Jim said.

"Yeah, sure."

"Would you like a paper bag with that? It'll be ten cents extra."

I never resorted to violence, but I wanted to punch this man right in his big nose. Couldn't he see that I was in a rush? What was with all these goddamn questions? I hated coming to places like this.

"Plastic is fine," I said.

"Someone doesn't care about the environment," Jim mumbled to himself as he placed the boxes into a plastic bag and *finally* rang me out. "That'll be one hundred sixty-eight dollars."

I pushed my card into the card reader and tapped through the buttons on the screen. Once the receipt printed out, I shoved my card back into my wallet, grabbed my plastic bag, and practically ran out of CVS.

Man, that guy was annoying as hell.

When I slipped into the car, it was nearly five o'clock already. I never came home after four, which meant that Dad was waiting for me. I didn't have time to read the back of every box to figure out which one would be best.

So, I sped home in a daze and parked in the driveway of my family's home. We didn't live in the slums, but on the outskirts of the ritzy billion-dollar section of Redwood. The two-story house was big enough to live comfortably in. And while it might not have been the size of a mansion, this place felt too big for just three people sometimes.

I stepped out of the car with my backpack slung over my shoulder and the CVS bag in my hand, then hurried toward the front door. I needed to slip past Dad before he had the chance to stop me and ask where I had been.

After stepping into the dark house, I turned the living room lights on so I could head to my bedroom to take this stupid pill without Dad or Mom noticing. If she found just a single one, she'd snatch it up from—

"Surprise!"

I screamed and jumped up as my entire family popped out from behind couches and under tables with balloons and gifts in their hands. My heart pounded against my rib cage, threatening to freaking break it apart.

Dad had thrown a surprise birthday party. For me. After I had just climbed onto my professor during detention and gotten railed for the first time in my life.

Everyone stared at me, catching me red-freaking-handed with a CVS bag in my hand.

I was screwed.

8

sakura

BEFORE ANYONE COULD NOTICE, I gripped the CVS bag tightly and pulled my hands behind my back. If I didn't get this to my room *fast*, then all the nosy relatives would ask what I had gone to the store for.

But I couldn't be rude.

So, I giggled nervously, replaced my shoes with slippers at the door, and stepped into the room, forcing myself to smile at my family members.

We weren't supposed to have a party until this weekend.

Why did Dad ask everyone to come over tonight?!

Birthdays weren't even *that* special to us. We didn't celebrate the way other people did.

Usually.

I didn't know what the heck had gotten into Dad tonight, but I wished it hadn't.

"Happy birthday, Sakura!" Auntie Yua said.

I squeezed my eyes closed. *Oh fuck, I am screwed.*

Yua's daughter and my favorite cousin, Ichika, grinned and

handed me a stack of my favorite green tea cookies that she had made and wrapped with a cute cloth bow. I gladly took them from her and sent a thankful smile her way.

At some point tonight—once I took this goddamn pill—I needed to talk to her. She worked as a gynecologist in downtown Redwood. I needed to ask her to help me get on birth control because there was no way in *hell* that I'd ask Dad.

Before I could greet my other family members, Ichika grabbed my wrist and leaned close to me. "Do you have Plan B in your CVS bag?" she whispered into my ear. "You can see right through it."

Cheeks flushing, I gave her a worried smile. "Y-you can?"

She grabbed it from me and tucked it behind her back. "I'll bring it to your room, but once you greet everyone, we need to talk." She stood all serious for a moment, then giggled. "And I want to know all the details."

I didn't even know if it was possible, but my entire face grew warmer. Quickly, I nodded to her and continued to greet the other family members who had shown up, which was pretty much everyone on Dad's side. Mom wasn't even here.

When I finally wriggled through the crowd to Dad, I gently squeezed his shoulder. Dad wasn't one to show much physical affection ever.

He smiled up at me. "I hope you had a great birthday."

Oh, you don't even know.

"A great day," I said, glancing around again. "Where's Mom?"

He looked away from me and grimaced. "Just out tonight. Don't worry about her. I'm sure she'll be back by tonight to wish you a happy birthday."

But she hadn't remembered my birthday for five years now, which I guessed was when Dad had started sorta, kinda hosting small gatherings for my birthday. But definitely not this size with all my cousins and family members.

"It's okay," I said to him.

I hadn't expected her to come this weekend for the scheduled party. I wasn't surprised that she wasn't here now. She was probably urging some of her pharmacy friends to go to happy hour without her so she could toss a couple of pills into her purse without anyone noticing.

After sighing, I slumped my shoulders and peered toward the hallway. I wished things could've been different with her, but they'd been this way for years now. At least she still lived here—for the most part—and *sometimes* still tried.

"Were you studying after school?" he asked. "I thought you'd come right home."

Memories of earlier rushed through my mind—the feel of Mr. Avery's hands all over my body, his mouth on my neck, his cock buried deep inside my pussy. Feeling his warm cum spill out from inside me.

"Oh, I was just"—*fuck, what do I say?!*—"getting some extra credit."

"Good." He nodded. "I hoped you weren't doing anything too rebellious for your birthday."

I laughed nervously and stepped backward. "No, of course not."
Just fucking my teacher—that's all.

"Which class?" he asked as I desperately tried to make a run for my bedroom.

"Literature."

Dad pressed his lips together, as if he didn't approve of getting extra credit for *the arts.*

"Well," I said, taking another step toward the hallway, "I'm going to drop my backpack off in my bedroom, and then I'll be back out. Thank you for, um, setting up this party again." *Not really,* but I didn't want to break his heart.

Once I finally made it out of the crowded living room, I sprinted toward my bedroom, dumped my backpack on the floor, and locked the door behind me. My chest heaved up and down as realization finally hit me.

Ichika sat on the bed with her hands posted back on the mattress and a wicked *tell me all* grin on her face. She handed me a box of

Plan B. "They'll all do basically the same thing, but you should take this one."

I tore the box open, popped the pill into my mouth, and swallowed it whole without any water. Adrenaline rushed through my body at everything that had happened today—Mr. Avery, seeing Vera at the CVS while I'd bought Plan B, and this damn surprise party.

"So," Ichika started, sitting crisscross on the bed, "tell me everything!"

After glimpsing back at the bedroom door, I took a deep breath and jumped onto the bed with her. Since I had been a child, I'd always told her my deepest, darkest secrets. But this ... this was way more personal than anything we had talked about.

"I, um ..." I leaned forward and lowered my voice even more. "I need you to help me get on birth control."

She grabbed my hand and squeezed it tightly, shaking it up and down. "Tell me you did not lose your virginity!"

Eyes widening, I ripped my hand away from her, slapped my hand across her mouth, and tugged her down onto the bed so we were both lying on the mattress. I turned to my side and slowly removed my hand. "Can you not scream it?! Everyone is here!"

Her eyes twinkled with excitement. "With who?!"

My cheeks flushed again, and I glanced away. "With someone at school."

There was no way in hell that I would tell her about *him*. Telling her I had lost my virginity was one thing. Telling her that it had been with a teacher was completely different! He was my professor, for God's sake.

"Who?" she urged.

"I'll tell you sometime. Not now. But I ... I really need you to help me get on birth control."

After playfully rolling her dark brown, almost-black eyes at me, she nodded. "Sure. I have availability tomorrow morning, but you'll have to skip school. I can get you a copper IUD that starts working immediately."

I stared up at the ceiling and blew out a breath, thanking the Redwood gods that Ichika had something that'd start working immediately. Because I didn't know how the hell I'd be able to stay away from him.

Detention or not, I hadn't been able to stop thinking about Mr. Avery for weeks now.

9

sakura

AT SEVEN O'CLOCK, after cutting the white sponge cake and opening small gifts, I sat at the dining room table and listened to the family gossip with each other. I sank my fork into a slice of cake and glanced at my phone, hoping that I'd get an email from Mr. Avery.

Usually, he sent an email to his students with a reminder about the homework, especially if he had been distracted in class. And today, I'd learned that he definitely had been because he was watching *me* glide my thighs together.

The thought of making him—a married man—hard enough that he had to stop class …

I knew that it was beyond wrong, but he never once spoke about his wife, like the other teachers at Redwood did. He never shared what he did at home with her, their goals or vacations or pictures. Nothing.

But every night, at precisely seven o'clock, I'd get an email. An email I looked forward to. One that I always responded to, showing appreciation for the reminder even though I usually finished the homework hours ago.

Tonight … nothing.

Unable to stop myself, I opened my school email and refreshed my inbox.

Still nothing.

Getting desperate, I messaged the only person whose number I had in Literature. I already knew what the homework was—I had finished it in class—but I wanted to know if Mr. Avery had taken me off his email list.

Maybe he was … regretting what had happened.

Me: Hi, Maddie! It's Sakura from Literature with Mr. Avery. Have you received his nightly email about homework yet? I didn't write down during class what's due for tomorrow.

I waited. And waited. And waited.

Anxiously chewing on my lip.

Nerves zipping through me.

Maddie: Email?

Maddie: I never get emails from him.

Maddie: But the homework is to just finish what we were assigned in class.

I stared at my phone in shock, warmth gathering between my legs.

Mr. Avery didn't send other students a nightly email? I had been receiving emails from him since the beginning of this school year. Did that mean that he was only sending them to me, only thinking about *me*?

Maddie: Also, btw, happy birthday!

Me: Thank you!

Quickly, I tabbed back to my school inbox and scrolled through the tens of emails he had sent me these past few weeks and all of my responses. If these were all to just me, then where was my email tonight?

He didn't have anything to say after fucking me during detention, using my body, stealing my virginity, and coming deep inside me? I rubbed my thighs together underneath the table and bit back a whimper.

Without anyone noticing, I slipped a hand underneath the table and pressed it against the front of my skirt, hoping that the ache would disappear. I glanced around nervously, ensuring that everyone was busy, then slipped my fingers even lower.

My clit throbbed as I pressed two fingers against it. Mr. Avery had had his fingers here today, rubbing the needy little bud, whispering filthy things into my ear. He had been thinking about me for a long time now, especially if he had only been sending me emails.

Every night.

Every single … night.

I pressed my lips together and forced myself to smile at Auntie Yua as she gushed about her son who was now in medical school. Pressure rose inside my core, but I rubbed myself even faster underneath the table.

Had he been thinking about me as long as I had thought about him? What would he do if he found out I was rubbing myself off and thinking about earlier today? Would he bend me over his desk and dump his huge load into me again?

Pussy pounding, I grabbed my phone and refreshed my inbox again.

Nothing.

Whimpering so softly that nobody could hear, I opened a new email and started typing out a message to him while grinding my thighs together. I needed to talk to him, to see him, to feel him inside me again.

It was dishonorable, but nobody had touched me like that. Nobody knew how to make me come so easily. With a flick of his thumb across my clit. With those dirty words in my ear. With him inside me.

Wrong.

We were so wrong.

Just as I was about to send the email to him, the front door opened. Mom walked into the house with her purse hanging off her arm and a strained smile on her face. The room suddenly fell into a deadly silence.

When she spotted the entire family here, she tightened her smile even more and glanced around at Dad's relatives. "What's everyone doing here?"

Dad clenched his jaw. "It's Sakura's birthday."

Mom peered at me, confusion on her face for a moment, and then she nodded. "Yes, of course!" She stepped backward to the front door. "I think I left your present in the car. I'll be back with it."

After she disappeared outside and shut the door behind her, the hushed whispers started up. I turned back to my phone, knowing that she wasn't coming back in until everyone left.

She didn't have a present for me, but that didn't matter.

I had already gotten the best present there was today—Mr. Avery's cum.

I chewed on my lip, tearing off a piece of skin, and stared down at the email I had carefully crafted to Mr. Avery. While I didn't know if it was crossing the line, I couldn't help but press Send.

10

callan

STEAM from the shower filled the master bathroom. I unbuttoned my shirt, let it hang off my shoulders, and stepped into the warm room. After pulling my phone from my suit pocket, I set it on the bathroom counter, faceup.

As I unbuttoned my pants before I stepped into the shower, an email notification popped up on the screen through my school email from none other than Sakura Sato with the subject line *Today's Detention.*

After tossing my shirt into the hamper, I opened the email.

Mr. Avery,

You usually send a nightly email out to all students about homework. I didn't receive one tonight and wanted to make sure that you were … getting along all right with everything at home. I know things can get pretty hard sometimes, especially after today.

I've thought long and hard about my actions in class today that led to my detention. The memories of my punishment haven't been easy to deal with, as they've brought me much … pressure in places.

After careful consideration, I've decided that I have done nothing wrong. I will eagerly accept any further detention you give me because of my illicit actions while you're trying to teach. I don't plan on changing.

Sincerely,

Sakura Sato

I drew my tongue across my teeth, my cock twitching inside my briefs. Sakura wanted to play. She wanted me to punish her. She planned on rubbing those thighs together during my lectures whether I wanted her to or not.

After dropping my pants, I opened the shower door just an inch to let some steam out before I stepped into the water and washed Sakura off me. I clicked my tongue and shook my head. It was dangerous to flirt with her over school email, but she had started it.

And I never left anything unfinished.

Sakura,

Apologies for not sending you an email about homework sooner. I believed you were paying attention and didn't need the reminder, but it seems you were distracted during class today, hmm?

In case you wanted to know, I've been busy cleaning up the mess you made in detention this afternoon. I've had a long, hard problem since then that I'll be taking care of while thinking about your punishment for tomorrow.

Don't be late to class.

Sincerely,

Mr. Avery

After I hit Send, I tossed the phone onto the marble countertop and stepped into the shower. Hot water pounded down onto my shoulders, running down my back. I gripped my hard cock in my hand and leaned against the shower glass wall, stroking myself and washing away Sakura's blood.

My balls hung heavily, filled up with warm cum that I wanted to spill inside her. Her pussy was unused and hungry to devour all of me, desperate to be full with my cock and my cum. She had pulsed around me so hard, over and over, milking out every last drop this afternoon.

I stroked myself faster from base to tip. For her being a virgin, she had taken it so well.

And her mouth. I growled. *That fucking mouth …*

She'd fastened her pouty lips around my cock, swallowing it whole and taking it deep in her throat. If I hadn't stopped her, she would've sucked me dry right there without me slipping inside her.

Grunting, I tilted my head back against the glass wall. She wanted to be a little brat with me too. She wanted me to punish her, to dump my cum into her tight holes and then hammer it deeper and deeper inside.

Fuck, I hadn't missed the way her pussy clung tighter around me after she said she wasn't on birth control and I told her that I wouldn't stop. That tight little cunt begged me to explode inside of it.

And once I had—my eyes rolled back—her walls had gripped me so tightly as I pulled out of her, like she didn't want to be empty, like she needed me inside her. I closed my eyes and grunted at the thought of pushing my cum back up into her.

I wanted to call her over to my desk in the middle of class while everyone worked, come all over her thighs and up that pretty little skirt of hers, and draw *slut* on her body with my cum.

She deserved it.

Especially if she wanted to disobey me.

Cupping my heavy balls, I stroked my cock even faster at the thought of her and listened to my school email notification ring through the bathroom. My cock twitched in my hand, my entire body tensing.

I knew that the email was from Sakura.

Which only made this fucking orgasm feel so much better.

After groaning in pleasure, I came onto the glass shower wall and stroked the last few drops from my dick. I imagined Sakura in the shower with me, so desperate to take my cum that she'd swipe it off the wall and thrust it into her tight hole.

God, she was driving me fucking crazy.

Once I gathered control of myself, I snatched a towel, stepped out into the steamy bathroom, and grabbed my phone to read her email.

Mr. Avery,
We'll see about that.
Sakura

11

sakura

WITH A METAL SPECULUM spreading my vagina lips apart, I lay back on the bed the next morning, completely tense and beyond nervous for what Ichika was about to shove up into my uterus. While Mr. Avery had been deep inside me yesterday, I hadn't felt *this* kind of pressure.

The bad kind.

"Relax, Sakura," my cousin said, gently patting my knees. "This might hurt a little."

"That is such a contradiction," I whimpered, grasping the bedsheets tightly in my fists.

"If you weren't a slut yesterday, we could've gotten you on something easier, like the pill."

I scrunched my nose and stared up at the ceiling. "I was not a slut."

She giggled and moved her fingers up my thigh, preparing me mentally for when she'd thrust an IUD deep into my pussy, which would stay there for, like, seven years. "Fine, not a slut. A horny slut."

"Ichika! I was not a—"

While my pussy lips were spread, I felt something metal being shoved up into my vagina. Then, there was immense pressure suddenly deep inside me. I groaned out in pain and squeezed my eyes shut.

A moment of pure agony later, Ichika sat back. "All done! See, that wasn't bad."

Still in lingering pain, I narrowed my eyes at her and flared my nostrils. "I hate you."

As she pulled the speculum from my vagina, she laughed again. "You're welcome."

I wriggled up to a seated position, the pain slowly subsiding, and crossed my arms. "Thank you for putting me in so much pain, Ichika. You're the best cousin ever. What would I do without you?"

Raising a brow at me, she walked to the sink to wash her hands. "Get pregnant."

"Wow."

"Like I said, Sakura, you're welcome. Now, when are you gonna tell me who it was?"

I threw my feet off the side of the bed. "Never."

"Since it's your first time with an IUD, I can prescribe you some pain meds," Ichika said, humming, twirling around in a swivel chair, and grabbing a prescription slip from the cabinet. "You might get some cramps throughout the day."

When she handed me the prescription slip, I hesitantly took it and glanced down at the paper. I had seen one too many of these at home because of Mom. Not only did she work at the pharmacy, but she was also always at the doctor's office with another excuse for being *hurt*.

After my cousin turned back around to write a couple of notes in my file, I crumpled the prescription up and stuffed it into my pocket. I didn't care if I had cramps today or not. I didn't want to become addicted, like Mom.

I hated her for it.

Everyone did. Even Dad did, but he refused to divorce her.

"Make sure to bring that to the pharmacy," Ichika said, opening the door. "They should have it ready in, like, fifteen minutes or so, and then you can go home or to school. But I'd recommend you stay home."

While I appreciated her advice, I couldn't miss many more classes. I had already missed one period earlier in the semester because I had to talk with my advisor about college. Today was already three periods wasted.

Which meant ... I'd missed Literature.

Once I waved good-bye to Ichika, I hurried to my car, slipped into the driver's seat, and pulled my phone out of my backpack. As I'd suspected, nobody had texted me, asking where I was today or if I was sick.

But I didn't care.

At least not about anyone else, except *him*.

Scrolling to my school email, I spotted three new emails. One from my History teacher. One from Calculus. And one from ... Gym. I sighed and slumped my shoulders forward.

Gym? Why the heck would gym class need to send me an email?

Grumpily, I shoved my phone into my backpack and drove to Redwood Academy. I steered through the staff lot of parked cars, spotting Mr. Avery's black car with tinted windows in his designated spot.

Whenever I stayed after with another teacher, I always saw him leaving in it. I wasn't too good with car names, but it was sleek and dark and mysterious, just like him. Something that I could see myself inside of, in the backseat, letting him thrust into me during lunch.

I blew out a deep breath and found my parking spot in the student lot. After grabbing my backpack, I walked up the sidewalk to the main entrance and then into the main office, listening to the secretaries chatter about how *sexy* Principal Vaughn was.

I nearly puked in my mouth.

"Hi. I need a late pass," I said.

The lady glanced up at me and readjusted her glasses. "Name?"

"Sakura Sato."

After she began typing into the computer, the office door opened. A tall, slender, and inherently creepy Principal Vaughn walked into the room with a fake smile on his face and thinning gray hair that looked like he'd tried to dye it multiple times without luck.

Giggling, the secretary stopped everything she was doing and leaned forward. "Principal Vaughn, the staff meeting is the third door down the hallway. I can take you there, if you'd like me to."

Hold it together, Sakura. Don't puke in disgust.

"I'm fine," he said, peering down at me. "Are we late today, Miss Sato?"

"Just had a doctor's appointment."

"Ahh, I see. You know, I never …" he continued speaking, but I couldn't focus because the door opened again and the Physics teacher walked in with Mr. Avery beside him.

When Mr. Avery glanced up at me, I froze.

Dressed in a dark gray wool sweater, Mr. Avery sported messy, dark hair and the same stubble that had tickled my neck yesterday afternoon. Warmth gathered between my legs as his eyes darkened with fury.

I had missed his class today. And he was mad.

"Right, Miss Sato?" Principal Vaughn continued.

But I didn't know what the hell he had said, so I nodded along and watched Mr. Avery walk down the back hallway toward the staff meeting today. His back was taut and tensed against his sweater.

Just as he was about to enter the room, he peered back at me with those devilish eyes that promised he'd punish me later.

12

callan

SAKURA HAD SKIPPED MY CLASS.

I sat in the teachers' meeting room, listening to Vaughn go on and on and fucking on for the past three hours. All the department heads were required to attend this bullshit meeting, and I couldn't get her out of my head.

This meeting had better be finished before the end of the day.

My phone lit up on the table, a notification from *Bitch*, my dear wife, on the screen. As Vaughn talked away about something, I unlocked my phone, ignored her message altogether, and opened my email.

I scrolled through all the unopened emails and spam, and then I stopped at my messages to her. An email chain of three messages last night, to and from Sakura Sato, her *teasing me*, telling me that she would be a brat from now on.

Minutes passed, and all I could do was stare at them, wait for her to message me, email me, do something. I had been waiting all day to talk to her after that little stunt she pulled last night, after having her as mine yesterday.

When the last bell rang throughout the room, I tightened my

hand into a tight fist and glared at Vaughn, hoping he'd hurry the fuck up. I had people to catch before they had the chance to slip out the exit doors and leave Redwood Academy for the night.

Once Vaughn finally shut his mouth ten minutes later, I stood up from my seat, grabbed my notes, and walked to the exit, growling to myself. We had sat in a three-hour meeting, and he couldn't even let us go before the day ended for everyone else.

I hated him.

For more than just that reason.

"Callan," he called from inside the room.

Fuck.

Deciding that I had nothing better to do, especially because Sakura had to be long gone by now, I turned around on my heel and faced him. She had no reason to stay past the end of the day unless it was for another class. No other teacher would give her detention.

"Can we do this another time, Vaughn? I have a wife to get home to."

Fucking lie, but who cares anymore?

"I wanted to talk to you about Sakura," he said. "She's in your class, right?"

What the fuck does he want with her?

"Yes," I said, keeping myself in check.

But on the inside—on the fucking inside—I wanted to rip him apart for even speaking her name. He rarely spoke about students other than some of the girls on the cheerleading team. I didn't know what he wanted with her.

"Why?" I urged.

"She's top of the class," Vaughn said. "A *stellar* student."

I stared at him for a few moments, trying to figure out what kind of game he was playing. I didn't know what it was, but I didn't like the tone of his voice, the way he had said her name, or how he had called her a stellar student.

We all knew that already.

Did he find out about the detention? Did he know that my hands were all over her?

"She is," I said, tapping the edge of my notebook against a table. "And?"

"I'm sure she excels elsewhere too," he continued.

Holding my tongue, I nodded. "She has told me about the volunteer work she does."

"Hmm … *volunteer.*"

After examining the scrawny, balding principal once more, I took my notebook again and walked to the door. The more he talked, the more fucking weird it got. Vaughn always had that creep vibe to him, but I didn't know what he was getting at.

Nor did I want to stay to figure it out.

Skipping pleasantries with the other teachers who had stayed behind to talk in the office with some of the secretaries, I gritted my teeth and walked out of the office and toward my classroom to snatch my car keys.

Yet when I turned the corner, Sakura bounced up and down on her toes right in front of my door, distracted by her phone. I walked up to her from behind, glanced around to make sure nobody was watching, then seized her by the back of the neck.

When she sucked in a sharp breath, I shoved her into my classroom and locked the door behind us. I'd spank her ass red for sending me that email last night, for skipping my class this morning, for pressing those thighs together and smirking at me when I'd seen her in the office.

Sakura would pay.

13

sakura

WARMTH EXPLODED through my pussy as Mr. Avery shoved me into his classroom and locked the door behind us. I wriggled out of his hold, turning around to face him and clutching my books to my chest—like this wasn't what I had wanted.

After I put a couple of feet between us, he immediately closed the distance, slipped between my legs, and pressed me against his desk. He snaked his hand around my throat and forced me to look up at him.

"You skipped my class."

I spread my legs a couple of inches wider, letting him nestle himself between them and grind his bulge against my pussy from underneath my skirt. He trailed his free hand up my sheer stockings until he reached my hip, bunching my skirt up by my waist.

With his dick pressed against my aching cunt, I couldn't think of an appropriate response. All I could imagine was him inside me already, him pushing his fat cock between my wet pussy lips, filling me.

"I … I know," I said.

Which wasn't the answer he was looking for.

He growled and strummed his fingers up the column of my throat. "Why?"

Not knowing what to say to him—because I would *not* tell him that I had a gyno appointment to get an IUD stuck up my uterus for the next seven years—I shifted.

"M-Mr. Avery," I whispered, "I … I'm just here to get the notes I missed during class."

Chuckling darkly, Mr. Avery shook his head and lifted my chin. "You're not here for your missed notes, Miss Sato. You're here for your punishment for skipping today." He dipped his other hand between my legs and cupped my pussy. "I can tell by how wet this pussy is for me."

When he drew the tips of his fingers against my clit, over my panties and stockings, I gripped on to his shoulders and stared up at him, whining softly, "N-no. I'm not here for … for *that*."

"Yes, you are."

Spreading my legs even wider, I slid onto his desk and pushed my hips as close to the edge as possible, wanting and needing to feel his bulge against my entrance. He thrust it against me a couple of times, taunting me with it.

A whine escaped my mouth. "Please …"

He curled his lips into a devilish smirk. "Please what?"

I didn't want to say it. I still couldn't get past how *wrong* this was.

"Please what, Miss Sato?" he asked again, his fingers slowing down, threatening to stop completely.

"Please, punish me," I whimpered.

He didn't know how long I'd imagined him inside me. I hadn't been able to get him out of my mind, to stop craving the feel of him inside me again. I had thrust a couple of fingers up into me, but nothing as big as him.

Nothing had ever felt as good as him either.

After sliding his hand further up my throat, he gripped my jaw and peered down at my lips. I clenched, the heat rushing to my core, and started moving my hips up and down against his bulge, desperate for him.

"Please," I begged.

Before I could stop him, Mr. Avery twirled me around and bent me over his desk. Pressing himself against me from behind, he leaned over me and grabbed a notebook and pen from his desk, placing it in front of me.

"Write *I will not skip Literature with Mr. Avery* a hundred times."

"Write it?" I repeated, wondering why he wasn't giving me a different punish—

He slipped both hands underneath my skirt from behind, found the seam of my stockings between my legs, and tore a hole into them to give himself better access to *me*. Once he undid his belt, he pressed his head against my entrance.

"Start writing, Sakura," he ordered.

Aching for him inside of me, I grabbed the pen, opened to a clean page, and wrote.

I will not skip Literature with Mr. Avery.

I will not skip Literature with Mr. Avery.

I will not skip Literature with—

My pen veered off the page in a squiggle as Mr. Avery plunged himself inside me. I tilted my head back and clenched around him, moaning out in pleasure. He slithered one hand around my waist and between my legs, finding my clit. He placed his other hand on the desk beside the notebook.

"Continue," he growled.

I will not skip Literature with Mr. Avery.

I will not skip Literature with Mr. Avery.

He rubbed my clit through my stockings and thrust himself up into me over and over, driving me wild. After pushing some hair behind my shoulder, he dipped his head and sucked on the column of my neck.

"You feel your pussy tightening around me?" he murmured, steadying his thrusts.

Pulling out of me slowly, then filling me inch by inch.

Pulling out of me slowly, then filling me inch by inch.

Torture. Pure fucking torture.

I focused on the sheet of paper, writing as quickly as I could. He rubbed my clit faster, pushing me closer to the edge until I was about to tumble over it and come all over his cock. But then he stopped.

"You don't get to come until you learn your lesson. Continue writing."

When I started writing again, he pumped inside me faster than before, his thrusts erratic. I desperately tried to hold my pen steady, but the higher he pushed me, the harder and harder it was for me to write legibly.

I will not skip Literature with Mr. Avery.

I will not skip Literature with Mr. Avery.

I will not skip Literature with Mr. —

"Rewrite the last five," he growled into my ear. "I can't read them. And if I can't read them, then you're not learning a thing."

Whimpering, I crossed out the last five sentences I had written and rewrote them, my handwriting only a tiny bit better. I could barely write a thing steadily with Mr. Avery grunting into my ear and pounding inside my pussy.

"P-please …" I whispered, brow furrowing. "I'm so close."

"Then, you'd better start writing faster."

"Mr. Avery …" I moaned.

"Write."

I will not skip Literature with Mr. Avery.

I will not skip Literature with Mr. Avery.

I will not skip Literature with Mr. Avery.

As if he could feel my body tighten the way it had before I came undone, he rubbed my clit hard and fast. "Don't you fucking come," he growled. "I'm going to push you past your edge, and you'd better hold yourself together and finish writing."

My pussy clamped down on his dick as I continued to write. Moments … I was damn moments away from coming. And he wanted me to hold myself together?! I placed a shaky hand on the notebook so it wouldn't move with me and pressed my pen harder onto the page.

With his free hand, Mr. Avery seized my nipple and tugged. Hard.

I bit down on my lip so harshly that I drew blood, all to stop myself from coming.

I will not skip Literature with Mr. Avery.

I will not skip Literature with Mr. Avery.

I will not skip Literature with Mr. Avery.

"Don't come," he growled.

But the more he said that, the closer and closer I came to exploding around him.

"Don't come."

I clenched harder.

"Don't come."

"Mr. Avery!" I cried out, finishing the hundredth sentence. "Please! I learned my lesson!"

He continued pumping into me. "Don't come."

"No!" I wailed. "Please, I'll do anything. Anything."

"Anything, Miss Sato?"

"Yes," I panted, fingertips turning white on the desk. "Anything."

"You get to come around me on one condition," he said, pumping into me. "After I come inside your cunt, you drop to your knees, stare up at me like the desperate little slut you are, and suck your juices off my cock."

"I'll do it! Now, please, can I—"

"Come for me, Sakura."

I threw my head back and moaned louder, my entire body trembling. Ecstasy exploded through my pussy. I doubled over the desk as my core pulsed around his throbbing cock. He slammed into me one last time and came deep in my pussy.

When he pulled out, I dropped to my knees, stared up at my professor, and wrapped my lips around his dick. I bobbed my head back and forth desperately, trying to take all of him inside me. I needed to please him. Badly.

Once my lips met the base of his dick, I gargled on his cock and swallowed around him. A few last drops of salty cum rolled down the back of my throat. After I flicked my tongue across his balls, I pulled back and collapsed against the desk, chest rising and falling quickly.

"I … God, I want more."

I scrambled to my feet, leaned against the desk, and gazed down at my creamed pussy. Needy. Desperate. Aching. Mr. Avery stepped closer to me, wiping the head of his dick against my pussy lips.

I shoved my hand between my legs and pushed all his cum back inside me.

Mr. Avery clenched his jaw and growled, "Only desperate little sluts would shove my cum back up into them like that." He seized my wrist as I was about to pull my fingers out of me and pounded them inside, getting deeper and deeper. "You're a bad girl, Sakura. A bad, bad girl."

Pressure built up inside me again, my pussy tightening around him.

"My fingers are too small," I whimpered. "They can't push it up all the way."

He grunted, "Fuck, you're getting me hard again."

"Please, push it up inside me," I pleaded, pulling out my wet fingers and grabbing on to his hand, guiding it toward my entrance. "I need it deeper inside me—as a punishment for skipping your class, Mr. Avery."

"*Fuck*," he growled, the sound guttural. "I got something bigger for you."

Instead of pushing his fingers inside me, he lined himself up to my entrance and plunged himself deep into my pussy. I clamped down on his dick and moaned out in pleasure, my legs trembling.

"Push it deeper inside me, Mr. Avery!" I moaned. "Please! Deeper!"

He gripped my waist and pounded himself into me, pushing his cum deeper until he nearly reached my cervix. Leaning down, he buried his face into the crook of my neck and gently sucked on my sensitive skin.

I wrapped my arms around the backs of my knees, holding my trembling legs apart so he could get as deep as he possibly could, pounding his cum deeper inside me with his throbbing cock.

"You're the sexiest fucking thing I've laid my eyes on," he murmured into my shoulder.

Clenching, I tilted my head back and whimpered, "Harder. Fuck me harder."

After wrapping his arms around my body, he pulled me into the air. Biceps rippling against me, he lifted and dropped me on his cock over and over. I wrapped my arms around him, sank my fingernails into his shoulders through his shirt, and dragged them down his back.

He growled against my collarbone, "Harder."

I scratched his back harder and tugged on his hair with my free hand, pulling his head back so he stared up at me. "Please," I whimpered. "Come inside me again, Mr. Avery. I haven't been able to stop thinking about you since last night."

"Promise me you won't miss another one of my classes."

"I-I promise!"

One last time, he slammed himself up into me and groaned in pleasure. I exploded around him, wave after wave rushing through my body and making me tingle all over. My juices drenched his dick.

14

callan

ONCE SAKURA HAD WRITTEN *I will not skip Literature with Mr. Avery* one hundred times across a sheet of paper and taken two loads of my cum, I set her on my desk, tucked myself away inside my pants, and leaned against the whiteboard to catch my breath.

With every single word she had written, I'd fucked her harder. I couldn't help myself.

After telling me that she'd continue to be a brat and continue to tease me at school, she'd decided not to show up for my class this morning while attending her others. And that deserved more than this punishment.

I wanted to decorate her ass with red handprints, make her whimper for me to stop and beg me to let her come already. But if I kept her in here any longer, the janitor would show up and catch us. Whether I locked this door or not, he had keys to the entire place.

Doubled over the desk, she took uneven breaths and pressed her shaky thighs together.

Taking the notebook from the desktop, I opened my messenger bag and stuffed it inside. If she wanted to tease and taunt me during class, I would do the same to her. Whenever she wanted to grind those knees together, I'd hand her the notebook to warn her that if she didn't stop, I'd do that to her in front of the entire class.

And I wasn't kidding.

Anyone in Redwood could be paid to keep their mouth shut.

Sakura readjusted her skirt and collapsed in her assigned seat in class. Leaning forward in her seat, she placed a hand over her stomach and whimpered slightly, her straight black hair falling into her face.

"What's wrong?" I asked.

After a moment, she sat up straight, shook her head, and whispered, "It's nothing." When she stood, she winced again and gripped on to the desk to support herself. She tugged her backpack over her shoulder and peered up at me. "I'm fine. See you tomorrow in class."

Cheeks much paler than they had been moments ago, Sakura walked right by me to the door. She must've thought I'd believe her and let her off the hook that easily. She seemed as if she was about to pass out.

I grasped her elbow and stopped her. "You're driving home?"

"Yes."

"Like that?"

Pressing her lips together, she stared at the ground and nodded. "Yes."

"No," I said, snatching her keys out of her hand. "You're not driving anywhere like that."

Georgina would've snatched the keys back and ground her teeth at me, but Sakura just slumped against the wall and slid all the way down to the floor, grasping her stomach. Tears welled up in her big eyes.

Fuck.

I crouched down to her level and furrowed my brow. "Did I hurt you?"

"I have really bad cramps all of a sudden." She curled into a ball and pulled her knees to her chest. "They hurt so much. I should've gone home." She whimpered into her knees, shoulders trembling. "I'm sorry."

After lifting her off the ground, I walked with her to my swivel desk chair and set her down so she wasn't lying in the middle of the floor, which was littered with dirt, fake nails, pieces of dyed hair, and whatever the fuck kids these days tracked into school.

"Did I hurt you?" I repeated, unsure if *I* had been the one to cause her pain.

She shook her head. "No."

Once I retrieved some pain meds from the closet, I shook two out into my hand and opened her water bottle. "Take these," I ordered.

With a shaky hand, she grabbed the pills and stared down at them with worry in her eyes. "No, I … I can't take them." She shoved them into my hand and looked away. "I-it's fine. I'm fine."

"Sakura," I growled. "You're not fine."

"Yes, I am."

Though she didn't move from the seat.

I clenched my jaw and stared at her.

"I'm sorry," she whispered, pulling her knees to her chest again. "I know you probably have to get home to your … to your wife." She stood shakily again and gripped on to my desk for support. "I need to get home anyway."

"You shouldn't be driving."

"Mr. Avery," she whispered, "I can't stay here all night. The janitor would get suspicious."

"Can you have a friend pick you up?" I asked.

If she drove home like this, she'd get into an accident—or worse …

Sakura chewed on the inside of her cheek and shook her head. "No. I … I don't have many friends," she whispered, glancing down at her thighs and frowning. "And I can't call my parents. They don't know that I got an IUD."

My eyes widened. "An IUD?"

Mirroring my expression, she sucked in a sharp breath, then winced and looked away. "Yes, I got an IUD today. That's why I missed class. I was relatively fine during classes today, but it ... it's hurting really badly now."

Before a smug smirk could cross my face—because Sakura had started birth control *for me*—I pressed my lips together and grabbed my keys from the desk. "Then, let me take you because I'm not letting you drive like this."

She snapped her head up. "Are you crazy?! You can't bring me home!"

"Not home," I said, drawing my tongue across my lower teeth.

I knew that I shouldn't bring my student to my house. But I had fucked her. We had broken far too many rules already, and this wasn't even a bad one. Not yet. Not until someone found us.

"Come on. I'll bring you back here to pick up your car once you're feeling better."

Gazing up at me through big eyes, she whimpered, "But Mr. Ave—"

"Now, Sakura."

When she stood, I held the door open for her and headed down the hallway. Georgina wouldn't be home for another week at the very least. Taking Sakura back to my place wasn't going to hurt either of us.

15

sakura

"I DON'T KNOW if we should be doing this," I murmured, staring out Mr. Avery's tinted passenger window and at all the mansions we drove past in Redwood's ritzy area. "What if someone sees us?"

Another lingering cramp squeezed at my insides, throwing me into a world of pain. I doubled over in the seat, rested my head against the door, and whimpered. Ichika had said I might get cramps, but not like this.

Curse IUDs. I hate them already.

He glanced over at me and drove a bit faster. "Nobody will see you."

I dropped my head to deal with some of the pain and shut my eyes, focusing on breathing deeply. Usually, my period cramps were bad, but this was worse—so much freaking worse. I sure hoped that childbirth didn't feel like this.

Because I would one hundred percent cry.

When we finally turned a corner a few moments later and pulled into a driveway, I fluttered my eyes open and gazed at his home, which seemed to grow bigger and bigger the closer we drove to it. I sat up slightly, eyes widening.

With enormous black-trimmed windows, an extended patio made of stone, and a wooden exterior, the house must've been three times the size of mine. He tapped a digital button on the dashboard that opened the black paneled garage door.

"Are you sure this is okay?" I whispered.

"No."

Yet he continued driving into the garage, then parked. When he stepped out of the car, I followed him, walked into his home, and slipped off my shoes at the door, my heart pounding against my rib cage.

I shouldn't be here. I shouldn't be here. I shouldn't be here.

My stomach twisted again. Those pain pills would've really helped.

But I couldn't take them.

The short hallway opened up into a large mahogany-accented living room with white couches, a fireplace, and a view of the infinity pool in the backyard that must've been heated if he still had it opened in late September.

Not that I would ever even *want* to go near that thing. I might've lived near the beach all my life, but any huge body of water freaked me out ever since I had almost drowned when I was five.

"Follow me," he said, heading toward another hallway.

Nervously, I followed after him and into a large bedroom with a connected bathroom.

"Lie down," he said, nodding to the bed. "Get comfortable."

"Is this your ... bedroom?" I asked, spotting a pair of diamond earrings on one of the nightstands.

Jealousy boiled inside me, the thought of whoever his wife was having her hands all over him making me angry.

It shouldn't have. I was the one in the wrong, sleeping with a married man.

But I couldn't help myself.

"Yes," he said, guiding me to the bed. "Rest."

I smelled her perfume all over the blankets, so I froze and balled my hands into fists. "No, I want to lie down on your couch. Not here." I stared at the hamper filled with thongs and bras that were sized much bigger than any of mine, chest tightening. "Please."

After eyeing me for a moment, he nodded and guided me back through the big house to the living room. Once I dumped my belongings on one side of the couch, I collapsed onto it, my stomach still aching, and closed my eyes.

Mr. Avery disappeared into another room, and I turned on the couch and pressed my lips together. Mr. Avery was married, and here I was—one of his students—lying on his couch while his wife's perfume was doused all over the place.

I felt bad for her. But at the same time, I wanted her out of the picture.

I wished he weren't married. I wished that he didn't have *anyone* in his life.

A couple of moments later, Mr. Avery reappeared in the living room with a heating pad and a mug full of what smelled like peppermint green tea. I slowly pushed myself to a seated position, eyes widening as he handed me both the items.

"These are for me?" I asked.

"Relax, Sakura," he said, heading to the other couch with his messenger bag and pulling out a stack of exams.

Warmth spread through my chest, and I sipped the tea, lay back down, and placed the heating pad on my stomach, hoping the pain would fade away soon.

Three hours passed as I lay on the couch while he graded exams from last week's class. And slowly, the pain had faded. I'd texted Dad a while ago, telling him that I was hanging out with a *friend*— I'd have to figure out *who* later before I saw him.

But I needed to get home to catch up on my schoolwork. I couldn't stay here forever.

What if his wife showed up? What would I do? Hide?

I gently moved off the couch and walked to the other side, Mr. Avery watching me every step of the way.

"You want to go?" he asked without me saying a word.

"Yes."

After gathering my stuff, I followed him to the garage in silence. I didn't know what to say to him besides *thank you*. So, I slipped into his car. He pulled out of the garage and began backing down the driveway, then stopped halfway.

"Fuck," he cursed underneath his breath.

I glanced in the rearview mirror and spotted a man in a black suit. He had parked his car at the end of the driveway, blocking us in, and was now walking toward us. My eyes widened slightly. I didn't know who he was, but I sensed nothing good.

"Mr. Avery," I whispered.

If someone found us together, my life would be over.

He placed one hand on the steering wheel, the other on my thigh. "Don't say anything."

When he approached the driver's side, Mr. Avery stared emptily out the windshield and lowered his window just a couple of centimeters. My stomach twisted in knots, but thankfully *not* the cramp kind.

"You know not to show up at my house," Mr. Avery said, not sparing him a glance.

"You haven't shown up."

Shown up? To where?

"What do you want?" Mr. Avery asked the man.

"We have work for you," the man said, slipping a note through the cracked window. It floated down onto Mr. Avery's lap, and then the man just walked back to his car without saying another word.

Along with Mr. Avery, I stared at the guy in the rearview mirror and watched him drive away. When I flickered my gaze back to my professor, he folded the note in his hand. I swallowed hard, knowing this wasn't anything good.

"D-do you want me to put that away for you?" I asked, reaching for the glove compartment.

"Don't worry abou—"

Without letting him finish—because I was a nervous wreck after almost getting caught and witnessing whatever *that* was—I opened the compartment without permission. Sitting front and center on the stack of car manuals was a fully loaded gun.

16

sakura

I SLAMMED the glove compartment shut and stared down at my thighs through wide eyes, hoping he hadn't seen me just gawk at the gun for who knew how long. Swallowing hard, I pressed my lips together.

But why does he have a gun?! Does it have anything to do with that guy?

"Sakura," Mr. Avery said, not moving the car.

"Please, can you take me back to my car?" I whispered, wanting to get out of here ASAP.

"Sakura," Mr. Avery repeated. "Look at me."

After biting back my fear, I glanced over at him and gripped the ends of my skirt. My stomach twisted into tight knots, squeezing the life out of me. "Y-yes?" I murmured, voice so quiet that I couldn't even hear it over my pounding heart.

He stared at me with those corrupt, sinfully dark eyes. "You didn't see anything."

"No," I breathed out, pushing some hair behind my ear and peering back toward the glove compartment. "I didn't see anything."

Lie. Lie. Lie. Lie. Lie. Lie. Lie.

I just didn't want him to use it on me.

What was I even thinking, coming home with him? I didn't know the first thing about my Literature teacher. *Why would I ever think that going to his house and sleeping with him was a good idea?! What is wrong with me?!*

His gaze burned into the side of my face. "Good."

Gulping again, I turned my legs toward the window and hoped he didn't ask me anything else, hoped he didn't bring the gun back up or use it on me. Nerves zipped up and down my arms and legs.

"Please," I whispered. "Drive."

Mr. Avery continued to back down the pavement, then pulled out of his driveway and onto the road. I stared out the tinted window at the mansions we drove past.

What can he possibly use a gun for?!

Who is Mr. Avery?

Ten minutes later, or maybe it was longer—I couldn't quite tell anymore—we drove into the desolate Redwood Academy parking lot. He parked in the very back, where it was known that Poison had disabled all the cameras.

When I reached for the door, Mr. Avery growled, "Wait."

My heart dropped, and I peered over my shoulder at him. "Y-yes?"

"I expect you to be in class tomorrow. Don't skip."

"I promise ..." I glanced at the glove compartment. "I won't."

He tightened his hand around the steering wheel, following my gaze. "Don't worry."

"How can I not?! You have a gun!" I exclaimed, speaking when I shouldn't have. Immediately, I covered my mouth and wished that I could take it all back. I didn't want him to hurt me, nor did I want to get in trouble for this.

He pressed his lips together.

"Sorry," I whispered in a hurry, yanking on the door handle to get the hell out of here.

But before I could slip out of the car, he seized my wrist. I sucked in a sharp breath and froze, nerves zipping through my body. I didn't turn back. Fear froze me to the fucking spot.

Why did I decide to come with him?

"Are you okay to drive?" he asked me after a second of silence.

I stayed quiet for a few moments, then nodded. "Yes, I'm fine."

Once he released my wrist, I hurried out of his car and speed-walked to mine. I shuffled through my backpack, pulled out my keys, and unlocked the doors, leaping into the car as soon as I could. I tossed my backpack into the passenger seat and sped out of the parking lot.

Sure as hell, I couldn't go home now. My mind was racing, and I probably looked like a ghost. Dad would definitely know what was up if I stepped a single foot into the house. He'd know I hadn't been with a friend.

After driving through the ritzy beach sector that had upscale boutiques and charged upward of two hundred dollars a plate at the restaurants during the summer months, I aimlessly headed toward the beach.

I didn't know where I was going or where I would end up.

But I needed air. I needed to breathe.

How can Mr. Avery have a gun?! A freaking gun! Has he used it on anyone? He didn't seem like the type of person to go hunting, and that definitely wasn't one of those hunting rifles that I saw in the movies.

Speeding through the desolate roads near the beach, I didn't even stop. My mind was racing. My heart was racing. I didn't know who the hell I was anymore. I was sleeping with my teacher! *Me!* The good girl who never got in trouble.

Once I made it through the beach without getting stopped by the Redwood Police—they usually hid down here for traffic stops—I took a couple of deep breaths and headed toward the first parking lot that I saw.

I needed to calm down. I couldn't go home like this.

A sign for Walmart glowed against the dark-blue night sky. I parked in the very back and pulled the key out of the ignition, breathing heavily. After inhaling sharply, I blew out a long gush of air. Head clearing.

Hands clutched on to the steering wheel, I closed my eyes and gently banged my head against the headrest.

What the hell was I even thinking? Sleeping with a married man and my professor? Going to his house? Finding his gun?

"I need to stop," I whispered. "God, I need to stop."

But he felt so good. So fucking good.

No! He can't make me feel good. He's married.

Yet I couldn't stop thinking—

Someone knocked on my window. I snapped my eyes open and sat up in the seat, scrambling around to lock the car and see who was standing outside in the darkness. The knock came again from my passenger side.

Gunther Zurn.

17

callan

FIFTEEN MINUTES after Sakura left the parking lot, I still sat in my car and stared through the windshield with my gun sitting on my lap. She was never supposed to find this. I should've fucking hidden it better.

The note that Rick Santos had slipped me earlier lay on the passenger seat. After unfolding it, I dragged my hand over my face and grunted. One of these fucking days, when Georgina was out of my life, I'd fucking leave the mob. I hated working for them.

On the paper, there was a single name.

Cortez.

A cop.

They wanted me to kill a fucking cop, and I just wanted to teach.

My phone buzzed nonstop in my pocket. Without checking who it was, I yanked it out and hit Answer. I needed a distraction from Sakura tonight or else I'd figure out where she had gone off to and follow her.

It was a FaceTime call from my wife, who was in bed at the five-thousand-euro-a-night luxury hotel room in the heart of Paris. She had on nothing but a lacy navy push-up bra and panties, not even our wedding ring.

Not that I wore mine anytime she wasn't with me.

"What're you doing out so late?" she whined. "Where are you?"

"Out."

She giggled incessantly. "I went out tonight too."

"Great. Listen, I got to—"

When she rolled over in the bed and rested her head on someone's bare chest, I gritted my teeth. Then, from behind her, another man draped his arm over her breasts and squeezed one.

I pressed my lips together and flared my nostrils. I hadn't loved her in years, but the damn nerve of that woman irked me. I didn't give a fuck if she cheated on me, but at least try to fucking hide it.

"What's wrong, sweetheart? Don't tell me that all you did was teach at that boring school of yours, come home, and grade papers. All you do is work, work, and work. You never have the chance to spend time with me, and I—"

Before she could get another word out of her whore mouth, I ended the call and turned off all notifications from her. I thought about blocking her number completely, but if she told her father that I had done that …

He had the money to pay off the entire mob, if he wanted. Get me killed.

Every time I even mentioned breaking it off with her and finalizing a divorce, she hung this over my head. Which was why I was even in this mess to begin with. If the mob trusted me enough to get shit done, they wouldn't kill me.

Someone knocked on my window, jerking me back. I cursed to myself and glanced over to see Principal fucking Vaughn standing in the dark in the desolate parking lot. I turned off my phone and rolled down my window.

"Yes?" I asked.

He folded his hands. "You're here late, Callan."

"I had to come back to class. I forgot a couple of exams that I'm grading tonight."

God, what the hell is he doing here this late?

He usually left Redwood Academy at four in the afternoon, not eight at night. As far as I knew, all the admin meetings were in the mornings anyway.

"Did you get them?" He rocked back on his heels, the wind blowing his suit pants against his skinny legs.

"Hmm?"

"Did you get the exams?" he asked again.

Fuck.

"Doors were locked," I lied through my fucking teeth to my boss.

He nodded toward the doors and stuffed his hand into his pocket, pulling out a silver ring of keys. "Come on. I'll let you in, and we can talk. I have much to ask you about, seeing as you ran out of our meeting yesterday pretty quickly."

After turning off my car, I gritted my teeth and followed him through the empty parking lot toward the main building on the high school campus. Wind burned my face, the biting fall temps chillier than usual.

"Why'd you park so far away?" he asked.

He knows something.

And I didn't have any answers for him. I could lie all I wanted about why I was here, but why had I parked in the back lot, where there were no cameras? I couldn't get around *that* unless I was trying to hide something.

"Just felt like it," I said, as it was the best fucking response I could fabricate.

"Hmm ..."

When we reached the doors, he shoved the key into the lock and pushed the door opened. A single automatic light turned on in the hallway. The school looked so different at night. I stepped into the building and walked with him toward my room.

"As I was saying in our meeting, you have an astonishing student in your class," Vaughn said, stopping when we reached my classroom. "I mean, Sakura Sato is amazing, even outside the classroom. Wouldn't you say?"

I pressed my lips together, wanting to ignore him, but I couldn't help but feel off. That same eerie feeling washed over me from the last time I had spoken to him about Sakura. And I couldn't fucking shake that he was talking about more than just her studying and volunteering.

"Sakura is great," I said in as monotone of a voice as I could. "Why?"

"Smart. Pretty. Caring. She's got everything going for her, hmm?"

He wanted me to agree for some fucking reason. Had he caught us? Was this him trying to get me to admit to sleeping with one of my students and enjoying it? No, Vaughn wasn't that much of a saint. His pockets were stuffed with dirty dollar bills from the rich.

"Why?" I asked with my back turned, walking toward my desk.

"Some of these seniors ..."

I shuffled through some papers on my desk. "What about them?"

He chuckled. "I don't know how you do it."

"Do what?" I asked, not wanting him to actually find out that I didn't have any exams.

After a couple of moments of complete silence, I glanced up to find him still by the door, shaking his head.

"Ah, that's a story for another time, Callan. If you ever want to get a drink at Escape, I'll tell you about it."

Escape? One of the Redwood mob's hangouts?

"Yeah, sure," I said, stuffing some papers into a manila folder. "Sounds great."

But I'd never take this asshole up on his offer. He was too interested in Sakura, had commented on her looks, and suspected me of something. I didn't know what the fuck he was getting at, and I wasn't sure I wanted to ever find out.

18

sakura

I DIDN'T KNOW what the hell I had agreed to, but for some reason, I was now walking through aisles in Walmart and dropping things in my cart that I didn't need while Gunther—*yes, Gunther from Literature*—stood next to me.

Turning into the chip aisle, I pushed my cart to the Doritos, stared up at them, and nervously chewed on the inside of my cheek. I wished that I had just kept my window rolled up in the parking lot and decided to just go home.

But it was too late. I had been too nervous.

And now, a guy that I had barely said a few words to was grabbing chips from the top shelf.

"I, uh, wanted to ask you something," he said, setting the chips into the cart.

Fuck! Please don't ask me to go out with you. Please don't ask me to go out with you.

After tightening my hands around the cart, I walked to the end of the aisle with my gaze trained on the food in front of me. If anyone saw me out with Gunther at night alone, my life would be ruined. Rumors would spread like wildfire through Redwood.

How will Mr. Avery react once he hears them? The thought made me warm between my legs, my heart pounding. I squeezed my eyes shut and shook my head. *No, no! I can't think shit like that! He had a gun!*

"Are you okay?" Gunther asked.

I stopped in my tracks and pushed some hair off my flushed cheeks. "Yeah, sorry. Um, sure, you can ask me whatever."

He paused and flipped some longer hair off his forehead. "You okay? Really?"

"Yeah, I'm fine. Why?"

" 'Cause ..." He shrugged half-heartedly at me. "You seem nervous in Literature."

Double fuck.

Eyes widening, I looked away. "I'm totally fine. You don't have to worry."

"Is Mr. Avery—"

"Mr. Avery is great! My favorite teacher!" *Fuck, I am so nervous.* "Don't worry, really."

I didn't know what to tell him. I didn't want him to ask me anything else because I feared that I'd either blush harder than I was now or I'd completely blurt out everything that had happened during that detention.

Anxiously, I glanced around Walmart and spotted Akio, a nice senior from Redwood.

"You sure because—"

"Akio!" I shouted, waving like a maniac even though I had barely spoken to him. I pushed my cart in his direction and glanced over my shoulder at Gunther. "Sorry. Akio is my cousin. I'll, um, see you in class tomorrow."

Once I left Gunther alone in the chip aisle, I speed-walked to Akio, who stared at me quizzically.

He stood in front of the freezer of boxed pizzas with a bunch of sweets in his basket. "We're not cousins."

"Shh!" I whisper-yelled at him, peering over my shoulder to watch Gunther leave. Once he disappeared from my view, I turned back toward Akio. "Sorry, didn't mean to push that on you. I just didn't want to continue talking to him."

"It's fine."

"Long night?" I asked, glancing into his cart again at all the sweets.

"Uh ..." He scratched the back of his head. "Sorta. Long story actually."

While I didn't know Akio *that* well, he worked as an intern under Mom at the pharmacy. I didn't want him to ask me any questions about her because I didn't even want to start to answer them. It wasn't my fault that Mom was an addict.

"Well, um ... have fun with that," I said.

After he flashed me a nervous smile and scratched the back of his head—like seriously the same way any guilty main male character in all the anime that I watched did—I steered my cart toward the checkout lines.

I felt bad, walking through the store and putting everything back where I had found it, so I guessed that meant I would be buying all this food and junk that I didn't need and probably would never use.

Just as I turned the corner to the checkout, I spotted the same man from earlier at Mr. Avery's house waiting near the exit. I swallowed hard and froze, knowing that he hadn't seen me through Mr. Avery's tinted windows, but fearful that he had.

Quickly, I turned back around and walked to Akio, who still stood in the frozen pizza section. "Actually, I know that this is a stupid request, but could I shop with you until you're ready to check out? I, um ... don't feel comfortable walking outside alone."

Akio paused for a long moment, glanced down the end of the aisle just as the man passed by us—like he had spotted me and followed—and then nodded. "Sure, I don't mind. I'm almost done anyway."

My stomach twisted in knots. I couldn't wait to get out of here and go home.

Between the IUD, going home with Mr. Avery, finding his gun, and walking around Walmart with Gunther, today had been the craziest day of my life. And I only expected tomorrow would be even crazier.

19

callan

I PACED AROUND my classroom the next morning with a whiteboard marker in my hand and Sakura on my mind. Last night, I hadn't been able to think. Even after I had my hands covered in blood from working with the mob, I couldn't get her out of my fucking head.

She'd better show up today.

While she had promised not to miss class, I wasn't so sure what she'd do after spotting that gun in my glove box.

Students for the third period began flooding into the classroom. Every time the door opened, I glanced over and hoped it was Sakura. But the desks began filling with uninterested kids until there was only a minute before class.

Growling to myself, I uncapped the marker and began writing today's lesson.

Sakura was *never* late.

After glancing over my shoulder again at the unoccupied desks, I gritted my teeth. And she wasn't the only one missing from class today.

Surprise, surprise, Gunther wasn't here either.

Fucking punk.

Fifteen seconds before the late bell rang, Sakura rushed into the room, wearing a pair of reading glasses, with her hands clasped around her backpack straps. "Sorry I was almost late," she said, trying to catch her breath.

Gunther walked in after her.

I clenched my jaw and held myself together. They hadn't been doing anything together. Sakura must've been talking with a teacher or had a class in another building on campus, or maybe she had been in the restroom. *With him.*

As if that kid knew what he was doing, he smirked at me.

Averting my gaze, I glared at the whiteboard and continued writing today's lesson. Gunther was screwing around, trying to piss me off, wanting to get under my skin. That fucking brat never liked me.

"Did you find what you were looking for last night?" Gunther asked Sakura.

With the marker in my hand, I froze halfway through writing notes on the whiteboard and tensed. *Where the fuck did he see Sakura last night?* She had been with me for hours after school ended. *What have they fucking been doing together?*

"Um ... yeah, I did," Sakura responded.

After forcing myself to finish the notes, I set the marker down and walked back to my desk with my hands balled into fists by my sides. Sitting down, I cut my gaze to him and Sakura, who sat next to each other.

On the outside, I was calm. I was so fucking calm.

But inside ... I wanted to bash that kid's brains out.

Tonight, I'd find that punk kid after school and make sure he didn't lay a hand on Sakura. Fuck getting Blaise to do it. If Gunther wanted to taunt me in class, then *I* would be the one to warn him to stay away.

"Good," he said to her, leaning forward.

And I couldn't fucking handle it anymore.

"We're changing seats today," I said through gritted teeth. "Stand up."

Murmurs erupted throughout the class. We had just started the year a bit over a month ago. There was no obvious reason to switch seats, and I'd had no plans to, but I couldn't handle them together anymore.

Everyone grabbed their belongings and hurried to the walls to make space in the center. I didn't know who the fuck I would place where, but Sakura would be as far away from Gunther as I could get her.

"Sakura," I announced, knocking my knuckles against the desk closest to mine. "Here."

I walked diagonally across the room to the back and tapped the desk. "Gunther."

Gunther walked over to me and clenched his jaw. "What are you doing?"

"Sit," I growled quietly.

It was childish to be fighting with a fucking eighteen-year-old, but he needed to learn his place. This was my classroom, and he didn't get to flirt with her in front of me. He didn't even get to look at her from now on.

Sakura watched me closely as I assigned everyone a new seat, making sure she was surrounded by girls and not a guy even two seats near her. Something deep inside me wouldn't allow it.

Never again. Never fucking again.

Once I approved of the new seats, I walked back to my desk and opened my Literature book. "You should've read the chapters assigned last night. We'll begin on the next chapter. Sakura, why don't you start reading?"

After gazing at me for another second, Sakura readjusted her reading glasses, straightened herself out, and flipped to the next chapter, beginning the section. As she read, she crossed her legs, her skirt riding up.

My gaze traveled from her knee to the hem of her skirt, and I cursed.

She was fucking killing me with these outfits too.

When the bell rang through the class, all the students—who had packed up fifteen minutes ago—jumped up from their seats and hurried out of the room. I glared at Gunther lingering in the back, but he quickly disappeared out the door too.

Sakura grabbed her backpack and walked up to me.

"Whatever you're going to do to Gunther …" Sakura started, chewing on the inside of her cheek with her brows pulled together. She peeked over her shoulder at the last few students exiting the room. "Please don't hurt him."

"Why not?"

"Because," she whispered.

"Where were you last night with him?"

Her eyes widened. "What?"

"Where. Were. You. Last night? With him?"

Never in my forty fucking years had I ever been this possessive, this controlling, this toxic with Georgina. I didn't give a fuck about what she did or who she was out with, but with Sakura … I didn't want another man laying a finger on her.

Nobody would touch her.

Sakura crossed her arms. "Why do you need to know? You have a wife."

I gritted my teeth, attempting to keep my cool. "Don't play with me right now."

"Well, if you can't tell me why, then I can't tell you where we were or *what* we were doing."

A low snarl escaped my throat. I drew my tongue across my bottom teeth. "*Sakura.*"

"What I do with Gunther is none of your—"

Before I could stop myself, I shot up from my desk, wrapped my hand around her fragile throat, causing her to suck in a surprised breath, and pinned her to the whiteboard. "It is my fucking business, Sakura, because you're *mine.*"

20

sakura

HIS.

I was his.

He didn't take it back. He didn't look like he regretted a single word he had just spoken.

After placing my hand atop his that was fastened around my throat, I squeezed it gently and stared up at him. My pussy pounded in pleasure at the sound of my professor so recklessly admitting that *I* was his.

All my fears from last night had flown out the fucking window when his hand wrapped around the front of my throat and he had called me his. But I didn't want to give him that satisfaction yet. He had to promise not to hurt anyone for me first.

Just as I was about to respond, someone jiggled the doorknob. Mr. Avery dropped his hand from my throat and stepped back, cutting his glare to the door. A kid from the next period opened the door and walked into the room.

Mr. Avery gritted his teeth. "Please, wait outside, Calix."

Calix, the tall senior, grumbled and walked out of the room.

When the door closed, Mr. Avery walked back to his desk and

sat in the seat, staring up at me and curling his finger in my direction. "Come here."

I crossed my arms. "I-I'm not yours," I whispered breathily, heat gathering inside me.

"You'll do anything I ask of you, which means *you're mine*," he said. Not in a matter-of-fact or condescending tone. But as if he were stating an undeniable fact.

My mouth dried. "No, I won't."

"Sit on my desk and spread your legs."

Warmth pooled between my thighs. I pressed my knees together to ease the lingering ache and knitted my brows, desperate to hold myself together. I didn't want to give in to him so easily, especially if he planned on hurting Gunther.

I didn't like the kid, but I didn't want Mr. Avery to kill him.

After gathering all the courage I had, I shook my head. "No."

He chuckled darkly and set his lips in a scowl. "On my desk. Now. Or I won't touch your aching pussy, Sakura. I'll make you go all day without me being inside you. And by the way you keep pressing those legs together, you can't wait until tomorrow."

Glancing between him and the desk, I pursed my lips and whimpered.

This wasn't fair. After what he had done to me yesterday afternoon and the day before during detention, he knew that I needed it. He knew that I couldn't stop, that one taste wasn't enough, that I couldn't last a day without coming anymore.

"No," I pushed myself to say.

But I stood in front of him, grinding my legs together and shifting from foot to foot. My clit was aching so badly for him to touch me, the need inside me growing with every single moment he wasn't inside me.

Instead of bending me over his desk and forcing me to do whatever he wanted, he leaned back in his seat and crossed his arms over his chest, his muscles bulging through his thin dress shirt.

My gaze dropped toward his biceps. *Fuck.*

They were so big. I could only imagine him picking me up with his strong arms and doing whatever he wanted with me. My gaze slipped lower and lower to the bulge in the front of his pants. He didn't even look completely hard yet and …

And he was already huge.

"Mr. Avery," I whispered.

Yet he didn't move, just continued to stare at me with those dark, daring eyes.

"Don't do this," I whimpered, grinding my thighs harder together.

No response.

"Please …"

When he still didn't make a move to grab me, pull me forward, and punish me, I slid onto his desk in front of him and spread my legs for him, placing each of my feet on either side of his armrests. I couldn't handle it anymore. I needed him to touch me so badly.

"Touch me, please," I pleaded.

He unfolded his arms, pulled his seat closer to me, and placed his hands on either of my knees to spread them even farther apart. "That wasn't so hard, was it, Sakura?" he asked, sliding his hands up my thighs, inch by inch. "Now, where did you meet Gunther last night?"

I sucked in a sharp breath and stared at him through wide eyes, impatiently waiting for him to touch me all over, like he'd promised he would. My legs trembled, my entire body tight, breath held.

"I'm going to get it out of you either way," he said, drawing the tips of his fingers across my clit through my underwear.

My legs jerked into the air, and I whimpered, letting him do it again and again.

"I'd prefer you told me willingly."

"Mr. Avery …"

"Callan," he growled. "You call me Callan from now on when we're alone. Understand?"

"Yes."

He moved his fingers faster against my clit. "Where did you meet him?"

After pressing my lips together to hold back a moan, I gripped the edge of his desk and furrowed my brow. I didn't want anyone outside the classroom to hear me screaming his name, but the pressure was building up too quickly inside me.

"Sakura," he demanded. "N—"

Unable to handle the pressure anymore, I threw my head back. "Walmart! I drove to Walmart after I left your place last night because I ... because I couldn't go back home. Not being as flustered as I was. That's all, Callan. Now, please, don't stop."

"He didn't touch you?"

"No," I said breathlessly. "He didn't touch me."

"You'd better not let him lay a single finger on you."

"I-I ..." Pressure rose inside me, sending me so close to the edge. "I promise I won't."

"You're mine," he growled. "Say it."

"I'm yours," I cried out softly.

"Next class, you're going to wear a skirt short enough for me to peek up while I teach. No stockings. No panties. Legs spread, just like this." He continued to rub my pussy in small, torturous circles. "Bring a toy to sit on."

My eyes widened. "A ... toy?"

Massaging my clit with his thumb, he dipped two fingers into my pussy. "To stuff this hole full. I want it plunged deep in your cunt. You'll clench on it, try to hold it inside you, and hope it doesn't slip out of your pussy and drop to the floor in front of the entire class. It would be a shame for everyone to see *my* star student using a toy on herself in the middle of class."

"Such a shame," I whispered, legs trembling around him.

When he flicked my clit, I slapped a hand over my mouth and screamed out into it. Pleasure rushed through my body, and I tried desperately to stay quiet, but Mr. Avery—I mean, Callan—made that so hard for me.

Once I finally came down from my high, I pulled my hand from my mouth and focused on breathing evenly. Lifting the same thumb he had used to rub my clit, he pushed it between my lips. I sucked on it gently and stared at him, pleasure rushing through me. He gazed down at my lips and grunted.

"You're going to be a good girl for me, right, Sakura?" he asked, voice soft.

I nodded in a daze. "Only for you."

21

sakura

"WELCOME TO PLAYTHING PLEASURES. Can I help you?"

Cheeks flushing, I pulled my hat down so the man at the counter couldn't see my face and quickly walked into an aisle of dildos. "Um, no thank you," I said, hoping that he didn't recognize me.

I had driven three towns over to go to my first sex shop. I needed a toy to use for tomorrow during class, really wanting to please Mr. Avery. I wanted something almost as big as him that I could stuff up inside me and ride—even after class was over.

Walking through the aisle, I stopped at the extra-large dildos that were basically, like, twice the size of *any* human dick. They looked like they'd belong to a monster or alien or a creature from out of this world.

After deciding that I wouldn't be putting that up inside me, I stopped in front of the large dildos and pressed my thighs together. Long, thick, and with ridges. God, I wanted Callan inside me so badly right now.

I didn't know if I could wait until tomorrow to stuff this inside me and touch myself at the thought of him. I bit my lip to hold back a whimper and grabbed the biggest one as close to his size as I could find.

It looked like an actual dick with veins and ridges and even had a suction cup at the end.

Shuffling up to the register, I slid it across the counter and didn't look him in the eye as he scanned the item. After pulling out a hundred-dollar bill—because I wasn't putting this on a card—I handed it to the man.

Once he slid a bag and my change across the counter and told me to have a good day, I hurried to my car and slammed my door shut. After stuffing my new toy into my glove box, I blew out a deep breath and pulled off my hat.

———

Thirty minutes later, I sat in a booth at Mustang Ranch with a vanilla milkshake in front of me. Ichika was supposed to meet me for dinner at six tonight, and I had gotten here way too early. I just didn't want to be home when Mom finished work. She was supposed to be off early tonight.

Kicking my legs back and forth under the table, I sipped on my shake, finished the last bit of homework I had for Calculus on my laptop, and pulled off my computer glasses. After stuffing them into their case, I closed my laptop and set my phone down on top of it.

Callan drifted through my mind. I knew nothing of the man. But I sure as hell wanted to.

Because I couldn't help myself, I picked up my phone, typed *Callan Avery* into Google, and clicked on Images. After pictures of him at Redwood Academy, there were a couple of him and his wife, dated from five years ago.

Long strawberry-blonde hair, petite, bright green eyes, Georgina Harleen-Avery was perfect. Not to mention, she had curves in all the right places—breasts, hips, and even her goddamn lips. This picture pinned them as the *it* couple.

Me compared to her? Ha.

The only thing I sorta had were wide hips. My ass? Flat. My chest? Flat. My face? Not as interesting, kinda boring and average compared to hers. Why would Callan ever cheat on her with someone like me?

A guy like him could have *any* woman.

I scrolled further down the search results and spotted another picture of Callan and Georgina, pictured with Ethan Harleen—billionaire and the father of Redwood's bad boy, Blaise Harleen. My eyes widened slightly when I realized that Ethan and Georgina were related. Maybe even siblings. They both had that same money-hungry sneer.

"Looking at pictures of him?" Ichika hummed as she walked up to me, a huge grin stretched across her face.

Cheeks warming, I shoved my phone into my purse and shook my head. "No!"

"Let me see him," she teased. "Please!"

My cheeks flushed, and I shooed her away. "No! Not now. I promise, one day."

She sat down across from me and took a menu from the center of the table. "Is there a reason you don't want to tell me who it is? You know, I know, like, nobody in your grade. And I've spilled all my dirty secrets to you."

Swallowing hard, I furrowed my brow.

If I lied, she'd see right through me.

She grinned like a maniac. "There is, isn't there?! Is he, like, a bad boy or something?"

No, Ichika, he is my freaking teacher!

"Ichika, please," I whispered, glancing around. "I can't tell you here."

After she stared at me for a moment, her smile dropped. "This is *serious*, serious."

"Yes," I whispered. "It's *serious*, serious."

Ichika leaned forward and lowered her voice even more. "Is it a teacher?"

I pursed my lips and stared down at my milkshake, nerves

building up inside me. I didn't want her to tell anyone, especially my dad. Everyone would judge me for this because what I was doing was wrong.

It was all so wrong. And I hated myself for it, but I didn't want to stop.

Callan Avery was the only person to ever give me attention like this.

"Sakura," Ichika scolded me when I didn't answer. "Are you serious?"

I grabbed her hand from across the table and held it in both of mine. "Please, don't tell anyone. I know I need to stop this. I know it can't happen again. I know it's so wrong. But don't tell my dad, please."

"You both can get into so much trouble," she whispered. "What are you thinking?"

"I'm not thinking. At all! Please, don't tell anyone."

She shook her head. "I won't, but please, be careful. Tell me if anything happens, if you need me for anything. And know that, at some point, it will have to end. You can't date this guy, whoever it is."

Dropping my gaze, I stared at the table between us. I couldn't date Callan. I had known that from the very start, but ... part of me wanted to. He had become so jealous, so possessive of me, especially in class.

But we would never ever be able to be together like a normal couple.

22

callan

GUNTHER ZURN HAD another thing fucking coming to him.

I tried not to ignore him, like Sakura had requested, but the more I paced my empty house alone tonight, the angrier I became. Gunther knew he was pissing me off, and he was doing it anyway. He *continued* to spite me.

After parking my car at the skatepark, where I knew that punk would be, I tucked my gun into my waistband and gritted my teeth when I spotted him in the rearview mirror. He skated alone down a rail and stopped at the bottom of a slope.

Unable to control myself, I stormed out of the car and up to him, grabbing him by his shirt collar and shoving him against a metal fence. He dropped his board, eyes widening, and shoved me back.

"What the fuck—" When he spotted me, he smirked. "Mr. Avery."

"You need to back the fuck off Sakura," I growled.

"Why? Do you like her? Is that why you gave her detention when she did nothing?"

I gritted my teeth and took him by the collar again. "I'm not fucking playing around with you, Zurn. You're going to leave her the fuck alone. Don't follow her around. Don't talk to her at the store. Don't look at her in my class."

"She's too pretty not to stare at."

Instinctively, I balled my hand into a fist. I wanted to slam it into his face so badly.

Give him a taste of what it'd feel like if he even looked at my gir—

At Sakura.

Because she wasn't my girl. She could never be my girl. Not like that.

"Don't get me wrong; your wife is hot, but Sakura?" He whistled. "I'd fuck h—"

After whipping my gun out of my waistband, I shoved it against his abdomen. "Finish the fucking sentence, Zurn, and see what fucking happens to you."

Suddenly, Zurn's bratty mouth snapped shut. I wasn't playing around anymore.

When he didn't say anything for a few moments, I growled, shoved him back, and tucked the gun away. Gunther kicked up his skateboard, tossed it over his shoulder, then stormed out of the park, disappearing through the thick brush of trees surrounding this place.

I clenched my jaw and glared at the fence. I'd fucking hated that kid the moment he walked into my class. Nobody got to fuck Sakura. Nobody got the privilege of even *thinking* about fucking her.

After shaking my head, I turned around and scanned the skatepark to ensure that punk didn't come back. But my gaze landed on my nephew from Georgina's side, Blaise, the bratty, entitled asshole.

"What're you doing with Gunther?" Blaise called, sauntering up to me.

I cocked a brow up at him. "None of your business."

After rolling his eyes, he hopped on his board and skated down the halfpipe ramp. "Fine."

"You don't tell anyone what you saw," I said to him, stalking closer and stepping underneath the dim overhead light that illumi-nated the skatepark after dark, noticing that Blaise's eye was black and swollen. "And what the fuck happened to your eye? You get into a fight?"

He stopped his board inches from my feet and kicked it up, staring me right in the eye, almost as if he was looking for a fight. But while I had wanted to slam my fist into Gunther's annoying fucking face, I wouldn't hit Blaise. And he knew that.

"None of your business," he said through gritted teeth.

"You should be at home."

"*You* should be at home with your *lovely wife*," he said, spitting my words back at me.

We both knew that my wife—his dad's sister—was a spitting image of Blaise's father, absent from everyone's life, except her own, and didn't give a shit about anything other than how much her shoes cost.

She was an annoying fucking bitch that Blaise knew not to talk about.

Pissed off that he had brought her up, I gritted my teeth.

"What happened to Vera Rodriguez?" I asked back, remem-bering that I'd spotted them together in Blaise's car the other day.

If he wanted to piss me off, then I'd throw his love life back into his face. Stoop down to his level, which I had never done until I started sleeping with Sakura.

She brought out something ferocious in me.

"Shut your fucking mouth," Blaise growled, storming away from me.

While I wanted to go after him and piss him off more, my mind was racing a million miles a minute, and I couldn't get the thought of Sakura with Gunther out of my head. I didn't have time to fuck around with Blaise.

I needed to see her. I needed to touch her. I needed her to tell me that she was mine.

And only mine.

I didn't know if I could wait for class tomorrow.

23

sakura

AFTER DINNER WITH ICHIKA, I took a long drive around Redwood. Mom didn't have to work late tonight, which meant that she'd probably be home by now. I knew Dad didn't *love* being around her by himself, but I couldn't get myself to go home.

Instead, I drove to the beach, through the slums, and even … into the rich sector.

Down his road.

To his house.

Rain drizzled down upon the windshield. I turned on my windshield wipers and lights, glad that the sky had darkened since I'd left for dinner with Ichika. If anyone saw me here, I would be absolutely screwed.

I wanted to stop myself, to turn back, to drive away. But something kept me there.

The need to see his wife in real life. I wasn't going to stand in front of his house and peer into his windows or anything, but I wanted to see if she was home with him. Jealousy pooled inside my flesh at the mere thought of her.

What I was doing was wrong. All of it.

Yet I couldn't stop.

Parking on the side of the road across the street, I turned off my lights and pulled the key out of the ignition.

I shouldn't be here. I shouldn't be here. I shouldn't be here.

But I wanted to see her because I hoped that it would give me enough courage to stop this.

Enough to convince myself that this was wrong.

No lights were on inside the house. No cars in the driveway.

I chewed on the inside of my cheek. I should go.

A car approached mine with its left blinker flashing, and I held my breath. *Is this her?*

Instead of turning into Callan's driveway, the car slowed down, turned off its blinker, and drove closer to me. My eyes widened as I realized that it wasn't his wife or any of his ritzy neighbors, but him.

No!

Scrambling to start my car, I shoved the key into the ignition and quickly put the car in drive. I slammed my foot against the accelerator and hoped that he didn't see me. It was way too dark to see into my car, right? Especially through tinted windows like his.

With his window rolled down, he peered over at me the entire time I drove past him. I wanted to turn away, to stare at the road ahead of me, but I couldn't stop myself from looking back at him.

Nerves bubbled inside my stomach.

What is wrong with me? I shouldn't have come here! Why am I looking back at him?!

After I passed him, I glanced into the rearview mirror and spotted him turning around in his driveway and now following me. He kept his distance. But when I turned around a corner, he turned. When I drove onto the main road, he followed. And when I parked in front of the Overlook, he parked behind me.

Rain poured. I stared into my rearview mirror. He wouldn't get out of his car to see me, not in this weather. He wouldn't come over and ask what I had been doing at his house. He—

He opened his car door and stepped out into the pouring rain without an umbrella, the wet soaking through his dress shirt and making it cling to his muscles. I pressed my thighs together and thanked the Redwood gods that nobody was here tonight.

The Overlook was a popular place for people my age, but after almost drowning years ago in this very ocean, I never thought I'd come here.

Especially not with my Lit professor.

24

sakura

ONCE CALLAN REACHED MY CAR, he thrust his hands into his pockets, slightly tilted his head to the left, and stared at me. I peered up at him and rolled down my window, rain splattering into the car and onto me.

"Can I ... can I help you?" I asked.

"Get out of the car," he said between gritted teeth.

My eyes widened at his harsh tone. Was he mad? Obviously, yes. His wife could've seen me spying on her, or a neighbor could've spotted an unusual car lingering by his property. I shouldn't have gone to his neighborhood.

Why am I this freaking stupid?

"Sakura," he growled. "Out. Now."

After quickly shutting off the car, I unclasped my seat belt and scrambled out of the car. Rain poured down upon us and dripped off his wet hair. He shoved me up against my car and snatched my chin in his large hand.

"I'm sorry," I whispered. "I shouldn't have gone to your—"

Before I could get out another word, he buried his head into my neck and sucked on my sensitive skin. I inhaled sharply and plastered myself against my car door.

"You're not angry?"

"Angry?" he repeated, hands all over my body. "The fuck would I be angry for?"

"B-because …"

He leaned down, wrapped his strong arms around my knees, and picked me up into the air. After he walked to the front of my car, he set me down on the hood and moved his mouth down my chest, his hand slipping underneath my skirt.

For a moment, I thought he'd pull out his cock to fuck me, but instead, he ripped off my panties and buried his face between my legs. I yipped at the sudden pressure between them, nobody ever having touched me like this.

"C-Callan!" I whisper-yelled. "What are you doing?!"

"Relax, baby," he murmured against my cunt, making me clench.

Baby? Warmth exploded through my core, and I whimpered. *Did he just call me baby?*

He peppered kisses up and down my pussy lips, circled around my pounding clit, then up my stomach. I watched his lips move against me, breath catching in my throat. I wanted his lips on mine, his tongue sinking deep into my mouth.

All this time together, and he hadn't kissed me yet.

Kissing was intimate—too intimate for a couple of measly hookups. Maybe he thought if he kissed me, then things would change, or if he kissed me, then it wouldn't be the same between us. I didn't know, but I wanted to find out what would happen if he did.

My lips ached for his to be on mine.

"Please," I whispered, wanting to finish with *kiss me,* but unable to say the words.

When his lips found my clit again, he really began flicking it in circles. Not stopping. Pushing me closer and closer to the edge. Pressure rose up inside me, my pussy aching to be filled with his cock.

"We're out in public," I whispered, pushing on his head between my legs.

It wasn't that I wanted him to stop, but the pressure was rising faster than it ever had in my core, building me up higher and higher. I feared that if he didn't stop now, he'd tip me over the edge with just his mouth, and I'd scream out his name in pleasure.

"So indecisive tonight," he murmured, shoving two thick fingers inside me. He pumped them in and gently curled them around my G-spot on the way out. "Pleading for me, then pushing me away. Tell me what you want, baby."

When he flicked my clit again, I held my breath and tensed. So close …

"Sakura …" he hummed, looking up at me.

"Don't stop," I begged. "Please."

He sucked my swollen clit between his lips. "Has anyone ever eaten you out before?"

"N-no."

"I'm your first everything then?"

"Yes," I whispered, legs jerking into the air. "You are."

He had taught me how to give a blow job, eaten my pussy, and stolen my virginity.

But he hadn't kissed me. Yet.

"Good," he growled, the sound vibrating my clit. "And I'll be the only one."

I pressed my hand over my mouth to hold back my moans before I … before I …

Callan pinched my nipple through my soaked blouse, and I fucking lost it. Back arching hard, I pressed my hips up and against his mouth and moaned out his name through the rain. Wave after wave of pleasure crashed over me.

When he finally pulled away, I tugged my thighs together and whimpered softly. The orgasm was so much more intense than my others with him so far, the feeling of him willingly giving me pleasure without taking any for his own …

God, it did something to me.

Callan wrapped his hand around my wrist and tugged me to my feet, twirling me around and pressing my front side against my wet car. Pressing himself against my backside, Callan took a fistful of my hair and pulled it to the side to give himself better access to my neck. He drew his nose up the column of my throat, his stubble tickling my skin.

I tightened and dug my fingers into the hood of the car until they whitened. His lips moved up and down my neck, leaving sloppy, wet kisses all over. When he kissed my jaw, I sucked in a deep breath and clenched.

God, I need him to kiss me.

But I didn't have the courage to ask or to turn my head and kiss him myself.

If I made it weird, he might not want to do this anymore. And that couldn't happen.

I had become obsessed, needy, dependent on him being inside me.

I didn't care about the consequences, and part of me didn't even feel bad.

Breathing heavily, he fumbled around with his zipper and pulled himself out of his pants. I arched my back and ground my wet pussy against the head of his cock, desperate for him to be inside me again.

"Please," I breathed. "More. Give me more. I need more."

He rubbed the head of his cock between my pussy lips, then plunged himself inside me. With each and every thrust, he shoved me up against the car and sucked on the column of my neck, hard enough to leave a bruise.

"Callan," I breathed out. "Nobody can know about this."

But he didn't stop sucking on my sensitive skin, which only pushed me closer to the edge. I dug my fingers into the car and tilted my head to give him better access. Moans and whimpers escaped my mouth.

After grabbing a fistful of my hair again, he tugged it back and trailed his nose to my ear, his lips brushing against it. "You're my good fucking girl, Sakura. I will do what I want with you, what I want to you, and what I want for you. And right now … I want you to come."

Almost on command, I exploded all over him.

25

callan

"WOULD you happen to have an extra shirt?" Sakura asked, chewing on her inner lip and staring into her car. "I don't really want to drive home in soaked clothes. I don't have any extras here. I really should do that ..." Her voice quieted toward the end, as if she was talking to herself.

Long-sleeved shirt clinging to her braless body, Sakura crossed her arms and shivered in the rain. I tore my gaze away from her—because if I didn't, I would probably shove her up against the car again and take her—and took her hand.

When I reached my car, I opened the back door. "Get in."

"But I'm all wet."

"Get in, Sakura. You're freezing. I have a shirt in my trunk."

After Sakura finally shuffled into the car, I shut the door, retrieved an extra shirt of mine from the trunk, and slid into the car from the other side. She wriggled out of her long-sleeved shirt, her nipples hard from the cold, and pulled my large shirt over her head. I tore off my shirt because it was soaked through, too, and left the pants because I didn't have a spare.

"Thank you," she said, inhaling deeply and shutting her eyes. "This is so much better."

I took her wet shirt and tossed it into the front passenger seat so the water wouldn't soak through my books. I had a mess of literature back here that I had been meaning to bring into the house, but I hadn't wanted Georgina to comment on them.

All the books we had in the home library were for show. She hadn't read any of them, and I doubted that she ever would. But that bitch always had to sneer at my personal books, had to comment on them somehow.

"You have so many books," Sakura said, picking up one. "You have Kayleigh Stone?! She's my favorite!"

"Is she now?" I sprawled my arm across the back of the seat and smiled softly. "I read a lot."

She handed it to me. "Read me something."

My eyes widened. "You want me to read you this?"

She turned her body toward me and laid her head against the headrest, cheeks rounding. "Read it, then do that cute little analyzing thing you do after every paragraph in school."

Warmth exploded through my chest.

Sakura thought it was ... *cute*?

Georgina would laugh in my face if she saw me do such a thing.

"I don't know if you want me to read you this book," I said, chuckling. "This is a romance book that I—"

"A romance book?!" Sakura giggled, placing her hand against her heart. "Mr. Avery—the most prolific, well-spoken reader at Redwood—likes smut?! I have never heard of such a thing!"

I cut my gaze to her, lips curled into a small smile. "It's for my sister's daughter."

The more she giggled to herself, the faster my heart raced.

She gently pushed on my arm. "It's okay. You can admit it, Callan. But which do you enjoy most? The ones filled with filthy smut or the meet-cute romances that leave you with butterflies?"

"Neither," I said. "Because all romance books end happily."

A decade and a half ago, I'd fucking believed in love. Now? That thought was laughable.

"You don't believe in romance and love?" she asked, suddenly quiet.

"I believe in love, but not everyone's story ends in smiles. Sometimes, it's just fucking …" I sucked in a deep breath and stared emptily at my Literature student sitting in the backseat of my car, dressed in my T-shirt, and thought of how empty my life had been.

How fucking *sad* my life had been.

I'd resorted to sleeping with a student to feel something, and, fuck … I felt more than I ever should've. And deep down, I knew that I would never be able to truly have her the way I wanted. We would always be sneaking around, always a secret.

"Sometimes, you're not meant to be happy," I whispered.

Sakura stared at me for a few moments, then dropped her gaze. "You're right."

We sat in the back of my car, listening to the rain patter against the roof. I peered over at her and rested the side of my head against the headrest, my breath steadying. This silence wasn't heated silence, like when I was with Georgina.

She gazed at me and mirrored my pose, head resting gently against the seat. My textbooks for teaching and fiction books that I read in my free time lay at our feet. She glanced down at them again and chewed on the inside of her cheek.

"You should get home before your wife finds you out here with me," she whispered.

A low sigh escaped my lips. I didn't want to think about her tonight.

"Don't speak of her," I said.

"We shouldn't be doing this, and you know it."

Even while she was out of the country and sleeping with a handful of French men, Georgina was still fucking up my life. She had her claws so deep into me that I couldn't shake her off. Now, Sakura was the one speaking of her.

I balled my hands into fists. "You're the one who showed up at my house tonight."

Unable to look me in the eye anymore, she turned her head away and stared out the window. "I know," she whispered, staying quiet for a few moments. "It was a mistake."

A mistake?

We'd had made too many of those for me to care anymore.

"It wasn't a mistake," I said.

If Sakura and I were a mistake, then Georgina had made hundreds of mistakes since I'd married her a decade and a half ago. It wasn't a mistake. It was a decision. I didn't give a shit what Sakura thought of my non-fucking-existent relationship I had with my wife.

Sakura was now *mine*. Even if we had to be a secret.

"I can't do this anymore," she said, shaking her head and pursing her lips.

But nobody had ever shown me the attention that she did and made me feel wanted. She didn't get to choose if she could or couldn't do this anymore.

"We need to stop."

"No," I growled. "You're mine."

"You have a wife."

I gritted my teeth. "She means nothing to me."

"I bet that's what you'd tell her about me, if she found out about us," she said.

"That's not true."

"Yes, it is. If Georgina—"

I seized her chin and pulled her closer, raging on the inside. "Don't say her fucking name. I hate that bitch, Sakura. She does nothing but—" I stopped myself before I could tell her what my wife had done to me all these years.

All the fucking abuse I had gone through with her. All the late nights, wondering where she had gone when we first married. All the early mornings, hoping that she wouldn't send her father after me for making her cry when I threatened divorce.

It made me feel like less of a man, weak.

"Fucking forget it," I said between gritted teeth.

I hated myself for everything that Georgina had put me through. The emotional abuse, the cheating, the not giving a shit about me …

I didn't want to think about her. Ever.

When I was with Sakura, I didn't have to think about fucking anything. I didn't have to put up the facade of a happily married man, like I had to at work, in front of colleagues, family, and friends. Because truthfully, I was a miserable asshole who wished he'd never met Georgina.

With Sakura though … I could read and teach literature, do what I loved without the constant shaming and bashing. I didn't have to pretend like I cared, didn't have to feel weak for once in my fucking life.

"Please," I whispered, voice softening. "I don't want to think about her when I'm with you."

Eyes widening, she gulped and nodded. "Okay. I'm sorry."

Thunder rumbled above us. And I found myself staring down at her lips as she spoke, then back up into her eyes, heart pounding inside my chest. She sucked in a sharp breath and glanced down at my lips, furrowing her brow.

Gently, I released her chin, trailed my hand up her jaw, and sank my hand into her hair. I brushed the pad of my thumb against her cheekbone and cursed myself for these feelings that I couldn't control anymore.

Her breath hitched as she stared up at me through the most curious, biggest eyes I had ever seen, her fingers resting on my chest. When she glanced down at my lips again, I pulled her toward me and kissed her.

26

sakura

I GENTLY LAID my hands upon Callan's wet chest and moaned softly against his mouth, warmth exploding through my body. He sucked my bottom lip between his teeth and slipped his tongue between my lips.

Pressing my thighs together, I moved closer to him and found myself crawling into his lap. I straddled his waist and sat on his thighs, taking his face in both of my hands. While I had never kissed anyone and feared that I was doing it all wrong, Callan continued to kiss me.

"God, Sakura," he groaned into the kiss.

My heart pounded as my breathing became more ragged. I wanted to kiss him forever.

He placed his hands on my hips and curled his fingers against my waist, deepening the kiss even more. His mouth moved hungrily against mine. And what had started as a simple brush of our lips turned into something more.

This wasn't just a kiss.

This was my first kiss, my first taste of him.

Callan had been my first everything. I just hoped he wouldn't be my first heartbreak too.

After a few more moments, I pulled away to catch my breath and rested my forehead against his. My chest heaved up and down. I dropped my hands to his muscular shoulders and smiled softly, a giggle bubbling up in the back of my throat.

What we had was physical, but it felt like … more.

Our heavy breaths filled the car. Callan closed his eyes softly, and they stayed closed, his fingers still digging into my waist. He drew his nose up mine until our lips met again, but even gentler this time.

"Sakura," he murmured.

I pulled away slightly and cupped his chin in my hand, lifting it so I could gaze into his eyes. Lightness fluttered in my stomach, and I wondered how it'd feel to be with him as an item. Not just … like this.

Would the sex still be the same? What about his kiss? His touch?

He lifted his head so he stared right up at me, a soft and almost-vulnerable expression on his face, one that I had never seen before. No stress lines. No angry, furrowed brow. No disappointment.

Ease. Peace. Serenity.

While I had made him look up at me, the moment I stared into those deep eyes, I froze. I didn't want to say the wrong thing and fuck this all up, nor did I want to make him regret kissing me. Right here, right now … it was the most I'd felt alive.

"You look so calm," I whispered, gliding my fingers across his forehead to push his hair off his face.

Staring up at me, he followed my gaze with his eyes. And somehow, his expression softened even more. "I am," he said, pulling my waist closer to him so our bodies were flush together. "I don't get many nights like this."

"What? Sitting in the back of your car at the Overlook?"

He chuckled. "No, Sakura. Without constant nagging, screaming, shouting. This is nice."

Screaming? Shouting?

Callan had only raised his voice to the class a couple of times. I couldn't imagine him yelling at anyone. But maybe ... he was talking about his wife doing that to him.

Is that why he has been sneaking around with me? Has she hurt him?

"I'm sorry," I whispered, not wanting him to become upset.

I didn't even want him *thinking* about her.

When he didn't respond, I sat back against his thighs and gazed out the window.

Always ruining things, Sakura.

Rain pounded against the windshield, lightning shooting through the sky. I didn't want to go, but it was getting late.

"I should get going," I whispered.

He tightened his grip on me slightly, then looked over my shoulder at the dash. "It's late."

But as I reached for the door handle, he stopped me and sat me on the seat beside him. He popped his trunk and scurried back to it, rummaging around in the rain. A moment later, he opened an umbrella, then my door.

Quietly, he walked me back to my car, holding an umbrella over my head and letting himself get soaked yet again.

After he opened my car door, I slipped into the driver's seat and smiled up at him. "Thank you."

He nodded, then held out his hand. "Give me your phone."

I slipped my phone into his hand and watched him type in his number.

He handed it back to me. "See you at school, Sakura."

My smile turned into a full-on grin that I couldn't hide. "Bye."

Once he shut the door and walked back to his car, I started the engine and pulled off the curb, heading in the direction of home. Thoughts were racing through my mind, my stomach fluttering with all sorts of giddy emotions.

When I reached a stoplight, I hummed to myself and glanced out the driver's window, lost in my own little world. A motorcycle pulled up next to me, and Kai Koh—a member of Redwood's most cutthroat gang—looked over at me and nodded.

Yes, nodded.

My gaze drifted from him to the girl sitting on the back of his bike. Her arms were tight around his waist, her coiled brown hair emerging from the back of a black helmet. She leaned closer to him to say something, and then the light turned green.

They whizzed ahead of me on the bike, but I didn't mind.

All I could think about was Mr. Callan Avery. My Literature professor.

I turned onto my street and drove toward the house. I didn't know how the hell I'd get inside with my hair and skirt soaked while wearing a shirt that my parents had never even seen before, but I'd have to find some sort of excuse.

After I turned off my car, I sat inside it and just smiled. I wished I had a best friend—besides Ichika—who I could talk to about this. I had so much to gush about, so many feelings to confess.

Callan Avery kissed me tonight. He kissed me!

And not the sorta heat-of-the-moment kiss, but softly and slowly.

Like that little moment had meant something to him.

27

callan

I NEEDED to get rid of Georgina.

After stripping my wet clothes and replacing them with new ones, I paced around my house and ran a hand through my wet hair, thinking about the way Sakura's lips had felt against mine. All of this was only supposed to be physical; I was never supposed to kiss her. She was my fucking student.

But I couldn't help myself.

I couldn't even fucking think straight when I was with her.

Her pure innocence the night I had given her detention. Her soft lips against mine in the backseat of my car. The way she had fucking giggled at the cheesy romance book, stuffed away with my literature books.

God, it was unreal.

Two headlights glimmered through the window and into the front room. A car drove up the driveway, and I stopped, wondering if it was Sakura back for more.

Part of me didn't even believe that any of this had happened. I feared I had hallucinated it all to get through the rest of my life with Georgina.

What if I walk into school tomorrow and it is all gone? What if Sakura doesn't look up at me in adoration anymore, but in fascination for the Literature material?

A low growl escaped my lips. I would fucking hate myself if that happened.

Someone knocked on my front door. I glanced over at the side table, where I had buried a gun in one of the drawers. If it was the mob, they wouldn't knock; they would barge right in. I should be fine.

When I pulled the door open, I sighed. Maybe I needed that gun after all.

"Callan," Jett Harleen said, placing a wrinkled hand on my shoulder and walking right into the house.

It was after ten at night on a weeknight, and here he was … now inside my house without a care in the fucking world.

"What're you doing here?" I asked, much ruder than I'd meant to.

But I'd just had the night of my life, and he had to come to my house and ruin it all. I didn't need to be reminded of the constant pressure to be the perfect husband and let Jett Harleen remind me of why I couldn't step out of line.

"Wanted to drop by to see how you and my daughter are doing."

Bullshit.

"Georgina is in Paris by herself," I said dryly.

And hopefully, one of the random men that she hooked up with would kill that bitch so I didn't have to get my hands dirty. I'd gladly kill her myself, if it meant I could be with Sakura and I didn't have to worry about the mob offing me.

"My son is in Europe too."

Oh great, so they're both cheating on their spouses together. How fucking fun. He should go, too, and make it a family affair. That would really be the cherry on Redwood's corrupt cake.

"That's great," I said, turning away from him and walking to the kitchen. "Drink?"

"I'll have a glass of whiskey," he said, following me.

I gritted my teeth and continued to the bar, wishing he hadn't even come over. But when Jett had a couple of drinks in him, he got straight to the fucking point. He had come here for a reason, and I didn't want to drag this out.

After pouring us each a glass—because I wouldn't be able to get through a conversation with him without one—I set his on the table and sat across from him. The bitter alcohol slid down the back of my throat, dry as hell.

"How are you and my daughter doing?" he asked.

"Couldn't be better," I lied. "She asked me to go to Paris with her, but I've been busy."

"With that job of yours."

"Yes, with teaching."

He knocked back his drink. "My daughter wants you to quit."

Fuck.

She fucking had to tell her daddy. She couldn't let me have this one fucking thing.

I balled my hand into a tight fist and stared blankly at the table. I fucking hated that bitch more and more every single day. She was free to do whatever the hell she wanted—and she did—but she hadn't been able to take this away from me.

Until now.

"What do you say?" Jett asked, cheeks reddening from the whiskey.

I say that it's not fucking happening.

"I'll have to think about it," I lied.

He leaned forward and chuckled. "Don't think too hard."

The last time we'd had a conversation like this with just me and him, he had convinced me to marry his daughter for an obscene amount of money. And a poor kid like me couldn't pass up on his offer. Even if I had tried, he threatened that he would off me. Anything to make his daughter happy.

But not this time.

No amount of money would convince me to leave my job in the

middle of Sakura's senior year. No amount of money would take her away from me. Not now. Not after I knew what her mouth felt like against mine, how she felt while sitting in my lap, giggling.

"Are you still making Georgina happy?" Jett asked.

I plastered that fake smile I'd perfected over the years onto my face. "Of course."

Neither of us was happy anymore, and I didn't know why Georgina hadn't divorced me already. We didn't have any kids or any pets. We were the damn definition of *no strings attached*, except we didn't have sex anymore. But she still had some sick fantasy of us together in her head.

"Good," he said, placing the glass down on the side table. "I hope it stays that way."

And I hope you get hit by a fucking car on the way home.

"Don't worry about that," I said, lying straight through my teeth and walking him to the front door so he would get the fuck out of here and stop threatening me just because I wouldn't quit my job.

In order to get rid of Georgina, I would have to dispose of her father first.

I needed to figure out a way. Something.

Anything to get out of this fucking family.

Jett walked out the front door to head back to his car.

"Jett," I called before he shut the door.

That asshole glanced over his shoulder with a wide smile on his aging face. He had once been the man all the girls threw themselves at for his looks. Now, he was just some old guy with a saggy dick.

"Nobody has called me that in ages," he said, smiling. "What is it?"

"You wanna get drinks Saturday night at Escape?"

"Is that the mob place?"

Look at him. Playing dumb. Like he hasn't hung the mob over my head for decades now.

"The one and only," I said, flashing him the smile that had won over his daughter years ago.

After a moment of hesitation, he nodded. "I'll be there at eight," he called over his shoulder, walking down the sidewalk.

28

sakura

FUCK! *I am going to be late to class!*

The next day, I hurried into a restroom stall, slammed the door shut, and pulled out the dildo from my backpack that I had bought last night. No way in hell would I put that thing inside me *during* Literature, so I had to do it now and try to walk normally into class.

Yanking up my skirt a few inches, I squatted down and placed the head against my entrance. After pushing on it and failing to shove it inside me, I wiped off some sweat from my forehead and let a wad of my spit fall onto the rubbery head of the dildo.

If anyone found out about this, I'd go straight to hell.

Right before I tried sliding it into me again, my phone buzzed. A text from Mr. Avery.

Callan: Don't be late, Sakura.

"Fuck," I whisper-yelled to myself, moving the head of the dildo back and forth against my entrance to wet it. After a moment, I stopped and slowly slid the first inch into me at this awkward-as-hell angle.

Once I forced myself to relax, I slid another inch inside myself and whimpered. How the hell would I do this the entire class? There was no way I'd be able to walk straight, never mind think clearly during Callan's class.

After sliding the rest of it up inside me, I pressed my thighs together and clenched so it wouldn't fall out of me while I walked down the hallway. The bell rang throughout the halls, and I cursed at myself.

I zipped up my backpack and scurried out of the restroom, limping so stupidly to Callan's class. I couldn't believe that I was actually doing this, but I had spent the money buying that toy, and I wanted to tease him today. After that kiss last night ... I'd do anything for him.

The halls were empty, and I squeezed my eyes shut when I reached his door.

God, I am going to hell.

When I pushed the door open, every single student looked over at me. Callan sat at his desk, lips curled into a small smirk.

"Sakura, you finally decided to join us," he taunted. "Why don't you have a seat?"

"Y-yes," I whispered. "Sorry for being late."

Trying to be as inconspicuous as possible, I scurried to my desk with my legs pressed tightly together. Mr. Avery's smirk widened even more.

"Are you okay?" he asked. "It looks like you're limping."

Once I finally collapsed into my seat, I cut my glare to him. "Just a pulled muscle."

Callan hummed to himself and dropped his gaze briefly to my skirt. I sucked in a breath and hoped nobody was watching, especially Gunther, as I pulled the fabric a couple of inches up my thighs to give him a better view.

I wanted him to see what I would do for him, how far I'd actually go.

No stockings. No panties. Just as he had asked.

After drawing his tongue across his teeth, he clenched his jaw and tore his gaze away to address the class. But by the way he kept taking peeks over at me, he had seen everything. He enjoyed it. He wanted more.

So, I curled my feet around the legs of my chair, spreading my legs wider.

He kept his gaze focused on the class and gulped. Hard.

I pulled my skirt up another inch. I'd bet his cock was throbbing inside his suit pants, bulging against the material. That was why he wasn't standing up in front of the class to teach, like he usually did.

Wetness pooled between my legs, and I clenched hard around the toy.

"Finish up the chapter," Callan started. "You have an essay due next Friday on the material. You can"—he dropped his gaze to my pussy, eyes lingering longer than they should've—"start working on it today. No partners. Work in silence."

My eyes widened. *Silence?!*

Today, I'd expected that he'd teach class and be up front, his booming voice muffling the sounds of my wet pussy stuffed with this toy. If we were all silent …

Damn it. I could already start to feel the toy slipping out of me.

I clenched harder to keep it still, but my pussy was too wet.

So, I opened my computer and hoped to distract myself.

An text popped up on my screen.

Callan: Having some trouble, Miss Sato?

Another inch slipped out, and I tightened even harder. I stared at the text, then peered up at him. This class was going to be way too long. Even if I tried to readjust it, someone might see. I either had to take a chance or … risk it falling out.

When I went to reach under my desk, another text popped up.

Callan: No touching.

Breath hitching, I typed a one-sentence text back.

Me: Callan, please!!!

Me: It's going to fall out!

The more I begged, the wider his smirk became. He stared at me from his desk, watching me with those sinful, dark eyes. I'd bet he was hard right now, watching me desperately clench my pussy to keep this damn toy inside me.

Callan: Clench.

Me: I'm trying!

Callan: Try harder.

Me: I can't! Please, I'm too wet.

When he read my last message, his eyes darkened, and he readjusted himself underneath his desk. I wished so badly that I could crawl underneath and suck him off until he was coming down my throat.

Callan: How easily do you think I'd slide into you while your little toy was plunged deep in your cunt? Do you want to be stretched out tonight, Sakura? Fucked until you really can't walk tomorrow?

After biting my lip to hold back a whimper, I clutched the edge of my desk and closed my eyes. *Fuck!* My pussy got even wetter, pulsing over and over on the huge toy inside it. When I reopened my eyes, I forced myself to type another message.

If he didn't stop playing around, it really would fall out of me.

Me: Please, let me readjust it.

Callan: No.

Another inch slipped out, and I had to reach between my legs.

Callan: If you even touch your toy, you don't get my dick tonight.

I snapped my gaze back to him and widened my eyes. *Why is he torturing me?!*

Another ten minutes—*yes, ten freaking minutes*—passed. I squirmed on my seat, sweat dripping down my back and my walls clenched hard on the inch of the toy left inside me. It was going to fall out. Right now. I didn't have much time left.

"You're free to go," Callan announced to the class, glancing down at the toy. "Sakura, please, stay behind."

Everyone stood and dumped their books into their backpack. I squirmed in my seat and pressed my thighs together, nervously watching students walk to the front of the class. Mr. Avery headed to the door, his bulge throbbing against his suit pants, and ushered the students out.

As soon as the last person left the classroom, he locked the door. I clutched the edges of my desk until my knuckles turned white and felt the last inch slip out of my pussy with a pop. It landed on the ground and practically suctioned itself to the tiles, sticking straight up and covered in my juices.

"Callan, please," I breathed heavily. "I can't do that again."

"Sakura," he murmured, taking my chin in his large, callous hand and lifting it.

I stood next to him. He peered down at the toy at our feet.

"How wet is your pussy for me right now? By the looks of your toy, you're soaked."

"Callan—"

"Answer me."

I tugged his free hand between my legs and let him see for himself. He clenched his jaw and grunted, his fingers sliding between my pussy lips and his tongue dragging across his lower lip, as if he was hungry.

He looked down between us. "Look what you've done to me."

Heat gathered inside my core as I gazed at his cock, pressed against his pants. God, he was so freaking big. I wanted him inside me right now.

"You know you're going to have to take care of it now, Sakura." He nodded down to my toy on the ground, sticking straight up. "Bounce on your toy until you come," he ordered, "while you take my dick in your throat."

My eyes widened. "Wh-what? Right here?"

"Right here, Sakura."

When he released my chin, I sucked in a sharp breath. I squatted down until the head of the toy grazed against my hole, my skirt bunching up to the top of my thighs. Staring up at him, I lowered myself even further and stretched my pussy out on it, whining softly.

Callan stepped closer to me and unbuckled his belt, then undid his button and zipper. His cock sprang out of his pants—thick, hard, and veiny. I tightened on the toy and bounced up and down on it, opening my mouth for his dick.

Once he slipped his head into my mouth, I grabbed his hands to help myself bounce up and down and slowly slid my mouth around more of his dick. Only a few inches deep, I gagged and pulled back.

"Come on, Sakura. You're better than that."

Not wanting to mess up again, I took him into my mouth once more and forced myself to suck every last inch of him. My pussy tightened around the toy. When I reached his base, I pressed my lips against his hips and stared up at him through watery eyes.

I gagged again. Then again. Then again. But I didn't pull away.

Spit and drool rolled down my chin and dripped onto the tiled floor. I bounced up and down on the toy.

He released one of my hands. "Slap your clit and come for me— now, Miss Sato."

I dropped my hand between my legs, gripped his tighter to hold myself up, then smacked my clit hard. Pleasure surged through my body, an orgasm ripping through me. Callan grabbed both my arms and lifted me into the air, then set me on his desk to finish riding out my orgasm.

He pulled the toy out of my pussy and lined himself up at my entrance.

"Open up," Callan said, holding the toy by its base and placing the head at the tip of my lips. When I opened, he slid it into me, inch by inch. "We have to train your throat so you don't gag on my cock anymore."

Halfway, I gagged. He slipped another few inches between my lips and down my throat, making me gag again. It was so big, but not as big as he was.

"It should slide down your throat without a problem. Understand?"

I nodded at him, hot tears building in my eyes as I took it. He pushed it even deeper until the base met my lips. He wrapped his other hand around the front of my throat and squeezed gently. I swallowed around the toy.

"Good girl," he praised. He took my hand and placed it on the base of the toy. "Now, fuck your throat with it."

Wanting to please him, I seized the toy and moved it in and out of my throat, slowly at first. But when he started pounding hard into my pussy, I thrust the toy as quickly as his cock thrust inside me.

A low groan escaped his lips. He rested his hand over mine, pressed the toy deeper into my mouth, and pushed some strands of hair off my face with his other hand.

"Listen to me very closely, Sakura. This is the closest that you'll ever be to having another man inside you."

My walls clung on to every inch of his cock sliding in and out of me. I sucked on the toy and stared up at him with eyes wide, hazily nodding. Heat rushed to my core and exploded throughout my body.

"Nobody will ever touch you the way I do."

I whimpered on the toy, about to tip over the edge again.

"And you won't even *think* of another man," Callan said, pumping harder. "Ever."

Slobber rolled down my chin, and I shook my head.

"You're mine." He pulled the toy out of my mouth, strands of spit hanging from it. "Say it."

"I'm yours," I breathed heavily, chest rising and falling. "All yours, Callan. All the time."

After setting the toy on his desk next to us, he snatched my chin in his large hand and pulled me toward him to kiss me hard on the lips. Pleasure surged through my body, and I moaned into his mouth, my pussy pulsing around him as an orgasm ripped through me.

Once he finally pulled out of me, his cock smacked against his thigh. He tugged me in for one last lingering kiss, then ironed out my skirt with his hand. His cum dripped down my thighs.

"Meet me back here for lunch today."

29

callan

"WHERE THE HELL ARE THEY?" I mumbled to myself on my break period before lunch. I walked up and down the grocery aisles of Stop and Shop, the closest grocery store to Redwood Academy, to pick up lunch.

"Can I help you find something?" a college-aged brunette asked, twirling her finger around a strand of her hair.

I suppressed an eye roll and gazed down the aisle. "Pickle-flavored chips?"

"Follow me!"

"Can you just tell me where they are?" I asked, wanting to get back to class before Sakura made it there.

If Principal Vaughn caught her standing out in the hallway during lunch, he'd be talking shit to me about her.

And after this morning's class, I didn't want *anyone* talking to or about Sakura.

She was mine.

"Right this way." When she turned around, I ran a hand over my face and followed her down the aisle. She stopped in front of a selection of chips and grabbed a green bag. "Pickle-flavored chips, just for you."

"Thanks," I said, twirling on my heel.

She grabbed my wrist. "I didn't catch—"

"Get your damn hands off me," I growled, not looking back once while heading toward the prepared food. I grabbed two containers, in case Sakura didn't have anything, and walked to the checkout line.

After scanning my items, I hopped into my car and headed back to the school. Once I parked, I grabbed my paper bag, filled with food, and started for the side entrance. I did not want to run into Principal Vaughn on my way over because he'd ask too many fucking questions.

What'd you buy? Why'd you leave the school grounds? You're going to eat two meals?

Grumbling to myself, I slipped into the building and walked through the empty halls to the staircase to head up to my classroom. Whistling echoed through the corridor, and one of the gym teachers nodded at me.

I pushed through the doors to the staircase and took two stairs at a time. When I reached the top, I sighed through my nose and headed to the classroom. I wanted to be out of these halls before the bell rang and the students flooded into the hallways.

Once I made it to my classroom, I shifted the paper bag into my left hand and opened the door. Inside my damn classroom was Blaise Harleen—the fucking punk—and Vera Rodriguez, who sat on my desk, both their cheeks flushed.

I arched a brow at Blaise. "What the fuck are you doing here?"

Vera scooted behind Blaise and stared at me in fear, as if I'd send her to the principal. And while I didn't like Blaise, I didn't want to get into it with his father and then Jett. I didn't want him making another unannounced trip to my house in the middle of the night.

"Just leaving," Blaise said, nudging Vera toward the door.

Vera shuffled out of the room and nearly sprinted down the

hallway toward the library, but I caught Blaise by the shoulder and yanked him back.

"We need to have a fucking talk," I said between gritted teeth.

"What do you want?" he asked, tossing his backpack over his shoulder and grabbing his skateboard off the ground. He jerked himself away from me and headed toward the door again. "I don't have time. I gotta get to class."

I grabbed his shoulder again and shoved him back. "Tell me you didn't fuck that girl in my class."

Blaise stopped walking and rolled his eyes. "Come on, Avery. It's not like you haven't fucked anyone in here before. I know Aunt Georgie isn't sucking your dick. She's out with her girlfriends every night, isn't she?"

Blaise was trying to get underneath my skin, and it was working.

I clenched my jaw and shoved him away. "You could've used any other fucking classroom, Blaise. Don't use mine next time, or I'll write you up and get you suspended."

His eyes widened, and then he smirked.

"No shit. You have fucked someone in here, haven't you?" he asked.

God, I hate this kid more and more by the fucking day. All the Harleens kill me.

He ambled around the room and shook his head, chuckling. "But who could it be? Definitely not any of the cheerleaders. I mean, not that you couldn't score them, but they're not really your type, just like Georgina isn't."

I gritted my teeth and placed my grocery bag down. "Get out of my fucking classroom."

"But I thought you wanted to talk," he taunted. "It's not Nicole or Jasmine or Aiza. Couldn't be Juana. She's probably your type but way too loud. And her voice ..." He scrunched his nose. "Too fucking annoying."

"Out. Now."

Suddenly, someone knocked on my door. I tensed and glanced over, my jaw clenched. A moment later, Sakura peered into the classroom with her hair still in those braided pigtails and a huge grin on her face.

"Calla—" she started, but then spotted Blaise in the back of the classroom. Her cheeks flushed red, and she quickly looked away and stood up straight. "I-I mean, Mr. Avery, you said that you wanted me to meet with you during lunch about an assignment."

After Blaise eyed me, he curled his lips into a smirk and sauntered to the door. "Would've never guessed, Avery. Is that why you were at the skatepark last night? Needed to take care of"—he glanced at Sakura, who quickly averted her gaze—"someone?"

Fucking Blaise.

I didn't want him to scare her away, and I definitely *didn't* need rumors about Sakura and me. Especially not when Jett and Georgina were still alive and thriving, apparently.

I drew my tongue across my teeth. "Sakura, give us a minute."

Sakura quickly scurried out of the classroom, keeping her head down the entire time.

When the door closed, I grabbed Blaise by the collar and shoved him against the wall. "If you speak a fucking word about this to anyone, I will fucking kill you. You understand?"

Blaise tilted his head—the same way his father and grandfather did when they were about to make a god-awful offer to me. "If you don't mention anything about Vera to Redwood, then your secret is safe with me."

Not as bad as I thought.

Growling, I pushed him toward the door and straightened out my suit. "Get the fuck out of my classroom and send Sakura in."

I had a lunch date with her that I didn't want to miss. And I didn't want her scurrying off to the cafeteria either.

Once Blaise found his way out of my class, he peered over at Sakura and smirked. "Have fun."

30

sakura

BLAISE HARLEEN HAD BASICALLY CAUGHT us!

I tried to calm my racing heart after Callan locked the door behind me for lunch, but my stomach was in knots.

What if he says something to someone? His father? What if Callan's wife finds out about it?

"Don't worry," Callan said, sitting at his desk.

After scurrying farther into the room, I glanced at the chair he must've placed across his desk. In front of it was a container of freshly baked food from what looked like Stop and Shop and a bag of … pickle-flavored chips?

"What's this?" I asked.

"Pickle-flavored chips. You had some in your car last night," he said sheepishly. "I saw them through the back window."

The chips had been in my backseat from my Walmart trip the other night, where I had just hurled anything into my cart because Gunther was with me. I hadn't realized what was in my cart when I checked out.

But if Callan had bought these for me, that meant …

"Do you not want them?" he asked.

My eyes widened, and I snapped out of my thoughts. I took the chips from him and smiled. "No," I said even though I had never tasted this flavor. "Thank you so much for getting this for me. I love them!"

A small fib, but I didn't want him to feel weird.

"Well … since you got me some chips, I brought you a book for you to read to me," I said, digging around inside my backpack for one of the many smutty books I secretly had at home from my all-time favorite author Kayleigh Stone. *Doesn't every nerdy girl have a secret collection of steamy books that they hide from their parents?*

He took the smutty book from me. "Where'd you find this?"

"Oh, you know, just lying on my bookshelf at home."

He flipped through the pages and chuckled. "You have porn books just lying around?"

"Excuse me!" I giggled. "It's *not* a porn book! There is definitely some romance in there."

"Buried under pages of filth."

I smirked and hmphed at him. "I would like you to read it. I'm having some trouble understanding some of it. And I mean, *you are* the Literature professor. I'm sure you can find some deep meaning in it."

He cocked a brow. "You have a hard time understanding a chapter titled 'Fucking 101'?" He continued to flip through the book. "What about 'Cock Riding'? 'Squirting'? Oh, and my personal favorite …" He smirked. " 'Throat Fucking.' " He gazed over at me. "This shouldn't be hard for you to understand, Sakura. You showed me how well you can do this last one today."

My cheeks burned, and I crossed my arms. "Well, maybe I just wanna hear you read it."

Something about a man reading a romance book *to* me …

Warmth exploded through my body, and I pressed my lips together to stop myself from whimpering. Callan had already fucked me senseless today, and then we'd practically gotten caught by his nephew.

"You read it to me," he said, handing me the book.

"What? No! I asked first."

"You want me to read the book to you because you don't want to say all these filthy words aloud."

"What?!" I exclaimed. "Totally not true!"

"Go ahead then," he urged. "Read it to me."

I snatched the book from his hand and took a sharp breath, staring at the dirty words scattered along the page. I glanced back up at that smirk on his face, like he was betting I wouldn't read a single word out loud.

So, that was exactly what I was going to do.

"Once about four inches were buried inside me, he stopped and peered down. 'Your fucking pussy takes cock so well,' he growled, dark, hooded eyes gazing down upon me. 'Tell me to push it deeper.' "

Cheeks reddening, I peered back up at Callan and pressed my lips together.

" 'Push it deeper, Professor Patton,' I breathily whimpered. 'Please.' "

"He pushed it another inch deeper and grunted. 'The way your pussy lips spread and swallow this toy whole, Sierra … ' Another inch. 'It gets me hard as fucking hell,' he growled, then slammed the rest of the toy into me."

God, I would never do this again.

I snapped the book closed and pushed my shoulders back, avoiding all eye contact with him. "Okay, that's enough for now. I have lunch to eat before my next period." I tore open the bag of chips and stared down at the green-dyed chips.

I hate pickles.

But I didn't want to read any more of that book.

After reaching into the bag, I pulled one out and reluctantly put it into my mouth.

He gazed over at me and chuckled. "You look like you've never tasted one before."

I scrunched my nose and swallowed it, a small smile stretching across my lips. I leaned forward and swung my legs back and forth. "Can I tell you a secret?" I asked, realizing that I wouldn't be able to eat any more of these god-awful chips. "I, uh, have never actually tried any of the things that were in the bags. I picked up that stuff while at Walmart because Gunther was … making me nervous."

Callan flashed me an embarrassed smile. "I … sorry about that."

When he grabbed my chips to toss them into the trash, I grabbed his muscular forearm and stopped him. "No, I really appreciate that. Nobody has ever thought about me enough to buy me something they thought I liked for lunch."

"I think about you all the time," Callan said.

And then, as if he hadn't meant to say those words aloud, he tugged his arm back and looked away. Sitting back in his seat, he scratched the back of his head. "For Literature, of course."

Warmth spread through my body.

Callan Avery—the cold and callous teacher who had given me detention—was blushing.

Blushing!

He could lie to me all he wanted, but I knew that he didn't just think of me as another one of his students, as the smartest girl at Redwood Academy who loved literature. Callan had thought about me outside of school, just like I had thought about him.

Butterflies erupted in my stomach.

What do I mean to him? Who am I becoming to him?

When I didn't respond, Callan looked over at me. I flickered my gaze to his lips and pressed my thighs together. Those little memories of last night had been burned into my head. I wanted to kiss him so badly again.

"For Literature," I teased. "That's all, huh? Well, that's the only time I think about you too."

A small smile crossed his lips again, cheeks rounding. His gaze dropped to my lips, and I inhaled sharply. He gently brushed his fingers against the bottom of my chin, lifting it and drawing me forward.

Somehow, I felt more frightened to get caught in these innocent little moments between us than when he was slamming into me on his desk. But I didn't want to move away. The door was locked, and I wanted more of him.

When our lips were centimeters apart, I sucked in a sharp breath.

"That's the only time you think about me?" he asked.

"Yep," I murmured. "The only time."

"Somehow, I think that's a lie."

"I guess we're both liars then," I said and then kissed him.

31

callan

IN THE MIDDLE of lunch with Sakura, someone jiggled the doorknob.

Sakura sucked in a breath and glanced over at it. "Are you … expecting someone?" she asked when the knob jiggled again, followed by a bang.

"Open the fuck up," someone said from outside the door, his voice gruff and angry.

I'd asked João Rocha, the leader of Poison, to meet me *after* lunch. I needed information, information that I couldn't get by myself.

But he was here early.

"One moment, Sakura."

I walked over to the door and unlocked it. Sure enough, João stood in the hall with his arms crossed over his chest and his lips curled into an ugly snarl.

"Heard you were asking for me. What the fuck do you want?" he asked.

After peering over my shoulder at Sakura, who wiped a napkin across her lips, I stepped out of the room and closed the door behind me. I didn't want her to hear. I was doing this for her.

Once the door clicked, I sucked in a deep breath. I couldn't believe I was asking the leader of fucking Poison to do my dirty work for me. But nobody could find out that I had anything to do with this.

Especially Jett.

"I need a personal phone number," I said. "And you can't tell anyone about it."

"For who?" João asked.

"Diego Fernandez."

João stared at me for a few moments, then laughed. "The fuck you want his number for? He's the holiest fucking cop in Redwood, would do anything to see any of these corrupt motherfuckers behind bars. You a snitch?"

"No, I'm not a fucking snitch, João. Can you do it?"

"I don't work for free," João said.

"I'll pay you a thousand for it."

João scowled. "A thousand fucking dollars? Fuck that. Make it two, and you have a deal."

"You want two thousand for a phone number?" I asked.

"You're lucky I don't ask for two million," he said. "Already had one sucker pay that for info." He leaned against the lockers and cocked his head, as if he was trying to intimidate me. "You know, Poison does the best work in Redwood."

"Fine," I said between gritted teeth. "Two thousand."

"Make it three, and we'll keep quiet about it too."

I growled and hardened my glare. This fucking kid. If anyone else had asked for three thousand to find a damn phone number, I would've laughed in their face. But Poison got the job done right on the first try. And I knew he would keep quiet if I paid him.

"Half now," I started. "Half once you give it to me."

"Deal."

"Wait here," I said to him.

I sucked in a deep breath and walked back into the classroom, where Sakura finished off the lunch I'd bought her. I didn't want her to know my plans. She couldn't get involved with this shit.

"Is everything okay?" she asked, looking over her shoulder at João, who stood at the open door with his tattooed arms crossed over his chest and a brow arched at her. She quickly averted her gaze.

Unlocking the bottom drawer of my desk, I pulled out a yellow envelope that I had filled with money before I stopped at Stop and Shop. There were seventeen hundred-dollar bills inside. It was more than half, but I didn't have time to take out the extra two hundred with Sakura here.

After walking back out the door, I yanked João out with me and shut it so we stood in private in the empty hallway. As soon as I handed him the cash, he tucked it away in his jacket and turned around to walk back down the hallway. But I grabbed him by his shoulder and spun him back around.

"I need the information by the end of tomorrow."

"You'll get it when I give it to you," João said.

That punk was about to walk away from me again, but I grabbed the back of his collar and slammed him against the lockers. "You'll get it to me by the end of the day tomorrow."

He shoved me away and straightened himself out. "Get your hands the fuck off me."

Once he walked down the hall, I blew out a breath and stepped back into my classroom. Sakura stood from my desk and grabbed both her and my empty containers of food, bringing them to the small trash in the corner of the room.

"I should be getting to my next class," she said, grabbing her backpack and averting eye contact with me suddenly. "I don't want anyone to see me walking out of your classroom, especially when the hallways are flooded with curious eyes."

But lunch didn't end for another five minutes.

Five minutes.

And she wanted to leave early.

I shoved my hands into my pockets and walked to my desk, spotting my phone buzzing on my stack of Literature books. Sakura glanced down at it, then up at me, grimacing at the name glowing on the screen.

Georgina.

"You don't have to go," I said to her.

"But I should," she said, swallowing hard, but not moving toward the door.

My phone buzzed again, and I wanted to hurl it across the room. Georgina stopped calling me and was now suddenly texting me in the middle of my workday, as if she didn't care that I was at school.

Georgina: You're fucking terrible.

Georgina: I hate you.

Georgina: You're the worst husband ever.

Georgina: You can't even come on a simple vacation with me. This is what you get.

After her final message, a string of images appeared on my phone. Dick pics of whoever the hell she was fucking in Paris. And even a fucking video that I suspected she wanted me to watch.

I gritted my teeth. Saturday couldn't come soon enough. I would fucking destroy her and her father. Her entire fucking family. I hated them all, except Blaise. He loathed his family just as much as I did.

And once everyone was taken care of, I would have Sakura all to myself.

While I read the messages from my wife, Sakura had turned around and walked to the door with her hands wrapped around her backpack straps. She had pulled her hair into a high, straight pony-tail today that bounced against her shoulders.

"Come over tonight," I said to Sakura before she slipped out of my class.

I shouldn't have asked her until Jett and Georgina were dead, but I did anyway.

"Come over? Like, to your house?" she asked, eyes widening.

"Yes, to my house. Eight o'clock. Please."

God, now, I sound desperate.

But I didn't want to spend another night alone in that empty house.

She paused for a long time, then nodded, a small smile creeping onto her face. "I'll see you at eight then."

32

sakura

AT EIGHT P.M. SHARP, I pulled up Callan's driveway. I hadn't been able to stop thinking about him since lunch today. Before I could even get out of my car, Callan appeared at the side door, dressed in a casual pair of jeans and the same sweater from school today.

"Didn't think you'd show up."

I stepped out of the car and grabbed my backpack. "Were you waiting for me?"

Instead of answering me, he hummed and followed me through the house to the kitchen and attached living room. "I'm just finishing grading papers," he said, looking down at the mess on the island counter.

"Oh good," I said, hopping up onto a stool. "I can finish my work then."

He paused. "Sure."

While I was determined to spend time with him and *not* have sex with him for once, fifteen minutes later, I was getting too antsy. So, I excused myself to use the bathroom and then wandered through his large house afterward to calm myself.

Since the last time Callan had invited me over, he—or maybe his wife—had removed most of her stuff. Maybe they were in the middle of a divorce? Maybe they separated and she was in the middle of moving out? Was that why he didn't mind me coming over?

When I spotted a single picture hanging in a side hallway of Callan and Georgina when they were younger, I froze and stared up at it. She was so pretty with long strawberry-blonde hair, full lips, bright green eyes. I wished that were me in the picture with him.

After stepping closer, I craned my head up to look at it more closely. I should've been heading back to the kitchen, where Callan was grading papers and I should be doing my homework, but I wanted to torture myself with this a bit longer.

Maybe I have a masochistic kink or something. Who knows?

"I thought you were just using the bathroom?" Callan asked from down the hall.

My eyes widened, and I jumped back. "Oh, um … yeah! I was just … looking around."

He glanced at the picture on the wall, then clenched his jaw and walked over. Before I could say anything about it, he tore it off the wall and tossed it into a spare room that I didn't dare go in.

"I don't come down this hallway often, or that would've been gone already."

"Oh," I said. "It's okay."

No, it freaking isn't. He's mine.

"Come," he said, taking my hand and bringing me back down the stairs to the kitchen. "I know it's late, but I haven't eaten yet. I have a Wagyu steak in the fridge downstairs. Let me make it for you."

Stomach fluttering, I gripped his hand tighter and followed him to the kitchen. Callan Avery was holding my hand. More like tugging me along so I'd get out of that hallway with the picture of him and his wife.

But still, *holding my hand.*

When we reached the kitchen, he pulled a steak and veggies out of the fridge, then a skillet from one of the cupboards.

I walked over to his side and peered up at him. "How can I help you?" I asked.

He widened eyes. "You want to help?"

"Of course!"

He tried to hold back a smile, as if nobody had asked to help him with anything around the house, but then he shook his head. "I want to cook for you," he said. "You can go sit down and finish your work."

"Are you sure?" I asked.

"Yes," he said after a slight pause. "Go sit down."

Twenty minutes later, Callan set a plate of hot food in front of me. He sat across from me and cut into his steak. With a five-o'clock shadow under the kitchen light, everything about him seemed so much more real.

He wasn't just my teacher or the guy I was fucking.

Last time I had been over, he hadn't looked comfortable in his own house at all. But now, everything about him seemed so light and airy, like he was relaxed for the first time in a long time.

I bit into my steak and swallowed a piece. "This is delicious, Callan."

"You like it?" he asked, smiling when I nodded. "I love cooking, but I usually don't get a chance to anymore."

"Why not?" I asked, taking another bite. "School?"

He stayed quiet for another few moments and gazed down emptily at his food. "School. A wife who loves to criticize everything I do. The steak is either not done enough, too well done, has too much fat on it or not enough. You know, the usual."

My lips turned down into a frown.

The way he had said it …

The sudden drop of happiness from his face …

It was the first time he was actually really talking about his wife without me asking. If someone made me dinner every night—or even just once in a blue moon—I wouldn't complain about it, especially if the cooking was this good.

How ungrateful could someone be?

"Sorry," he said, looking down at his food. "I shouldn't have said anything."

I reached across the counter and grabbed his hand. "No, I'm sorry," I whispered, chest tightening at the thought of how long Callan had stopped doing the things he loved because the woman he was married to didn't love him. "Nobody should have to go through that."

Instead of refuting everything and telling me that nothing was wrong, like any other toxic boy would, Callan stared at me in silence for the longest time. He continued to eat, and I thought he wouldn't talk to me for the rest of dinner.

But he peered down at his food again, then looked back up at me. "I want to leave her," he whispered. "I'm not happy with her. I haven't been happy with anyone for over a decade now. Not until …"

He paused.

"Until what?" I whispered, heart racing.

"Not until you."

33

sakura

BRIMMING WITH EXCITEMENT, I knocked on Callan's door Friday after school and glanced into the unlocked room. Callan looked up from his desk, eyes softening slightly when he spotted me.

"Sakura," he said, my name rolling off his full pink lips.

Instead of waiting for an invitation inside, like I normally would, I walked into the room, placed my backpack on my assigned seat in class, and pulled a chair up to his desk, where he had been working.

"What is it?" he asked.

"I kinda have a favor to ask you," I said, placing my hand on his knee underneath his desk, finally having the confidence to touch him at school. The door was shut, so … it should be fine.

Besides, Callan told me that he had been happy lately … *with me.*

He cocked a brow. "And what is that?"

"Do you think that maybe"—I gazed over at him while my fingers wrapped around his bulge through his pants—"with your permission, I could skip Monday's class?"

"You can rub me off all you want, Sakura, but I'm not going to miss an hour of seeing you," he said, making my stomach flutter.

"I'll still be in class," I hummed.

"You want to skip my class, but you're still going to attend? How does that work?"

"I'll be"—I gripped him through his pants, feeling his dick harden in my hand—"underneath your desk."

Callan's soft eyes turned playful, his lips curling into a smirk. "Is that—"

Suddenly, João opened the door, sauntered into the room and kicked it closed behind him with his foot, then gazed over at me.

"The fuck is she doing here?" João growled, his backpack slung over his shoulder.

My eyes widened. *What is* he *doing here?*

I glanced over at Callan, then peered down at my hand on his ... bulge.

Quickly, I pulled myself away and fiddled with the bottom of my skirt. "Extra help."

"Extra help on a Friday?" João asked, tugging out a pack of cigarettes and his lighter. He stuck a cigarette into the corner of his mouth and lit it, taking a long drag from it. "What does the valedictorian of our senior class need extra help with?"

My cheeks turned bright red as strands of my black hair fell into my face. I gazed down at the papers in front of Callan and tried hard to ignore João's stare. But, fuck, I did not know what to say.

Like, at all!

Callan pulled a yellow envelope from his desk, cleared his throat, and stood, his expression hard. "None of your business, Rocha." He walked over to João, then held out his hand.

After growling underneath his breath, João pulled a piece of paper from his pocket. "Where's the money?"

When Callan handed him the envelope—which apparently had *a lot* of money in it if he was doing business with Poison—João handed him the slip of paper. I stared through wide eyes at the interaction, my stomach in tight knots.

What the hell is this?!

Why is Callan doing business with Poison?! Does it have anything to do with that scary guy who showed up to his house the other day and almost caught me with him? Does it have something to do with the Harleens?

João peered inside the envelope, pulled the cigarette out of his mouth, and blew out a puff of smoke into the room. "Good. You know where to find me if you need more information." Then, he walked out of the room.

I kept my mouth shut until the door snapped shut behind him, and then I let out a long breath. Callan stuffed the slip of paper into his pocket and stood there, tense, for a few moments, his back muscles rippling against his sweater.

"This is one of those times, Sakura, where you don't ask questions," he said before turning back around. When he finally faced me, his eyes were hard. "And don't mention that I did business with João to anyone."

"You did business with who?" I asked, playing along.

But, fuck, I was nervous.

Sure, the guy at his house had looked scary, and Callan having a gun stuffed in his glove box was terrifying. But Poison?! *Poison!* They were three kids from Redwood who did shit that nobody ever even *talked* about.

Dealt drugs. Bullied teachers. *Killed people.*

What does Callan want with them? What does that slip of paper have on it? How much money did Callan give him?

The questions continued to pile and pile and pile. And I realized for the second time that I didn't know Callan at all.

How far deep is he in all this stuff? What has he done? Or more importantly, what is he willing to do to and for people to protect himself? Is his wife just like him? Will she pull a gun on me if she finds me with her husband?

"I just have one question," I whispered, unable to stop myself. "And that's it."

Callan sat back down beside me, staying quiet.

"Am I safe?" I asked, chewing on the inside of my cheek and

kicking my legs back and forth underneath the desk. My throat was dry, my stomach twisting. "You know … being with you."

Callan snapped his head toward me. "Of course you're safe."

"But you're in some … some shady stuff," I whispered.

The only reason I had asked was because … I didn't see this ending anytime soon. I wanted to be with him more than I wanted to be with anyone. And—Ichika was right—it wouldn't last forever.

But I was happy now. And it seemed like Callan was too. He wanted to spend time with me outside the *classroom*, besides all the sex. Heck, he had invited me to lunch with him yesterday, then to his house, where we didn't even do anything intimate. I didn't want to lose this.

"Sakura," Callan said. "Look at me."

Nerves zipped through me, but I peered up.

"I will protect you," he said, his voice strong. "From anyone."

34

"ARE you sure it's okay that I'm here?" I asked, staring at the neon-white Escape sign plastered against the rich brick wall. We stood outside a building down by the Redwood Beach on Saturday night. "Isn't this a bar?"

Ichika wrapped her hand around mine and pulled me to the entrance. "It's a bar, but they have food for you too." She opened the door and ushered me into the busy atmosphere with dim lights and a luxurious bar.

"Yeah, but I'm not twenty-one."

"Well, we'll sit at one of the high-top tables then. You're my designated driver tonight, right?" she asked with a wink, pulling me toward an empty high-top table near the round marble countertop bar.

I arched a brow. "Only tonight."

"Wait, really?" she asked, eyes wide. "Because there is this really cute waiter who works here, who I'm definitely going to flirt with to get free drinks."

"So, *that's* why we're here on a Saturday night when I can't even drink. You know, I would've much preferred some milkshake or pasta or even pizza. Not bar food and drinks that I cannot even consume!"

"God, you're so dramatic," Ichika said, sliding onto her seat.

Standing on my tiptoes, I hopped up onto the seat and set my purse down on the table near the wall. I scanned the QR code for the menu, set out between us, and hummed to myself.

"Welcome to Escape," a handsome twenty-something man said. Button-up shirt rolled up his muscular, veiny forearms, he placed his large hands on the small high-top table, towering over us. "You girls need more time with the menu? How about we start with drinks?"

"Do you have anything salty?" Ichika asked. "Sour?"

I looked toward the wall and held back a snicker behind my hand—because, come on, a salty drink?! I *wondered* what she *really* wanted.

"What're you in the mood for?" he asked, smirking down at her with his eyes. "I can have them make something *custom* for you in the back."

I scrunched my nose and bit my tongue because this was *way* too awkward. Ichika was years older than me, but, damn … I hoped I flirted with Callan a bit better than this. This was just … yikes.

"Surprise me," she said. Ichika looked over at me, giggled, and then gently tapped his arm—and, God, I swore she almost fainted.

And she called *me* dramatic. This girl was about to pass out in the middle of a bar, leaving her underage and helpless cousin here.

From my peripheral, I spotted him peering in my direction. But I couldn't look over at him without laughing out loud, so I stared down at the menu on my phone. "I'll do water with lemon, please and thank you."

And please get out of here now before I burst into a giggle fit.

"I'll be right back with that drink," the waiter said, knocking his knuckles on the table.

When he left, I turned back to Ichika and let myself go absolutely nuts. "Please, God, do not tell me that he is the waiter you came here for," I said, giggling. "Oh my God. You ... him ... I ..." I said between giggles. "I cannot."

"All right, it wasn't *that* bad," Ichika said.

"Oh, yes, it was." I snorted.

She playfully rolled her eyes. "Well, I don't see you flirting with anyone. Ever."

"Yeah, because all the boys just flock to me," I said, tossing my hair over my shoulder and completely joking around. "I don't need to flirt. They just come for my pussy. I don't know what to tell you, Ichika."

"Like that teacher?" she shot back.

My eyes widened, and I leaned forward, slapping my hand over her mouth. "Not out loud! Someone might hear!" I whisper-yelled at her, glancing around at the high-tops and bar beside us to make sure nobody had heard.

But when my gaze landed on the far corner of the bar, I froze.

Callan sat with a man I only recognized from pictures. His wife's father.

Jett Harleen.

My stomach twisted into knots, and I dropped my smile. *What is he doing here with him?* Yesterday, he had told me that he'd protect me from anyone. And the other night, he'd admitted his wife didn't make him happy, that only I did that.

For some stupid reason, I'd assumed that he meant he didn't want to be with anyone else. That he didn't want to be with his wife. That he'd leave her. But ... he was now laughing over drinks with her father.

Has he been lying to me?

Ichika seized my wrist from across the table. "You okay?" She followed my gaze and furrowed her brow. "Is that Mr. Avery from Literature? I haven't seen him since high school. You know, it's always weird, seeing teachers out of their classrooms."

"Yeah," I whispered, trying to peel my gaze away from him.

Though ... I couldn't.

"Is it something that—" Ichika started, but then she widened her eyes. "Is that *him*?"

I wanted to answer her, but I couldn't. My stomach twisted into knots, and I stared down at the table, eyes becoming warm.

Why did I assume that he'd leave his wife for me? What the hell is wrong with me?

"I ... I don't believe it," she said. "Mr. Avery was always so nice."

"He is nice," I whispered, hand clutched into a fist underneath the table.

"I mean, like ... he didn't seem creepy."

"He's not creepy," I said, still defending him even though I was hurt.

These feelings piling up inside me ... were all my fault. Yet I couldn't help but feel like it was all a lie, like I had believed the fabricated reality he spun for me. The detention. Sitting in the car with him. Lunch on Thursday.

Almost as if he could feel my gaze on him, Callan looked over at me. He clenched his jaw, eyes hardening at me like we hadn't spent the other night together, just relaxing, like he hadn't told me that being with me made him feel good.

When he turned back to Jett, I glared back at the table. It had been a lie.

A big, fat lie.

All of it.

35

callan

WHAT THE HELL *is Sakura doing here?*

I gripped my drink tightly in my fist and peered at Jett while he made some sexist joke about something. But I couldn't listen. I couldn't focus.

Why is she in a bar—a bar run by the Redwood mob? Does she know how much danger she is in, just being here?

After forcing myself to breathe, I clenched my jaw. Of course she didn't know the danger she was in or else she wouldn't be here. But all I wanted was to storm right up to her high-top table and drag her out of the bar, throw her into the back of my car, and bring her home.

Jett finished off his second drink and laughed at his stupid jokes, cheeks round and reddening. I lifted the glass to my lips and let the contents roll down the back of my tightening throat, then glanced back over my shoulder at Sakura.

She crossed her arms over her stomach and glared at the table. Her friend looked in my direction, and I gritted my teeth even tighter. Whoever she was with looked to be older, more responsible.

She should have known not to bring an underage girl to a bar like *this*.

Once I finished my drink, I turned back to Jett. This was going to be a long freaking night.

"Another two over here!" I called to the bartender.

The faster Jett got drunk, the quicker I could dump him back home and come back here to pick up Sakura and whoever she was sitting with. It wasn't only the mob I worried about, but—I eyed the bartenders behind the bar—the men here also disgusted me.

The waiter serving Sakura and her friend walked behind the bar and gently nudged one of the guys making drinks. "Ichika's friend is single," he said to the bartender. "See the girl with those pigtails and short red leather skirt?"

Fuck.

I growled underneath my breath and gritted my teeth.

I swear to fuck …

If he went over there to talk to Sakura, I'd kill him.

Instead of following the waiter, the bartender thankfully turned to us, setting two new glasses in front of us.

"I'm good for now," Jett said, shaking his head to the bartender.

"Come on, Jett," I taunted. "What happened to all those frat days you used to tell me all about? When you'd drink until you passed out on the front lawn? I know you still got a couple left in you."

He let out a low chuckle. "It's almost like you're trying to get me drunk."

Fuck.

I flashed him the charmer smile and laughed along with him. "I already have your daughter locked down. No need to convince you to let me marry her all over again. That's long gone. What would I get you drunk for?"

"To get out of those vacations she goes on," Jett joked, his cheeks reddening even more.

Good, the alcohol is working.

"You got me," I said, throwing my hands up. "If I get you drunk enough, will you let me get out of going on vacations with her twenty times a year? That's too much traveling for an old man like me."

"Old man?" Jett asked, calling the bartender back over. "Get these two old men over here more drinks." He glanced over at me. "If you make it to my age and see what I have, Redwood is the only place you'll want to be. That's why I've been pushing you and Georgina to travel. You have to see the world while you're young and stupid."

Stupid.

Ha.

That must be why Georgina had been going on those vacations since we'd gotten married.

Three hours later, Sakura was gone, and Jett was nearly passed out drunk at the bar next to me. I had never seen the rich bastard *this* drunk. This was almost going to be *too* easy. Almost fucking laughable.

"Why don't we get you home?" I said, pulling out my wallet to pay.

He shoved my wallet away and pulled out his own, like I had known he would. After he gave the bartender his card, he set the wallet on the bar top. I stared at it, needing to distract him so I could snatch it.

After cashing us out, the bartender handed Jett his card back. And Jett handed it to me.

"Put this away for me, son," he slurred. "I need to get my jacket on."

Perfect.

When he stood, he stumbled slightly but rebalanced himself on the chair. He took his jacket and struggled to put it on while absolutely shit-faced. I grabbed his wallet and card, slid it underneath the bar, and slipped his card *along with* Officer Diego Fernandez's name and number right behind the license.

Once Jett finally put his fucking jacket on, I grabbed his car keys from him and guided him to his car. "No driving for you," I hummed.

After stashing him into the passenger seat of his own car, I slipped into the driver's seat and drove him home.

Besides his more sexist and now racist jokes that he started making—typical old-money prick—the car ride was relatively silent. I drove up his gated driveway and parked his car in the garage.

I guided him out of the car and to his living room when he stopped.

"We have to go back," he said, slurring his words. "I left my wallet."

"Why don't you get off to bed?" I suggested because we couldn't go back until someone from the mob found that wallet and looked inside it. The bartenders might pick it up to steal the cash, but once they saw that slip of paper with the number for a Redwood cop—who wasn't corrupted—shit would hit the fan. "I'll pick it up in the morning."

He placed his hands on my shoulders to steady himself. "This is why we need you in the family, Callan. You're the best thing that has ever happened to Georgina. I know I put you through a lot of hell, but look how it turned out."

Like shit.

That was how it had turned out.

"It's perfect," I said, playing into his little fantasy.

"Perfect," he repeated, then fell straight back onto the couch.

Passed out cold.

"Thank fuck," I whispered underneath my breath.

I hurried out of the house and back to my car, opening the trunk and rummaging through it to retrieve the fake evidence I had put together about the shit Jett had on the mob.

Once the mob found the name and phone number, they'd search his house to figure out *why* he had a police officer's number. And when they found this file that had pictures and shit that the mob had done—shit I had collected over the years—sitting in his office ...

No amount of money could rebuild trust like that again.

The mob would order a hit on Jett. And I'd be the one to take it.

36

callan

AFTER DRIVING like a maniac through Redwood to Sakura's house, I parked my car two houses down, near some tall hedges, and gripped my steering wheel. It had been *hours* since she'd left Escape, and she still wasn't home yet.

I waited and waited and waited.

Until a car pulled onto the road from behind me, the headlights glaring into my rearview mirror. When she passed me, I pulled off the side of the road. Sakura paused for a moment, slowing down by her house and then continuing down to the next street. She parked on the side of the road.

Once I parked behind her, I stormed out of my car toward hers.

She yanked the key out of the ignition and stepped out of the driver's seat, brow furrowed in an angry stare. "What are you doing here, Callan?"

"What the hell were you doing at Escape?" I growled at Sakura.

She shouldn't have been there, shouldn't have put herself in that kind of danger. She might not have known that the bar was run by the mob, but she would by the end of the night, and she'd learn never to set foot inside again.

She crossed her arms and poked me in the chest. "Why are *you* at my house?"

I gritted my teeth and stepped closer to her. "I'm not playing right now, Sakura."

"Neither am I."

"Are you fucking serious?" I asked in a breath, stepping closer to her.

When she pursed her lips and glared at me, I remembered the way Georgina used to stare at me like that years ago during our arguments. That was way before she didn't give a fuck anymore and just started arguments with me anyway out of the blue for fucking nothing.

At the mere sight of that look, I tore my gaze away and sucked in a sharp breath. "I'm here because you showed up at Escape tonight, at a bar owned by the Redwood mob. I don't know who brought you there, but you can't show your face there again."

"What were *you* doing there, *Mr. Avery*?" she asked.

Gritting my teeth, I dropped my glare to the sidewalk between us. I wanted to ask her again, wanted to explode at her, run in that same toxic circle Georgina had trapped me in, but I ... I didn't like the way she was looking at me. I didn't care so much if I hurt Georgina anymore, but Sakura ...

But I didn't care about her like *that*, right?

"Sakura, listen to me," I said, finally raising my gaze.

I must've stepped toward her too harshly because she widened her eyes, sucked in a sharp breath, and stepped back. I stopped completely in my tracks and stared down at her, heart pounding and throat drying.

Do I ... do I scare her?

After crossing her arms even tighter across her chest, she pressed her lips together and stared at the ground between us. "You were out with your wife's father," she whispered. "And I've been so stupid."

"What the hell are you talking about, Sakura? You're not stupid."

"For believing in you?" she scoffed, though it wasn't angry, like Georgina's, but full of sadness. "I ... I thought that we ..." She shook her head and turned her head so she stared down the street. She lowered her voice. "Forget it."

I took another step closer to her, not wanting her to make a run for it and head back home. After spending hours with Jett, I just fucking wanted to be with her tonight. I couldn't spend another second thinking about him or Georgina. The mob would handle it soon.

"You thought that we were what?" I asked, breath catching in my throat.

"Forget it," she said, turning her entire body away from me now.

"Please, tell me," I whispered, stomach light.

Somehow, I knew the words that were about to come out of her mouth. Maybe it was because those were the same words that I had been aching to allow myself to *think*. She couldn't ... we couldn't ...

After growling under my breath, I shook my head.

Fuck Jett. Fuck Georgina. Fuck the life I have lived for the past decade and a half.

I didn't want that shit anymore—hadn't for a long time. But Sakura? I needed her to tell me that she really wanted this, too, that I wasn't just a monster for giving her detention, that she really, truly wanted me.

"Sakura," I whispered, desperate for her to tell me how much I meant to her. *Because, hell, she means more to me than anyone else ever has.* I couldn't even remember the last time I'd felt like this, felt this lightness inside me, this happiness. "Please."

"I just ..." Sakura looked over her shoulder at me, eyes filled with tears. "You were out with your wife's father. I thought that you ... that you didn't want to be with her anymore. I just feel like"—she turned toward me, brow furrowing in anger—"the other fucking woman!"

"You're not the other woman."

She paced around the sidewalk in front of me and wiped an angry tear off her cheek. "Don't lie. I know that I fucking am because I have no control around you. I know that all these little things you tell me … every guy like you does it. You've probably told me the same words you have with every girl you've cheated on your wife with. I'm so upset that I … that I fell for it!"

"You didn't fall for anything. I haven't been with another woman like I have with you," I whispered, desperate for her to believe me.

Sure, I might've slept with different women a handful of times in the past decade just to get off, but I hadn't slept with anyone more than once, hadn't …

Felt like this.

"Don't lie to me," she said again, suddenly stopping and holding herself. "I'm so weak. I can't even walk away from you right now. I don't *want* to walk away. All this time … I just wanted someone to care about me."

"I care about you, Sakura," I admitted. "More than physically."

"How? How can you care about me?" she whispered. "When you were just out with your wife's father, drinking and laughing together?"

"It was an act, Sakura," I said.

If I told her the truth—that I had planned to get Jett on the mob's shitlist—what would she think of me? She already feared me because of the gun I had in my glove box, because I had done business with João, the leader of Poison.

"Well, you're a great fucking actor," she said, pointing between us. "Is *this* an act?"

"Fuck no," I growled. "This isn't an act."

"Then, tell me what it is. Tell me why you … why you were out with him."

"Sakura …"

She gritted her teeth and shook her head, tears building in her eyes again. "Why can't you tell me? What is so wrong about it? If you have nothing to hide, if you really hate your wife the way you say you do, if you really want to be with me … you would tell me."

"It's not that simple," I admitted, knowing that I sounded like a complete ass. "You have to trust me. It's not all a lie. You're not some girl that I sleep with anymore. You … you mean something to me, Sakura."

She stayed quiet for a long time. "Prove it."

"Come home with me tonight," I said, holding out my hand.

It was a selfish ask, especially after our conversation, but I didn't want to be alone tonight. Not after tasting what freedom from that bitch felt like. Not after tasting what life could be with Sakura.

When she didn't place her hand in mine, I pulled my arm back. "I'm sorry. That was self—"

Sakura pushed past me and opened my passenger door. "Just one night."

37

sakura

AFTER I TEXTED my parents and told them I was staying over Ichika's place tonight, I stepped out of Callan's car and into his garage. My stomach twisted at the thought of staying with him tonight. I didn't know what to expect.

While we had just gotten into our first fight, I hadn't wanted to leave him. There was a possibility that what he had said to me was all a lie, all some fabricated story so he could keep sleeping with me.

But then why would he invite me back to his place? Why would he buy lunch for me?

Deep down, I knew he was serious, but I was scared. Scared of the other side of him, the side he hid from me, the side that had a gun and talked to Poison. Scared that my gut feeling was so, so wrong.

"Come," he said, holding out his hand for me.

I set my hand in his and followed him into the house, kicking off my shoes at the door. He headed straight for his bedroom, released my hand, and walked to a couple of drawers. He picked out some sweatpants and an oversize T-shirt, then handed them to me.

"Something for you to wear tonight," he said.

Once I took the clothing from him, I swallowed hard and gazed at the bed. "I expected you'd want me to wear something sexy or just sleep naked tonight," I said quickly, trying to lighten the conversation.

"I want you to be comfortable," he said, smirk tugging at his lips. "But if you want to sleep naked, be my guest."

For some damn reason, I blushed. It wasn't like he hadn't seen me naked before, but he was flirting. Usually, he just took what he wanted from me whenever he wanted it and didn't give me much of a choice.

After deciding to be comfy, I pulled off my clothes and tugged on the ones he had given me. He disappeared into his closet while I walked around his bedroom. Instead of snooping, like I usually did, I sat on his bed and curled up against one of his oversize pillows.

My heart pounded inside my chest, nerves zipping up and down my arms.

What if I said something wrong tonight? What if I fucked this all up? If everything he had told me was true, then he felt the same exact way about me that I felt about him. And I didn't want to let him go. I couldn't.

A couple of moments later, he walked out of his closet in a pair of gray sweatpants and nothing else. My cheeks flamed at the sight of him, my eyes widening. Most of the time that I was around him, he had been dressed for work or to go out.

Now ...

Fuck.

Sweats hanging low off his hips, muscles swollen underneath the dim light, and tattoos.

Tattoos!

I swallowed hard and glanced away from him, trying to calm my racing heart. *Since when does Callan have tattoos?! Has he been hiding them underneath his nice clothes since I met him?!*

"You look flushed," Callan said, crawling into the bed with me.

"What?!" I squealed, laughing nervously. "N-no, I'm not!"

"Do you need any—"

"When did you get those?" I asked, staring at the tattoos through wide eyes.

There you go again, Sakura. Can't keep your mouth shut!

"What?" Callan asked, leaning against the headboard.

He followed my gaze to the black tattoo across the left side of his ribs. I moved closer to him and drew my fingers across it, sucking in a sharp breath.

"These tattoos?" he asked.

"Yes," I whispered in a breath.

He chuckled. "I got this one when I was nineteen. It's faded a little. But I've got a couple of others since then."

My eyes widened. "More?"

Callan has more tattoos? What else does he have? What other little secrets is this man keeping from me? I wasn't sure, but I planned to find out.

38

sakura

I TURNED IN THE BED, pulled the blankets over my head, and whimpered, my eyes still heavy despite the sun flooding in through the sheer curtains. Cozying into a hard chest, I bent my knees and curled into Callan's body.

Breathing in his scent, I relaxed further into the blankets. I had never woken up in a man's bed with his arms wrapped tightly around me, with my head on his steady chest, feeling so … content with my life.

"You're awake," he said.

"Shh," I mumbled. "Still sleeping."

"I wanted to make you breakfast," he murmured, brushing some hair off my forehead and smiling down at me. I blinked my eyes open. The sunlight glinted against his eyes, making them a sea of hazels and browns. "But I didn't want to wake you. You looked too peaceful and relaxed."

"Are you saying that I don't look peaceful and relaxed anytime else?" I giggled.

"Not at Redwood. You study too much."

"That's because you"—I playfully poked him in his chest—"give too much homework."

"Too much homework?" He chuckled, his chest rising and falling unsteadily. "I barely give you anything, Sakura. Literature is the least of your worries for the semester. You're already top of the class."

I curled into the crook of his arm and gazed at his chest, thinking about … this.

About … us.

Whenever we had sex, everything went so quickly. I couldn't hold myself back, but now … I actually had time to appreciate him. The way his shoulders shook slightly when he chuckled, the dark and graying hairs on his chest, the sound of his voice in the morning.

"Hey," I said, smiling to myself. "Just because I'm in your bed doesn't mean you get to go easy on me. I earn all my grades and *not* because you like the way I ride your dick, Mr. Callan Avery. So, don't think it's the other way around."

Another deep chuckle escaped my lips. Then, suddenly, Callan's phone buzzed on his bedside table. Instead of answering it, he continued to brush his fingers through my hair and sighed softly to himself.

Buzz after buzz after buzz cut through the room from his phone.

"You should answer that," I whispered. "Or shut it off."

He grumbled to himself and reached for his phone, his delicious muscles rippling as he moved. He took one look at his phone and growled. I glanced over his shoulder and spotted *her* name on the screen, followed by about a hundred messages.

After lying back down, he scrolled through his settings and turned off notifications for *her*.

But when he jumped back to the messages, I froze at the vile comments. They were vicious.

Unable to stop myself and completely out of line, I snatched the phone from him and sat up in bed. Fury surged through me as I quickly scrolled through the messages from his wife, the insults, the images and videos of her sleeping with other men.

Tears welled up in my eyes, my chest tightening.

Georgina: I hope I get pregnant here. <3

Georgina: Give you someone else's baby. The baby you always wanted.

Georgina: Fucking prick.

"Callan," I whispered, voice cracking.

Was this really his wife? The woman who he had been married to for over a decade?

How can ... how can he live like this? How can someone be so cruel?

"Why haven't you ... left her?" I whispered, staring at these messages in horror. I tightened my grip around his iPhone until my fingertips turned white. I shook my head and hoped that my angry tears wouldn't fall. "Callan?"

"It's complicated," he said, reaching for his phone.

I scrolled up.

Georgina: You're fucking terrible.

Georgina: I hate you.

Georgina: You're the worst husband ever.

Georgina: You can't even come on a simple vacation with me. This is what you get.

These messages ... pictures ... videos?!

"Sakura," he said, taking my phone. "Please, stop reading."

I released the phone from my death grip and let him take it away from me. As he turned it off and tucked it away in the bedside drawer, I stared at him with tears wavering in my eyes.

Has this been going on for years? Does he ... Does he want children at one point, but his wife ...

When he turned back to me, he grimaced. "Don't pity me, Sakura."

"How can you let her talk to you like that?" I whispered.

I would ... never talk to anyone like that. I could never even imagine *anyone* saying that kind of stuff in real life to another human being. Sure, sometimes, Mom got too high off drugs, but Dad didn't talk to her like that. He tried to get her help.

When Callan didn't respond, I sat up.

"That's not fair," I said, crawling into his lap and straddling his waist. I pushed some dark hair off his forehead and took his face in my hands, fingers grazing against his stubble. "You deserve better than that. Why haven't you left her?"

"I already told you that it's complicated," he said. "I can't just leave her."

"Why ... why not?" I whispered, a tear slipping down my cheek. "She's abusing you."

"It's complicated," he repeated. "But I'm taking care of it. For you."

While his voice was soft, he ended with an edge. I tensed in his arms and shook my head, knowing that what he meant and what I *hoped* he meant were two different things altogether. He was taking care of her in ways that I wanted to know nothing of.

So, I didn't ask.

I couldn't.

Instead, I gripped on to him tighter and hoped that he wouldn't get in trouble, that he didn't get thrown in jail for whatever he planned on doing to her. But deep down inside me, I knew that I wouldn't feel bad for it even if he was doing this for me.

I just couldn't lose him.

Callan swiped my tear away with his thumb. "Don't cry for me."

While I wanted to stop crying—because I wasn't even the one being abused—I couldn't wrap my head around how someone could be so rude, so cruel to their husband. How could someone berate and insult the man she had vowed to love and support forever?

Wanting to stop crying, to be strong for him, I stared into his hazel eyes and asked a question I shouldn't. Because I couldn't keep my damn mouth shut around him ... at freaking all, it seemed.

"Did you want kids with her?" I whispered.

He stiffened and sat up against the headboard, staring past me and frowning.

My chest tightened, and I curled my fingers into his shoulder. "Do you want kids?"

"I wanted to have children," he said, looking away from me. "But after spending a couple of years with her—*the real her*—I'd never have a kid with that bitch. She'd be a terrible mother. Besides, I'm too old for that now."

A frown tugged at the corner of my lips. He stared at me through eyes that held so much pain. All I wanted to do was take it all away, show him that he … he couldn't stay with her, that this wasn't right, that he deserved to be truly happy.

Callan was wrong. It was never too late for anything.

39

callan

AFTER I COOKED pancakes for Sakura, I brought her home and dropped her off at the end of her street, like she had requested. She didn't have many—if any—friends, so she had told me if a car dropped her off in front of her home, her dad would be suspicious.

"I'll see you tomorrow at school," she hummed.

"Tomorrow at school, huh?" I asked, lips curled into a smirk. I took her chin in my hand and pulled her closer to me, kissing her on the mouth. "I thought you asked me for a pass from tomorrow's class."

She looked over her shoulder and grinned at me. "Maybe. Guess we'll have to see."

With that, she jumped out of the car, slammed my door, and hurried down the sidewalk toward her home. She glanced around, as if to look for neighbors outside in case she had to come up with an excuse as to why she had climbed out of an expensive car with tinted windows.

If we worked out, I didn't know how the hell I would tell her parents that I had been sleeping with their daughter. She was roughly half my age and my Literature student.

Talk about a parent-teacher meeting.

Once I watched Sakura stroll up her driveway to the front door and slip into the house, I switched gears from park to drive and headed back home. If anyone saw me lingering here for too long, they might get suspicious.

I had left my phone at home, so I was Georgina-free for the rest of the day.

Leisurely, I drove through Redwood without a care in the world. I hadn't gone back to get Jett's wallet last night, and I hoped to fucking God that they found it and didn't suspect me at all. Jett was an entitled asshole that I planned to eliminate as soon as possible.

Halfway to my house, I spotted a blacked-out SUV tailing me. I tightened my hand around the steering wheel and smirked. The Redwood mob had found the wallet and maybe even the evidence I had planted in Jett's home.

They wanted to talk because they thought I had information. Just as expected.

When I turned the corner, I spotted a second car behind the first. And when I drove onto my street, there were two more parked out front. I could only imagine how many were already in my house, trying to find whatever kind of information they could.

I turned into my driveway and parked my car behind three other SUVs. Before I could even turn the car off, someone ripped my door open, yanked me out of the car, and slammed me onto the ground.

With a thud, I landed on my stomach. I glanced back up in time to see someone hurl the back of a machine gun right into my temple. Then, everything went black.

"Jett Harleen dropped his wallet at Escape last night while you and he were out, having drinks," someone said, standing right in front of me.

I blinked a couple of times, the words drifting through my ears as I came into consciousness again.

"He had a card with Diego Fernandez's number."

"He's your wife's father," Yui said, crossing her arms and glaring at me.

"I don't know anything," I mumbled, slowly regaining my composure.

"You were out with him last night."

"He's my wife's father," I said, sitting back up. My wrists were bound tightly behind my back and to the chair, my ankles bound to each chair leg. "Of course I'm going to be out with him. He's been trying to convince me to fucking go with her on all her fancy little vacations to Europe." I yanked on the rope. "Yui, is this necessary?"

"Yes, it's necessary," Rick Santos said.

"I wasn't talking to you," I growled and stared at Yui. "You're going to let him talk for you? The leader of the Redwood mob is going to let some kid do her talk—"

She shoved her gun into my mouth and gritted her teeth. "Shut the fuck up, Avery."

When she pulled the gun out, I pressed my lips together—not because I was scared, but because I wanted her to think I was.

She pursed her lips. "If you have no part in this, then prove it," she sneered. "Kill Jett Harleen."

A smirk *almost* tugged at my lips, but I pressed them together. I had expected nothing less from Yui. She had played right into my little fabricated lies, into the *evidence* I had planted in Jett's wallet and home office last night.

"You want me to kill my wife's father?" I asked, eyes growing wide.

Playing the fucking part.

"Yes."

"What am I supposed to tell Georgina?"

"We all know you hate that bitch," Yui spit. "Kill her father."

"I'll kill Jett, but I want out."

"Are you fucking seri—" Ben, one of Yui's men, started.

"He's no use to us anymore," Rick Santos said. "We have the in at the school."

I furrowed my brow. *The fuck does that mean? At school? In with what?*

"We have as many girls as we need," Rick said to Ben, talking among themselves.

"We can have more," Ben said.

Girls? Girls for what?

"Quiet!" Yui said, commanding the attention of everyone here. She took a knife from her pocket and cut through my ropes. "You have yourself a deal, Callan Avery." She held out her hand for me to shake. "You kill Jett Harleen, and we'll release you from working with us."

40

sakura

"EXCUSE ME!" I pumped my legs hard and fast, pushing around students in the hallways. I elbowed a couple of football jocks who had decided to take up the entire corridor and shoved past them, heading for Literature.

The first bell had rung a minute ago, but I needed to get inside before anyone else.

After basically sprinting down another hallway, I stopped in front of Mr. Avery's room and sucked in a deep breath. When my breathing finally evened out, I pushed open the door and hurried inside.

Callan sat at his desk, one brow arched. "You're early."

I glanced around the classroom to make sure that nobody had come in yet, and then I walked over to his desk and dumped my backpack behind it. Callan rolled his seat back slightly, one forearm on the desk.

With his sleeves rolled up his muscular arms, he reached out for me. "Come here."

Warmth exploded through my core. I took his hand and walked toward him, sliding my ass across the bulge inside his khakis and then dropping to my knees in front of him. I crawled underneath his desk just in time for the door to open again.

Eyes widening, Callan glanced up. "Gunther."

Fuck, this is so wrong.

Sitting under his desk, I rested my hands on Callan's knees and slid them up his thighs to his zipper. My pussy tightened, and I bit my lip. After undoing his zipper and his button, I pulled down his pants enough to whip out his hard cock.

He leaned back in the seat, spreading his legs a couple of inches wider as more students walked into the classroom. His dick was veiny, swollen, and throbbing. And I couldn't wait to have it in my throat.

I took the head of his cock into my mouth and sucked gently, letting my spit slide down his shaft. Then, I slowly took him into my mouth, inch by inch. The late bell rang through the room, and I forced myself to take all of him until he was far past the back of my throat.

Callan started his lecture from his desk as I face-fucked myself with his huge cock. I forced it down my throat over and over. The heat gathered between my legs, and Callan's hips twitched.

After pulling back slightly, I stuck my tongue out and slapped his cock onto it, the noises drifting through the quiet room. Callan reached underneath the table, hand thrusting into my hair to shove me down onto his dick.

When he slid into my throat, I nearly gagged and sucked hard. But his dick was enormous, and my throat was so wet. I couldn't stop thinking about him shooting his load deep into me, whether in my throat or in my pussy.

Throat squeaking, I bobbed my head up and down on his shaft, forcing him to hit the back of my throat with every thrust. He curled his fingers into my hair and held me down onto his cock. I flicked my tongue against his balls.

God, I want him to come so badly. So fucking badly.

Callan continued with the class, talking to the students while I swallowed his cock. He reached underneath the table and played with my tits, his fingers grazing and pinching one of my nipples, bouncing my small breasts up and down in his palm.

Desperate to be touched and horny as hell, I pulled away from his dick and tugged my shirt over my head. Then, I undid my bra so I sat almost naked in front of him. He glanced down underneath his desk, dick twitching.

When he peered back up at the class, he clenched his jaw. Warmth surged through my body, and I took his cock in my mouth again. I wanted to break him, wanted him grunting and coming down into me while teaching.

I stared up at him from underneath the desk, eyes wide and mouth full. And because I couldn't stop myself, I reached between my legs and played with my aching little clit. I sank my mouth all the way down until my lips met his hips, and then I bobbed my head back and forth, tongue flicking against his balls.

He gripped my hair harder and held me still, almost as if to stop himself from coming.

But I wanted none of that.

So, I disobeyed my teacher and shoved him another inch deeper, sucking his balls into my mouth. Spit and drool ran down my chin and dripped onto the floor. I gagged and rubbed my pussy harder, on the brink of an orgasm.

He peeked down at me again, jaw clenched even harder. I furrowed my brow and gagged but held him inside my mouth. One day, I promised that I wouldn't gag on him anymore, but right now … in the middle of class … it was kinda hot.

Suddenly, he stiffened, and his cum shot into my throat, filling it up to the brim with cum. I gripped his thigh with one hand and rolled my eyes back, coming hard. Pleasure surged through my body, and I whimpered on him.

When I finally pulled back, my face a complete mess, I licked his cum off my lips and swallowed like a good girl.

41

callan

YUI: **Before you eliminate your wife's father, I have one last job for you.**

Yui: Take care of Lucas. He fucked up a job last night.

Growling to myself, I clutched my phone in my tight grasp and glared at my empty classroom. It was right before lunch, and I didn't want to do shit, but I needed to get out. I only had a couple more days left, a week at the most, before I could finally leave the mob for good.

Me: What'd he do?

Yui: A girl washed up on shore.

Me: A girl?

Lucas killed a fucking girl?!

Yui: One of your students. Skylar Walker.

When the last text rolled in, I pressed my lips together and hurried to the door.

Skylar Walker is dead? Fucking dead? She had been Blaise Harleen's plaything for the past three years, and now, she was dead?

This town would attempt to blame Blaise.

I walked into the hallway, arms crossed, while I scanned the crowd for my nephew. Blaise would be getting out of English right now, and I needed to at least warn him to stay out of as much trouble as he could these next few days.

When I spotted a skateboard thrown over someone's shoulder, I straightened myself out. "Blaise!" I called, but that punk ignored me. "Blaise!" I shouted louder this time.

He gritted his teeth and turned around to face me. "What?"

After I glanced around for anyone listening in the halls, I nodded to my classroom. Blaise rolled his eyes and followed me inside, slouching down at a desk.

"What?" he asked with annoyance. "Aren't you having Sakura Sato for lunch? Don't want to miss getting in one of your student's pants, huh? Make this quick."

I locked the door and clenched my jaw. "I'm not going to entertain you with my love life, Blaise. I doubt you'd really care for it anyway, seeing as you hate your father's side of the family just as much as I do."

Pissed, he rolled his eyes again. "Then, what do you want me for?"

I walked to my desk, placed my hands on it, and leaned forward, staring him down. "Where the fuck were you last night?"

"Out."

"Where?"

"Why does it matter to you?"

"Where?" I repeated, dead fucking serious.

He stood up and growled, "The Overlook. What the fuck is wrong with you?"

"You were at the beach?"

"No, the Overlook."

I ran a hand over my tired face and paced the room. "Same fucking thing, Blaise."

"Why do you want to know all this shit anyway? What's it matter to you?"

"Shit's happening in Redwood," I said. "Who were you with?"

"Who the fuck you think?"

"Vera?"

"Yeah. Now, are you going to tell me any shit or not? I have lunch."

After glaring at him for a couple moments longer, I stormed to the door, unlocked it, and pulled it open. Blaise tossed his backpack over his shoulder and walked toward me.

But I snatched his arm before he could pass. "Stay out of trouble."

"You too, Av. You fucking too."

Once he pulled himself out of my grasp, he stormed down the hallway to the cafeteria.

While I wanted to tell Blaise about the text I had just received, I couldn't say shit here.

After listening to the mob talk yesterday about having girls in Redwood—I still needed to figure out what the fuck that meant—I didn't trust anyone but Sakura around here. I didn't know which of the girls in my classes were connected with the mob and if someone had bugged my room.

Just as I was about to shut my door, Principal Vaughn walked over.

"Have you heard the news?" Principal Vaughn asked.

"What news?"

"Skylar Walker," Vaughn said, "is dead."

I furrowed my brow and stared at the principal. *How the fuck did he know about this before I did?* He had waltzed right into my classroom, as if he had known this all day, possibly even all night.

"She's dead?" I asked to see if I could get as much information out of him as possible.

"Murdered. Body washed up on the beach."

Fuck, this isn't good.

The mob obviously had some connection to it, but what the fuck did they want with her? In the beginning of the year, Blaise Harleen had hung out with her. He might have some information, something. I'd have to ask him tonight, where we could speak in private.

"It's a shame," Vaughn said, shaking his head. "She was a pretty girl."

I stiffened. *What the hell is he getting at?*

"Don't you think?" he asked.

"She was attractive," I said, cringing at the sound of my own voice.

I didn't find her attractive at all, but I needed info from him. He obviously knew something about the mob and maybe even what they meant when they talked about Redwood girls. I needed to fucking know before something happened to Sakura.

"You're awfully fond of Sakura Sato," Vaughn suggested. "She's a pretty girl too."

Behind my back, I balled my hands into fists. "She is."

Vaughn leaned against the window and stared out of it, lips curled into a small smirk, as if he hadn't just told me that a student at Redwood had been murdered. "Have you ever thought about … crossing the line with her?"

"What are you talking about?" I asked.

He chuckled and glanced over at me. "You know what I mean, Callan."

"I'd really appreciate some clarification," I said, peering at the middle drawer of my desk, where I kept my gun.

I didn't trust Vaughn at all. If he did have connections with mob—even deeper ones than I had—then I had to … protect Sakura and myself. No matter the cost.

After kicking himself off the windowsill, he walked over to me and placed a hand on my shoulder, squeezing. "Do you want to sleep with her?"

While I had known it was coming, I still stiffened. Vaughn had some balls, coming up to my classroom and asking if I wanted to sleep with one of my students. If he already knew about us, then I would have to *take care* of him too.

"No," I scoffed, pulling myself away from him and walking around my desk. "Why would you ask me that shit?"

"Because," he hummed, smirking like he had done nothing

wrong, "I can set it up for you, if you'd like. I have … *connections.*" He walked toward the classroom door and glanced over his shoulder. "Think about it."

With that, he walked out of the room.

Fuck. Fuck!

The mob had been using me all these years to get closer to the leadership at Redwood Academy. My stomach turned, and I slammed my fist down on the desk, papers flying everywhere.

If my suspicions were correct, then the mob was pimping out students from Redwood.

42

callan

SHIT HAD HIT the fucking fan after school yesterday. Blaise had been taken to the police station to be questioned by police who were trying to frame this on him. Redwood girls were gossiping nonstop about him. And I had barely been able to talk to Sakura for twenty-four hours, only a few words in class.

I ran my hand through my hair and hurried toward lunch period.

From what I had gathered last night from Lucas before I killed him, the police were trying to blame Blaise Harleen for this because his father had slept with the police chief's wife. Too much fucking drama for me. But I wasn't going to be a dick about it.

Whatever had happened, I needed to protect Blaise and his girl. Because this shit was getting messy, and now that I had become aware of what they were doing with girls at Redwood, I wouldn't let Blaise take the blame for this or let his girl fall into their hands.

Without Blaise to protect her, Vera was in danger.

And Skylar's friends were vicious creatures who'd do anything to hurt her too.

To my surprise, the first floor was eerily quiet. Then, I heard it—Vera defending Blaise.

"That's because he's been with me," Vera said from the cafeteria, her voice drifting down the halls. "He was at the library with me on Saturday night and went out for milkshakes with me on Sunday. Blaise Harleen is innocent."

"You're lying," someone said back to her, and I picked up my pace. I needed Vera to stay out of this mob business. "Blaise would never take you out on a date or hang out with someone like you. He was only around Skylar. They spent every night together."

"I'm not lying. I have proof."

"Then, where is it?" There was a pause. "So? Where is it?"

"I swear. I swear, we were together. You've seen us hanging out at lunch. Some of you have seen us in the hallways," Vera stuttered, and I jogged a few feet to the cafeteria door to get her out of this complete mess.

I cleared my throat as I hurried in. "You're right," I announced to the students. I draped my arm around her shoulders in the *nice, caring teacher* kind of way. "Vera doesn't know what she's talking about. She's been under a lot of stress in my class lately."

"But—" Vera started.

Because we both knew that she wasn't in my class.

"I know today has been hard on you all, so finish up your lunch," I said, guiding her toward the exit of the cafeteria, my grip on her shoulder tightening, my fingers digging into her muscle. I spotted Sakura sitting alone at a table, eyes wide. "I'll bring Vera to the nurse."

"Wh-what are you doing?" Vera asked, furrowing her brow once we stepped out of the cafeteria. She tried to stop, but I continued to push her along toward my classroom. "I'm not in your class."

When we reached my room, I guided her in and closed the door behind us. "You can't say shit like that aloud to the entire school," I said, clenching my jaw and staring over her shoulder at the door's window. "Bad people are trying to pin this on Blaise, and I doubt that he would want you to get involved."

"Bad people?" she whispered, eyes widening. "Like … like who?"

"I can't tell you," I said. "Let me figure this out. Stay under the radar."

"No, I'm already part of this. I don't want anything to happen to him."

"Nothing will."

"Nothing will?!" she asked, throwing her hands up into the air. "They're trying to blame her death on him. The police want him in jail."

"I'll take care of it," I repeated.

"How?"

She had so many questions, and I couldn't answer any of them.

"That's none of your business," I said.

"But what are you—"

Before she could say another word, someone opened the door behind us. João Rocha stood at the door and stormed into the room.

After eyeing me, João snatched Vera's elbow and tugged her to his side. "You're coming with me," he said through clenched teeth, dragging her out of the room.

"Wait, stop! What are you doing? I need to ask him questions. Mr. Avery—"

"No more questions," João growled, harsher than usual. "None for him."

43

sakura

"GREAT JOB!" I beamed at Tyler, the senior kid that Mr. Barnes, the Biology teacher, had requested that I tutor. I gathered up all our papers and set them in front of him. "Mr. Barnes will most likely include meiosis and mitosis on this test, so make sure to study a bit more."

Tyler groaned. "Why are we having another test?"

I shrugged and leaned toward him slightly. "That's Mr. Barnes for you."

"You don't like him either?" Tyler joked.

"God, no." I giggled. "I hate Biology."

"You hate Bio? But you have, like, the highest grade."

After picking up a pen, I twirled it in my fingers and leaned against the desk. "I'm more of a Literature and art kind of girl. The sciences have always bored me." I smiled to myself. "But that's a story for another day. Good luck on the rest of your homework."

Once he left, I gathered all my belongings and stuffed them into my backpack. Feet shuffled against the ground behind me, and I leaped up and glanced over my shoulder, my heart pounding against my chest.

Nobody was there.

But I didn't trust people in Redwood anymore. They fucking terrified me.

"Is someone there?" I called.

No response.

It's probably nothing. I am just paranoid.

Rumor was that Blaise Harleen—Callan's nephew—had killed Skylar. I didn't know Skylar, and I never wanted to hang around with her because she slept around with the entire town. But still, it was sad. When I had heard about her death after Callan's class, I'd tucked myself away in the restroom and cried.

Yes, cried.

Because how could someone just … kill someone else? Especially someone *my age*?!

My phone buzzed, the vibration jolting me again.

Callan: Meet me in my class when you're done.

Callan: I'm taking you home.

Me: I can't.

Me: My parents will be suspicious if I sleep over two nights in one week.

Me: Once they find out about Skylar, they will definitely want me back.

Callan: You're not staying over, but I need to see you.

Me: Only for a couple of minutes. I have homework.

Callan: No.

Callan: I'm being serious, Sakura. This town isn't safe.

Skylar flashed through my head again. Callan was right. There was a killer on the loose. Redwood wasn't safe. And Callan Avery had promised to protect me from anyone and anything that tried to hurt me. I was … safe with him.

He had promised.

Besides, I needed to ask Callan if he thought Blaise had actually killed her because I had seen him and Vera—one of the sweetest girls at Redwood—hanging out a couple of times in the hallway. I never thought she'd date—*maybe they aren't dating, but still*—a bad boy like him. And Callan *had* saved Vera from embarrassment during lunch. He must know something.

When I walked out of the classroom, I bumped into someone's hard chest. After steadying myself, I craned my head up to see Gunther staring down at me through urgent, wide eyes and giving me an uncomfortable smile.

"Sakura," Gunther said, "I need to talk to you."

My stomach turned. Something didn't feel right.

"Were you … waiting for me?" I asked, mouth suddenly drying.

Gunther scratched the back of his head. "I didn't want to bother you."

"It's an hour after school ended," I whispered. "Have you been here the whole time?"

"Yes," Gunther said, shaking his head. "But that doesn't matter."

Doesn't matter? That matters to me.

It had been less than forty-eight hours since Skylar had been murdered, the police hadn't caught the suspect, and a student who skateboarded like Gunther was their prime suspect!

What the hell did he mean that it didn't matter?!

I grasped my backpack straps as hard as I could. "I need to get home."

I didn't feel safe here.

Before he could say another word, I hurried past him. But Gunther grabbed my wrist and jerked me back. Fear shot through me, paralyzing me to the spot. If he tried to do something to me, I'd scream at the top of my lungs so Callan would hear me.

"Please, Sakura," Gunther said quietly. "I just need to know if you're okay."

"I'm fine," I snapped, yanking myself away from him.

"It doesn't seem like it."

"I'm. Fine." My words come out harsh because I wanted to get the hell out of here right this very second. If I stayed any longer, I didn't know what Gunther would do to me.

Did he kill Skylar? Why is he waiting for me? Am I next?

"You've been acting differently this year," Gunther said quietly, stepping closer to me.

How does he know what I acted like before senior year? I had been a loner, and I still was.

I twirled around on my heel, ready to sprint to the second floor.

Gunther cleared his throat. "Ever since Mr. Avery."

My entire body froze. *He didn't just ...*

"I know about you and him," he said to me, but I refused to turn around.

My cheeks burned as my heart raced. *How does he ... is he going to tell ...*

Maybe he was bluffing. Fuck, I needed to get out of here quickly.

Without answering him, I fast-walked toward the staircase and hurried up it, taking two stairs at a time. When I came to the landing, I glanced over my shoulder to make sure he wasn't following me.

Still, I continued hauling my ass to Callan's room because Gunther Zurn had been watching me. Gunther Zurn had been waiting for me. And worst of all, Gunther Zurn knew my secret.

44

sakura

AFTER TWIRLING my fork around the spaghetti that Callan had made for dinner, I nervously glanced up at him. When I had made it up to his classroom earlier, I hadn't had much of a chance to tell him about Gunther. He had wanted to leave right away.

But I didn't want to hide this from Callan.

Especially after Skylar's death, Gunther terrified me. I had barely said a few words to him my entire life, yet he had met me at Walmart the other day and forced me to walk around with him, he had been staring at me nonstop in Literature, so much so that Callan moved our seats, and now ... he had waited for me outside of the room where I volunteered.

"What is it, Sakura?" Callan asked.

I glanced up from my plate and swallowed a mouthful of pasta. "Um ... today, I was tutoring someone for Biology in the science wing after school. When he left, I packed up and was going to come straight to your room, but ... Gunther ..."

Callan stiffened, balling his hands. "Gunther? What the fuck did that punk do to you?"

"He had been waiting for me the entire time while I worked," I whispered. "He stopped me in the hall." I winced, remembering the way he had harshly seized my wrist. It was nothing compared to some stuff that went on at Redwood, but nobody had touched me with that much force and anger. "He ... he didn't just stop me. He grabbed my wrist and forced me to stop."

"Why didn't you tell me this earlier?" Callan growled, jaw clenched and nostrils flaring.

"Be-because I wanted to leave the school before he ... before he told everyone."

"Told everyone what?" Callan asked.

"That he knew about us," I whispered.

As if he had already known that Gunther knew about us, Callan pressed his lips together. "Don't worry about him saying anything to anyone. He knows what will happen to him if he does. But if he laid his fucking hands on you, then he's going to pay for it."

After dropping my fork, I moved around the table, climbed into his lap, and wrapped my arms around his shoulders, burying my face into his neck. "I-I'm sorry," I murmured. "I know that it's not a big deal, but I'm scared of him."

Callan wrapped his arms around my torso and pulled back so he could look into my eyes. "I told you that I would protect you from anyone," he promised. "Nobody will hurt you when you're with me."

I curled my fingers into his shoulders and knitted my brows. "B-but ..."

"I will protect you," he repeated. "From anything." He squeezed me a little tighter and pulled me a couple of inches closer to him, lowering his voice. "Tell me, Sakura, do you feel safe in my arms?"

Shifting slightly to straddle his waist, I gently took his face in my hands. "I do."

We stared at each other for a few moments, and then I leaned down and kissed him because ... well, it felt right. He slid his hands down to my hips and gently gripped them, slipping his tongue into my mouth and moving his lips with mine.

"I promise you, Sakura," he murmured against me, "I'll do anything for you."

After resting my forehead against his, I deepened the kiss and undid the first few buttons on his shirt. It seemed like every single time that I had been with him, we had been quick to pull off each other's clothes and hungry to devour each other.

But our kiss was slow, passionate.

He lifted me into the air and walked with me to his bedroom, then set me down on the center of the bed and crawled between my thighs. I wrapped my legs around his waist and my arms around his shoulders, not wanting to pull back.

"Sakura," he whispered into my mouth.

He slowly moved his fingers up the sides of my body, then strummed them against my breasts. I tensed, and my breathing hitched. Heat warmed my core, and I squeezed my thighs together. After tugging off my shirt, he kissed down my chest, his lips finding the end of my bra near my cleavage.

I lay back on his bed and grasped the satin sheets. He slowly pulled down the cups of my bra, letting my small breasts fall out of them. He sucked my nipple between his lips and tugged gently, his fingers disappearing between my thighs. Tingles ran up and down my body.

When he dipped his hand between my legs, I arched my back and moaned.

"You're so fucking amazing," he murmured against my tender breast.

The pressure in my core grew higher every moment. He moved further down the bed, hooked his fingers around the waistband of my skirt, and tugged it down my body. He sat between my legs and placed his hands on my knees, every muscle in his upper body flexing.

As he pulled my legs apart and gazed down at my wet pussy, he lay down on the bed on his stomach and dipped his head between my thighs. "You're mine, Sakura," he said, and then he pressed his lips to my cunt, thrusting a finger into me.

I ran my hands through his hair and tugged lightly. He massaged it in circles, each time a little faster. I gazed down at him, breathing unsteady, and clenched around his fingers. I loved being with him, more than anyone else.

He was the only person to make me feel safe, even in his messed up town.

"Please," I murmured. "I want you inside me already."

When he crawled back up the bed, I reached between my legs and undid the button and zipper on his pants. Once I finally pulled out his cock, I wrapped my hand around the base and whimpered, pulling him closer so he lined up with my entrance.

I stroked him a couple of times, his head rubbing against my wet pussy. "Please."

After posting his arms on the pillow on either side of me, he leaned down, pressed his lips to mine once more, and pushed himself inside me. I moaned into his mouth, the ecstacy already rushing through my body.

He pumped in and out of me slowly, tongue tangling with mine. Pleasure pumped through my body, and I curled my toes.

I love him.

My eyes shot open while I kissed him. *I didn't just ... I didn't just think that ...*

"Fuck, baby," he groaned into my mouth. "God, your pussy just got so wet."

Oh God, I really did just think that!

Do I love the way he feels inside me, or do I really love him?

45

callan

HALFWAY TO REDWOOD ACADEMY with Sakura—who had been acting weird since we'd had sex—in my passenger seat, Jett's name flashed across the screen of my phone. I stopped at a red light, ran my hand over my face, and groaned. I couldn't have one fucking peaceful night to myself. Either he or his daughter had to fucking ruin it with their bullshit.

But I needed to figure out where he had been hiding out. Because he wasn't at his house.

"I need your help," Jett said in a rush over the phone. "The mob is looking for me."

Surprise, surprise. I wonder why.

"Why would they be after you?" I asked. "You pay their bills."

"Look, Callan," he said. "They think I'm betraying them. I need you to talk to them."

I could only imagine him pacing around a mansion and running a hand through his electric-white hair. If he was calling me to ask for help, he must've been shitting himself about this all day.

"Sure," I said to buy myself time. "I'll talk to them. Stay put."

Fat fucking lie.

"Where are you?" I asked.

"Are you stupid?!" he shouted over the phone. "I can't tell you. You work for them, idiot."

Wonder where Georgina got her mouth from? I rolled my eyes.

"You're going to need to trust me, Jett." I tapped my foot impatiently. I wanted to get off the phone with him as soon as humanly possible. Sakura was with me. "At least tell me the town," I reasoned.

"White Beach."

Ahh, he was hiding out at the infamous Harleen beach house. Now, it'd be easier for me once I finally had the time to dedicate to cutting every inch of his body up, giving him the hell that man truly deserved for raising such a bitch.

"Sounds good," I said and ended the call.

Thanks for that fucking information.

While I'd wanted to put Jett six feet deep last night, I had spent the entire afternoon and evening trying to figure out what the fuck had happened in Redwood. Georgina had called her brother, and her brother had called me to let me know that Blaise was being questioned by police.

Over murdering someone.

Blaise Harleen.

Blaise fucking Harleen.

He might try to act tough, but he wouldn't have killed that bitch. He didn't have the balls. He probably even hadn't held a gun before, never mind thought about murdering some slut from Redwood Academy. I just couldn't get over the fact that they had questioned *him.*

No matter who had done it or why, I needed to keep Sakura safe. She was my number one priority.

Once I pulled up to the school, I parked in the back, where Poison had disabled the cameras. I wanted to bring Sakura home myself, but I knew that I couldn't. We would never be able to be together how I wanted. At least, not in this small, judgmental town.

Sakura leaned over the center console and kissed me. "Good night."

Just as she was about to open her door, a car pulled up directly behind us. Headlights glared into the car and reflected off the rearview mirror, royally pissing me off. I seized Sakura's wrist so she wouldn't move.

Who the fuck is this?

A moment passed. Then two.

"Sakura, hand me my gun."

Eyes widening, Sakura yanked open the glove box without speaking a word. With a shaky hand, she pulled out the gun and handed it to me, then looked behind us. "Wh-who do you think that is?"

"I don't know," I said, gazing into the mirror to get a better look. "Stay here."

"Callan," she cried, grasping my forearm. "What are you going to do?"

"When I get out, get into the driver's seat," I said, hoping that she would do as I asked. If I watched her get hurt by whoever the fuck this was, I'd fucking kill myself. "If anything happens, drive off and don't look back."

"But, Callan ..."

"Please, Sakura," I said harshly.

"O-okay," she whispered.

I opened my door, stepped out of the car with my gun drawn, and watched Sakura shift to the driver's seat. After I closed the door, I stepped forward and spotted Gunther Zurn standing in front of those high beams.

Fury rushed through me. Not only had this fucker waited an hour after school to talk to Sakura, but now, he was following us. He had some fucking nerve to confront me like this, especially after the skatepark.

"Leave Sakura," he ordered, voice shaking.

Gunther Zurn's voice *never* shook.

"Get back into your car, Gunther," I growled. "And go home."

"No," he said, pushing his shoulders back. "Leave Sakura."

My hand tightened around the gun, but Sakura was in the car. I didn't want to scare her.

I stepped toward him and shoved him back toward his car. "Leave now, Gunther."

He squared up to me, shoulders back and gaze strong. "If you don't leave her alone, I'm going to …" He stuttered and paused. "I'm going to …"

"You're going to go home," I finished. "And act like you didn't see shit."

"No," he growled. "Stop using Sakura, or I'm going to ruin your life. I'll tell everyone what I saw. I'll get you fired, thrown in prison …" He reached behind himself and pulled out a gun. "I'll kill you if you lay another hand on her."

Sakura shrieked from the car. "Callan! Callan, please, don't!"

Gunther ran his hand through his hair and paced back and forth. "She's fucking screaming. She's fucking screaming at you. You don't deserve her." He waved his gun in the air. "You don't fucking deserve her."

"Gunther, please, stop!" Sakura said, shuffling out of the car.

"Sakura!" I shouted. "Stay in there."

"You see!" Gunther said, barreling toward her. "She doesn't want to—"

Before he could come within five fucking feet of her, I pulled the trigger and killed him.

46

sakura

I SCREAMED at the top of my lungs as blood splattered all over my clothes. Callan kicked the gun in Gunther's hand away to a couple of empty parking spots and then turned toward me, saying something but I couldn't hear him.

Because Callan had taken his life. *His life!*

Dropping to my knees, I crawled over to Gunther, heart pounding and beads of sweat forming at the small of my back.

This can't be happening. This can't be happening. This can't be freaking happening.

"Callan! What did you do?!"

"Get up, Sakura," Callan said, taking my wrist. "Don't look at him."

After ripping my wrist out of his hold, I held Gunther's chest wound closed with my hands. Blood oozed between my fingers, coating them in a thin, wet layer. I pressed my hands down harshly against his chest, needing him to stay alive.

"Stay with me, Gunther. Please, stay with me."

"Let him go."

"Stay with me. God, please," I sobbed.

"He's dead, Sakura," Callan said.

But he wasn't. He couldn't be. It was slight—very slight—but I felt his chest rise and fall underneath my fingers. Or maybe that was just me shaking his body with my trembling hands. Either way, we had to try something!

I leaned down and listened to a very soft, strained breath. "He's alive."

"No, he's not."

Frantically, I shook my head. "You have to bring him to the hospital," I pleaded. "He's still breathing!"

"He's dead, Sakura."

"No! He's still breathing."

"There's no time."

"There's no time if you don't do anything!" I shouted at him.

"Sakura, get up," he said, grabbing my arm and jerking me to my feet.

"No!" I cried, shoving him back. "I told you not to hurt him!"

"He was waving a gun around you," Callan growled.

I shoved him again and again and again, pushing him back. And when he collided with his car, I slammed my fists into his hard chest, tears pouring from my eyes. "How could you? How could you kill him?!"

"Lower your voice," Callan said. "Or we'll both get in trouble."

Snapping my mouth closed, I stepped away and scowled at him. Furiously, I pushed the tears off my cheek so I didn't seem weak. But my knees wobbled.

How can ... how can he just shoot him like that? Why isn't he doing anything? Gunther was still breathing.

If he wasn't going to do anything, then I would.

"Leave, Sakura," Callan ordered me. "Find somewhere to wipe the blood off—"

After falling to my knees once more, I wrapped my arms around Gunther's heavy body, right underneath his arms, and attempted to stand. I opted for crouching because I couldn't completely lift Gunther and dragged him a couple of inches before

I tripped over my own feet and fell face-first onto the concrete on top of Gunther.

Callan seized my entire body, lifted me into the air, and walked with me to my car. I struggled against him to escape his hold, to get Gunther help, but he held me even tighter so I could barely move, trapping my arms between his stronger ones.

"Let me out!" I shouted. "Now!"

"No," he growled, shoving me into my car. "Leave."

"Callan!" I screamed. "Don't!"

"Leave, Sakura!" he shouted back. "There is nothing you can do for him."

Fury rushed through me as Callan tossed my backpack into the passenger seat and then grasped the door handle.

"I hate you!" I shouted right before he slammed the door in my face. "I hate you so much."

47

callan

WHEN THOSE THREE little words left her mouth, I froze.

"I hate you. I hate you so much."

My throat dried. I tugged on the door to open it again because I had done this all for her. She had been the one to tell me how she was terrified of Gunther. She had been the one to tell me that he followed her around. She was the only reason I was doing *any* of this.

But she shoved her foot against the gas and nearly ran over my toes. I leaped back and called her name as she squealed out of the parking lot and disappeared down through Redwood's dark streets.

She was emotional right now, but I hoped that she didn't slip and tell anyone what had happened tonight. If anyone even *saw* her covered in blood and found out that she had been with me, I would be in deep shit.

Not only with the police, but also with the mob. Because they hadn't released me yet, they would force me to dispose of her. No way would I fucking do that. I'd much rather take my own fucking life than do that to her.

"I hate you. I hate you so much."

My chest tightened. I didn't care how much she hated me. She wouldn't die.

Turning around, I dropped my gaze to Gunther, who lay in the middle of the parking lot. Blood pooled around him, his shirt dyed in it. I had no remorse for Gunther. He had been waving a gun around Sakura, out of his damn mind, and he had been stalking her.

Couldn't forget about what had happened to the kid's parents either. Murder-suicide that happened less than a year ago. It had been the talk of the Redwood mob for months since Zurn's father had been laundering money for them. Gunther hadn't been stable ever since.

I did the right thing. I did the right fucking thing.

Gunther lay across the pavement in a pool of his own blood.

"I hate you. I hate you so much." Sakura's voice rang out through my head.

My chest tightened. She was the only person that I had in this shitty town. She couldn't hate me. I … I didn't know what I would do without her, if she never got over this, if she hated me for all of eternity …

Growling to myself, I tossed Gunther over my shoulder and shoved him into the backseat of my car. I couldn't believe that I was doing this. After sliding into the driver's seat, I sped out of the student parking lot and toward the Redwood Hospital.

I should've been burying his goddamn body and cleaning up the blood.

If anyone else had asked me, I wouldn't have done it.

But I'd told Sakura that I would do anything for her. And I'd meant it.

So, now, this fucker hung on to life in the back of my car, his blood soaking into my leather seats. I gripped the steering wheel and slammed my foot against the pedal, flying right through red lights with my flashers blinking.

Though I had shot him to protect her, she would hate me even more if he died.

I whizzed by dirty cops who probably recognized my car from

the mob and squealed into the parking lot. Once I finally reached the hospital, I whirled up near the front exit, parked my car, and hurried to get Gunther inside for help. He lay in my arms, head dangling back, as I rushed through the lobby right to the front desk.

"What happened to him?" a nurse asked, calling for others.

Gunther was quickly taken out of my arms and into a back room by a handful of nurses and doctors.

I dropped my arms to my sides and gazed down at the blood covering my hands and shirt. "He was shot."

"Do you have any other information? His name?"

"Gunther Zurn."

"Is that al—"

"I have to go," I said, turning around and heading back to the front entrance. I needed to get out of here as soon as possible, head back to the school, clean up and fix all the shit I had broken with Sakura.

"Mr. Avery, what happened to you?" a parent I vaguely recognized said, hurrying up to me. When she reached me, I read her name tag fastened on her white doctor's coat—Dr. Abara. "There is blood all over you."

"A student," I said, stopping. "A student was shot."

Fuck, I hate this. I hate lying. I hate feeling like scum.

"Who?" she asked, brown eyes widening.

"Gunther Zurn."

After letting out a breath of relief, she placed her hand against her heart. "I'm sure they'll call me in, but you should get cleaned up. There is usually a change of clothes behind the front desk for situations like—"

"I have to go," I said, stepping away from her.

I had done worse to people, but this felt wrong. So wrong.

I hadn't wanted to kill. I had never wanted to be in the mob. Jett had forced me to join them, holding my life and his daughter over my head. I had done things I had sworn I would never fucking do, and now, I had hurt Sakura.

No more. Never again.

Without saying another word to Dr. Abara, I stormed back to my car and slipped into the driver's seat. I had cleaning supplies packed in my trunk for times like this. I had to get back to the school before anyone saw that blood.

But I vowed to make this right. I didn't care how long I had to stay with the mob to take them down. But I would do it, not only for Sakura, but also for myself. I would kill each one of them if I needed to, cut their throats and bleed them dry.

48

sakura

"ICHIKA!" I shouted, banging on her front door. "Please, let me in!"

All the lights were off in her house, but her car was parked out front, so she had to be home. I couldn't head back to my house with Dad. Not covered in blood like this. I was an emotional wreck right now.

"Ichika, please!" I sobbed. "Open up!"

A light turned on in the back room, and I sniffled, shoulders heaving.

God, what is going on? I still couldn't believe ... I couldn't even force myself to believe that I had just witnessed Callan kill someone.

When the front door opened, Ichika pulled a plush pink robe together and yawned. "Sakura, what are you doing here so late? I have a—oh my God!" She stared at me through wide eyes, pulled me into the house, and slammed the door shut. "What happened to you?! Why are you covered in blood?" She ran toward the kitchen counter, reaching for her keys. "We have to get you to the hospital!"

With tears pouring down my cheeks, I thrust myself into her arms and cried my heart out. "How could he?!" I cried, my words incoherent as I snotted and sobbed, unable to even think straight anymore. "He-he—"

I grasped on to Ichika's elbows to hold myself up because my knees wobbled. My entire body felt so weak, and I felt like … like I needed to—

I pushed myself away from my cousin and found the closest trash bin, puking up my dinner into it.

Ichika hurried over and held my hair back, wrapping it up into a ponytail. Bile continued to rise in my throat, and I forced myself to throw the rest up. When I finally came up for air, I wiped the tears from my cheeks. My stomach gargled again, and I clutched it.

"We need to get you to the hospital," she said.

"Th-this isn't my blood," I said, stopping her.

"Not your blood?! What the hell happened to you?"

I so desperately wanted to tell Ichika what had happened with Callan, but I couldn't … I couldn't betray him like that. I hated him for what he had done, but I couldn't see him in jail. Nor did I want the mob to find out and kill him.

If Gunther died … if he fucking died …

Another sob escaped my lips, and I toppled over onto my hands and knees. Tears poured from my eyes. How could I want him to live? Gunther had still been alive when Callan told me to leave. *Still alive!* And he had stopped me from bringing him to the hospital. It wasn't fair. How could Callan be so cruel? Sure, I had been afraid of Gunther because of the recent killing and he had been stalking me. But death?!

Shooting him right in front of me?!

"Why are you covered in blood?" Ichika asked on her knees, grasping my shoulders.

Sniffling, I stared at her through tear-filled eyes and shook my head. I opened my mouth to lie, but I couldn't get out anything. My words were caught in my throat, stuck there, never to move.

"Sakura, please," Ichika pleaded. "Talk to me. You're scaring me."

"I-I can't tell you," I stuttered, shaking my head. "I can't."

"Does it have to do with Mr. Avery?"

I tried to hold myself together, but when I thought about him, I burst into tears. Again, I wrapped my arms around her body and pulled myself closer to her. I buried my face into her chest and sobbed.

Ichika wrapped her arms around me and held me close, gently stroking my hair. She rocked me back and forth, not saying a word. I cried into her shirt. I had just watched someone die. *Die!* Right at my feet.

"Let's get you cleaned up," Ichika said, picking me up and pulling me into the bathroom.

When I collapsed onto the toilet, she peeled off my shirt and ran a warm bath. After tossing my stained shirt into the trash, she walked back over to me and dipped a rag into the water, then cleaned the large splotches of blood off me so I wouldn't bathe in as much.

Once she finished wiping, she undid my bra and pulled off my skirt. Usually, I didn't like being naked in front of many people, but I didn't mind Ichika seeing me like this. She saw tons of naked women for her job, and she was my closest cousin. Besides, I was far too gone to think straight anymore.

After I climbed into the tub, the water turned a light pink.

I leaned against the edge, pulled my knees to my chest, and sobbed. "What am I going to do?" I cried into my hands. "I can't believe he did that."

"It's going to be okay," Ichika whispered, shampooing my hair. "Calm down."

"N-no, it's not. It's not going to be okay."

Massaging the shampoo into my scalp, Ichika frowned. "I'm sure he had a reason for doing whatever he did, but I … the blood … I can't picture him doing whatever he did for nothing."

Through stinging eyes, I stared at the porcelain pink wall tiles and shook my head. This was my fault. I had told Callan that Gunther terrified me, that he had waited for me after school, and then … at Walmart, the way he had looked at me during class …

I should've kept it to myself. I shouldn't have said shit.

"Was he protecting you?" Ichika asked, scooping water in her hand and washing the soap out of my hair. She stared down at the small bubbles forming around my breasts. "Was he jealous? Can you tell me anything?"

I squeezed my eyes closed.

Whether he was protecting me or not, he had been wrong to kill Gunther.

"The other guy," I whispered, not wanting to admit it, "had a gun."

"So, he *was* protecting you."

"Yeah, but … he didn't have to … he didn't have to hurt the guy."

"Sakura," Ichika said, gently taking my shoulders, *"he had a gun. He could've killed you."*

I opened my mouth to disagree with everything that she had just said, but I couldn't. Ichika was one hundred percent right.

What if Gunther had killed me or Callan? If he had shot that gun and killed Callan, I would've wished Gunther to be dead.

I probably wouldn't have been in my right mind, and I'd have killed Gunther myself.

<h1 style="text-align:center">49</h1>

callan

AFTER I FINISHED CLEANING up the mess at Redwood Academy and then *taking care* of Lucas, who must've killed Skylar, I drove to Yui's home. Usually, I wasn't allowed inside, especially without an invite, but the guards outside her mansion were scrambling tonight.

I walked right into the foyer without a problem.

Sakura hadn't been home, so I found myself here, ready to search for any information that I could about the mob's business in Redwood as well as who had killed Skylar. I needed to keep Blaise out of this as much as possible.

"The fuck are you doing here?" Ben asked.

"What happened with Skylar?"

"None of your fucking business," he said.

"You're putting the blame on Blaise Harleen," I said, pushing past him to enter the house farther. Yui's office was on the second floor, overlooking the pool and with a beachside view. "It is my business."

Guards and men shuffled up and down the staircase. I pushed

my way through them and stormed right into Yui's office. She sat at her desk, glaring at her husband and shaking her head.

She gazed over at me. "Did you take care of Lucas?"

"What happened with Skylar? Why did you kill her?"

"It was a job," Yui said calmly.

"So, you put the blame on Blaise Harleen. He's my nephew," I said. "Still a kid. You can't blame him for this."

"In a couple of days, you won't be part of the family anymore," Ben said, cracking a smirk and chuckling with Rick Santos, who I wanted someone to fucking kill already. "It won't matter who we blame then. We could blame you."

"Ben!" Yui scolded, slamming her hands down onto the desk and standing. She glared at him. "You know that's not how we run things around here."

"We're hosting a sex trafficking ring with underaged high school girls," Ben said. "Do you think I believe you actually care about the rules around here?"

So, it is true. They are pimping out underage girls.

Yui growled, stepped forward, and grabbed him by the neck. "I'm the boss. You do as I say, and I say, stop harassing Avery. He's worked for us for nearly a decade and a half. Shut your mouth and respect him."

Once Yui released him, I stepped forward. "Stop blaming Blaise," I said. "Please."

"It's the police," Yui said. "Not us."

I wasn't sure if I believed her completely. What did the police have against Blaise? Maybe it was his father who had slept with the chief's wife a few years back? Had he really held a grudge all this time?

But ... still, Yui *had* to have had some hand in choosing Blaise to put the blame on. Jett was Blaise's grandfather, and *I* had made it seem like Jett had betrayed the mob. This was my fault that Blaise was where he was right now.

I didn't put it past Yui to blame him herself, just to get back at Jett.

"Before Lucas killed her, he sent messages from her phone to a *therapist*. Made her seem crazier than she was. Our backup was to frame this as a suicide, but Skylar's parents had doubts."

Fuck.

I grumbled to myself. This shit was getting messy quickly.

"Who ordered it?" I asked, needing *some* kind of information.

"You know," Yui started, "that's private information."

50

callan

THE NEXT DAY AT SCHOOL, Sakura didn't look at me all class.

Dressed in oversize jeans and T-shirt, she scowled at her textbook until the bell rang with her lips pursed and eyes puffy. I hadn't even expected her to come in today because if I were her, I sure as hell wouldn't have.

I didn't even want to fucking be here.

"Sakura, please stay behind," I called, hoping she'd hear me out. "We need to talk."

Instead of listening, she dumped her textbooks into her backpack and walked out of my classroom without speaking a single word to me. I stared at her from my desk and frowned.

God, she hates me. She really fucking hates me.

I'd screwed everything up between us, and I didn't know if she'd ever forgive me for it.

All the other students piled behind her, desperate to leave Literature. I just wanted the hell out of this school. I debated about finding a substitute teacher for the rest of the day and leaving, but someone knocked on my door. Through the small door window, I saw Blaise.

On the second knock, I opened the door and tugged him into the room by the collar, locking the door behind me.

"What information do you have?" he asked me.

I sighed through my nose and walked back to my desk. "You're in deep shit."

"I didn't fucking do anything."

"I know that."

"Well, who the fuck did it then?"

"It was a job," I said.

"You? You fucking killed her?!" Blaise asked, eyes bugging out of his head. "You?!"

"No, not me," I said, clenching my jaw. "The mob. I don't take jobs involving students."

"Why is the Redwood mob in on it? What'd they want with her?"

"It's a long fucking story that I can't talk about in school. There are people here that're in on it too. I'm trying to stop it."

"Wow," he said sarcastically, walking back toward the door to leave. "Great information. This was a really great use of my time."

I snatched his elbow. "I'm not finished."

"Well, this shit isn't my fault!" he shouted, ripping himself out of my hold. "You're connected with the mob. Do something about it. Tell them not to blame me because they're not going to win against my father's lawyers."

"They'll eliminate your father's lawyers," I said in a hushed tone. "This shit is serious. I'm doing everything in my power to stop this."

"Well, try fucking harder."

"They made it seem like a suicide. Sent text messages from her phone beforehand to a *therapist*. Made her seem crazier than she was," I started, leaning against the whiteboard and crossing my arms. "Her parents suspected that it wasn't a suicide, so the mob is scrambling."

"So, they need someone to fucking blame it on," he clarified.

"And because you had to fuck her ..."

"That's all that happened between us," he said through gritted teeth. "Nothing more."

"Yeah, but you were the only guy at this school that people saw her with."

"Well, tell them to blame it on my fucking father and mother. Not me. I didn't do shit."

"If I try to avert the blame away from you to your parents, your father is going to give me fucking hell," I said. "Not something I want to deal with right now. I have too many other people to keep safe and away from this."

"Like Sakura?"

I grimaced. "Yes."

"What, you guys are actually a thing now?"

"That's not any of your business."

"Not my business until I tell everyone you're fucking a student."

After balling my hands into fists, I drew my tongue across my teeth, pissed the fuck off.

"Take care of this, *Uncle*," Blaise said.

Once Blaise walked out of the classroom, I followed him into the hallway and blew out a deep breath. Between Sakura, Gunther, Blaise, and the fucking mob, I was beyond stressed the fuck out today.

Three of those problems were out of my hands right now, but I needed to do whatever I could to keep Sakura safe. And that meant finding out who the fuck was in this sex trafficking business at Redwood Academy.

Principal Vaughn strolled down the hall, nodding to the *female* students as they hurried to class. He stuffed his hands into his pockets and perversely watched them walk down the halls in skirts too short for this place.

I balled my hands into fists behind my back and called him over to me. I couldn't believe that I was fucking doing this, but I needed to do something. Sakura had taken all my free time lately, but now that she was ignoring me ... I could only think about how terrible my life was.

I needed something to make me feel like less shitty of a man.

If Sakura wouldn't talk to me, then I had to save any other girls that I could.

When the hallways were empty, Vaughn stopped in front of me and smirked. "Have you thought about my offer?" he asked, gazing toward the stairwell, where a couple of students were shuffling to class late. "I know she's not wearing those cute little skirts today, but Sakura would still be a—"

"Who else do you have?"

He widened his eyes. "Who else?"

"What other girls do I have to choose from?" I asked. "The thought of Sakura hasn't been doing it for me lately. Who else can I … sleep with? I'm sure there are other young girls from Redwood Academy who parade themselves around."

The thought of being with anyone besides Sakura made my stomach churn. I wouldn't touch the girls, but I needed to at least figure out who they were so I could help stop this shit from happening to them.

"There are plenty of girls to choose from, Callan. Meet me in my office after school."

"Great. I'll meet you there then."

Principal Vaughn walked down the hallways and disappeared into the stairwell. I blew out a deep breath and shook my head when I heard a sniffle behind me. I twirled around to see Sakura standing at the door for the girls' restroom, tears welling in her eyes.

She stared at me in agony, like she had heard everything I said.

51

sakura

"WAIT, SAKURA. SLOW DOWN," Callan shouted and started after me, hurrying down the hallway to catch up to me. "This is all a big misunderstanding. I don't want to sleep with someone else. That's not what I meant."

I rushed down the hallway, desperately trying to hold myself together.

Dumb. Why am I so dumb?

He sprinted after me, grabbed my wrist, and yanked me back. "You have to fucking believe me. What you heard … it was taken out of context. I don't want to fuck anybody else. I was trying to—"

After yanking myself out of his grip, I stormed down the hallway toward my next class. "Fuck you," I growled.

I didn't have time for this shit. I had been in the restroom, trying to gather enough confidence to go back into his room and apologize for the way I'd reacted last night. I knew he was just trying to protect me. Or at least, I'd thought he was. But what I had heard him talking to the principal about … I couldn't believe it.

Did I mean that little to him? One little fight, and suddenly, he wanted to fuck someone else? Maybe he had been doing that this entire time that I had been with him. How many other innocent girls had he given detention to?

"Leave me alone," I said between gritted teeth.

The bell rang through the hallways, and I cursed at myself. I was late. I was freaking late, and I was running away from the only thing that mattered to me. I had thought I mattered to him. But I had been nothing but a plaything to him.

A stupid, dumb plaything.

He continued to run after me, but I grasped the door handle to my next class and flung it open. I didn't care what people thought about me. Not now. Not after I had my heart ripped out and stomped on right in front of me. This wasn't fair. It wasn't fucking fair.

How could I be so stupid? What the hell is wrong with me?

"Sakura, you're here," my teacher said with a smile.

I hurried to my seat and slid into it, dropping my backpack to the ground. I yanked out my computer and opened it up, my lips pursed. When the door swung open again, Callan scanned the room wildly for me.

My teacher glanced over at him, eyes widening. "Mr. Avery, what are you doing here?"

He stood in the doorway, staring at me. "I need to talk to Sakura."

"Sakura, why don't you go out into the hallway with Mr. Avery?" my teacher offered.

I ignored her.

I straight-up freaking ignored her. I didn't want to go anywhere with him, especially after what I'd just heard him say. I didn't want him touching me, trying to convince me to stay with him, to ignore everything he had just said.

Callan had been my first everything, and I meant nothing to him.

Nothing.

"Sakura," my teacher said a little bit louder.

All the students looked over at me, patiently waiting for me to leave with the only man in this entire world that I now officially hated with my entire heart.

I peered up at her and swallowed hard, firmly shaking my head. "No."

Murmurs erupted through the classroom. Everyone stared at me in shock. I'd never once talked back to a teacher. I was at the top of the class, the sweetest girl Redwood Academy had ever known. This wasn't like me. But I didn't care anymore.

I couldn't care anymore.

I hated Callan. Tears welled up in my eyes. I really fucking hated him.

I wish I hated him.

Truth was that I refused to walk out into that hallway with him because I feared that I would let him lie straight to my face. I feared that I'd forgive him. I feared that I would wrap my arms around him and tell him that it was okay, that it was fine, that I didn't mind what he had said.

But I fucking minded. I wanted to hurt whoever the fuck thought they could sleep with him too. Callan had been—*was*—mine. And if he thought that something like that would slip by me without a second thought … he had another thing coming.

My heart clenched. My chest was tight. I wanted to scream at him, cry, ask him what the fuck was wrong with me. Why wasn't I enough? Why did he have to go fuck another girl? Was that what our relationship was all along?

"Excuse me?" my teacher asked, clearing her throat and straightening her shoulders.

I glared at my desk, tears threatening to spill over. I didn't even want to look at him, but I forced myself to show him that I wasn't going to be played with any longer.

I dragged my gaze to his. "I'm not going anywhere with you."

He probably had followed me in here and thought that I wouldn't put up a fight in front of everyone else. But he was wrong. He wasn't going to push me around anymore. Nobody was. I wanted this year to end. I wanted to be out of Redwood for good. I hated it here.

I had no friends, and he had taken advantage of that.

He stared at me with wide eyes that were filled with what looked to be tears. I glared at him for a few moments, feeling nothing but anger, rage, hate.

How could he do this to me? How could he do this to me and then look at me like he was innocent?

"Sakura," my teacher scolded, "you will either go into the hall with him or to the principal's office by yourself. You choo—"

"No," Callan said, stiffening at her words. "It's fine. I'll talk to her later."

Before my teacher could say another word, Callan walked out of the room and left. When the door shut behind him, I looked back down at my computer and frowned, holding back the tears. The cries.

He had been using me the entire time.

The entire time, and I wasn't good enough for him.

52

callan

AFTER THE LAST BELL RANG, I pressed my lips together and shut off the lights in my classroom, and then I headed toward Principal Vaughn's office. I scanned the hallways for Sakura, like I had done all last period while my class was working in the library.

When I reached his office, I closed my eyes and took a deep breath. *Fuck*.

I tapped on the Voice Memos app on my phone. I didn't want to be here, but I had no choice. Whatever the mob had been doing behind my back, I needed to figure it out. I didn't know how bad it truly was, but I knew I needed to stop it.

"Callan," Vaughn said when I walked in. "I didn't think you'd show up."

I closed the door behind me, really wishing that I weren't here. All I wanted to do was go find Sakura and apologize, force her to hear me out. But she wanted none of that. She barely wanted to even *look* at me.

He nodded to his desk, and I sat across from him and gulped.

"Who can I choose from?"

"We have plenty of girls," he said.

"Plenty?" I asked.

"Whoever you'd like"—Vaughn smirked—"we can get them."

"Who's we?" I asked, playing dumb.

He chuckled. "You work for them, don't you? Have they not told you about this?"

"The mob?" I asked, running my tongue across my teeth. "They've mentioned it briefly."

Not to me, but to each other. I had to figure it out. They had been using me all these years to get in with the principal? Was that what I had been for? I fucking hated them. One of these fucking days, I'd end them too.

"Who are you into?" Principal Vaughn asked. "What's your type?"

Swallowing hard, I dropped my gaze to the floor and clenched my jaw. I would have to tell him anyone but Sakura. I couldn't pull her into this. He already knew too much about us from the way I looked at her and maybe even about the way I felt about her.

I couldn't get defensive.

"So, who's it going to be?" he asked.

"What kind of girls do you have?" I asked quietly.

"Ahhh, any kind you want. Student athletes, cheerleaders, emo goth girls with huge tits, and those nerdy girls. So, who are you into —besides Sakura? Are you *sure* you don't want her? She'd be way too easy, judging by the way she looks at you."

I gritted my teeth. "No, I don't want her."

I need her.

"Do you have a list?" I asked. "So I can take my pick?"

After unlocking and opening his bottom left desk drawer, he pulled out an iPad and turned it on. Once he opened the Notes app, he handed me the tablet. On the list, there were at least fifty names of girls at Redwood Academy, both past and present students.

Some were even freshman. Fucking freshman students.

Even the police chief's daughter, Nicole, was on the list.

I scroll through each and every name, trying to remember them. I needed to help out however I could. I wanted to save these girls.

Not only would it give me something to do other than sit around and sulk about Sakura not talking to me, but also because what was happening was wrong. So wrong.

What I'd done to Sakura in detention was wrong too.

But these girls … they were being pimped out for money. And most of them were underage. These men and women in Redwood were raping these innocent girls. It was hypocritical as fuck of me, but I needed to stop it.

"How do I choose?" I asked. "What happens if I do?"

"You don't have to choose one right away. I can show you what they look like, see if you're really into them before you go ahead and take one home." He smirked. "I think you'll want to see it."

"See it? What do you mean? Do you have pictures?"

"Oh, Callan. We have something better than pictures." He nodded me over.

When he opened a folder on his computer, a bunch of videos popped up of surveillance around Redwood Academy. While a few cameras were in the hallway, some were in the restrooms, locker rooms, everywhere.

He scrolled through a couple of videos of girls getting undressed, football players showering, people having sex in the locker room and in the fucking staircase. I stiffened when I realized Blaise and Vera were among some of the couples.

I balled my hands into tight fists. I wanted to fucking puke.

What the fuck was wrong with him? What the fuck was wrong with everyone in Redwood? I hated this entire fucking town. I wanted to leave, to whisk Sakura away as soon as she finished high school, and leave this place for good.

"These are fucking amazing," I said, desperate to *not* seem suspicious.

My voice was stone-cold. I didn't want him to know how disgusted I was by all of this.

Though I wanted to die on the inside. Thank God he hadn't found anything on Sakura and me. I had been careful to fuck her in my classroom and nowhere else. But I wondered if he had cameras in the classrooms. Maybe he had seen us together.

And Blaise ...

Fucking Blaise had already been accused of killing Skylar. Now, this?

I needed to tell somebody about this, somebody that I knew would take care of this mess. But I couldn't get my toes too much into it. I was too close to the mob. If they heard that I'd found out about them, about this, they'd kill me.

53

AFTER SCHOOL, I had watched Callan walk into the principal's office. I'd been waiting in the hallway for almost an hour now for him to come out with his hair all ruffled and that stupid sex-smirk on his face.

I wanted to see the girl he had decided to fuck in my place.

Who is it? Nicole, the head cheerleader? Maybe it is another good girl like me?

Pacing the hallway, I held my backpack straps tightly in my hands and shook my head.

This can't be happening. This really can't fucking be happening.

He had to be in there with another student, fucking her the way he had fucked me.

Doubts about the past three weeks raced through my head. *What the fuck am I doing here? Am I really staying and waiting for him to come out? Do I really want to see that? No, of course not. I hate him.*

But I did want revenge.

When I spotted Poison walking out of one of the many side doorways, I sprinted down the hall toward them. The only thing I could think about was Callan, about what he was doing, about the catalog of girls he could be fucking right now.

My entire body ached, my throat closing.

"Kai," I said, catching up to them and grabbing his wrist. "I need a favor."

João arched his brow and pulled out a box of cigarettes, leaning against the side of the building and rolling his eyes. "Oh, this will be good. Another good girl coming to us with a *favor*. How fucking exciting."

Kai cut his gaze to João, then turned to me. "What is it?"

"Do you have a gun?" I asked.

The words had tumbled out of my mouth before I could even stop them, and I didn't even know why I had asked. *Do I really think I can hold a gun steady? What the fuck will I even use it for? Protection? To hurt someone?*

Tears welled up in my eyes at the thought. *Hurt someone? Is that what I am resorting to? Hurting Callan? How can I think such a thing?* As much as I hated him for shooting Gunther, he had protected me from him.

And now, I want to hurt him?!

"A gun?" Kai asked, eyes widening. He snatched my arm and tugged me to the side, away from João, who was now laughing his ass off at me. "What the fuck do you need a gun for, Sakura? Is something going on at home?"

If Callan had done all that to just use me, if he was fucking another girl right now in the principal's office, if I had been so stupid to believe that a man twice my age would actually like an impressionable girl like me …

I pressed a hand over my mouth to muffle a sob.

Why have I been so stupid these past few days? Why did I actually think he liked me and wasn't just using me for my pussy because his wife wasn't giving him any? Tears streamed down my face. *What is wrong with me?*

"Sakura," Kai said.

"N-no," I whispered. "I'm sorry. I shouldn't have asked."

When I turned away, he yanked me back by the wrist. "What is it?"

"Nothing," I said, pulling myself away. "Forget it."

"Is it something at school?" he asked.

"Please, drop it," I whispered. "It doesn't matter. Why do you even care?"

"Because you asked me for a *gun*."

"Forget it," João said to him. "Hurry this up. We have shit to do."

"I'm not going to just forget it," he said, shoving João back. "You know there's some shit going on in this town. And now, the valedictorian is asking me for a fucking gun." He turned back to me. "What's wrong? What happened?"

But I couldn't tell him. I didn't want to tell him. This had been a mistake, asking him for a gun. I wasn't even planning to use it. I didn't know what had gotten into me. I was so jealous. So fucking jealous.

It wasn't fair. None of this was fair.

It had been an hour after school. An entire hour.

"I can't tell you," I said. "It's just … it's my love life. My stupid fucking love life."

João took another long drag of his cigarette. "Avery? I knew Vera couldn't trust him."

Vera? I pushed my tears off my cheeks and glared back at the school. *Is he fucking Vera too?* She was the prettiest girl in all of Redwood Academy. I didn't know why the hell I'd thought she wouldn't do something like that.

Callan must've liked the smart, nerdy, geeky girls, like me.

Which meant he had a load of women to fuck—Allie Hall, Imani Abara, Vera Rodriguez, Maddie Weber, Astrid Hansen. The list went on and on and on and on and on. He had an entire collection of women to choose from if he wanted.

Kai pressed his lips together. "What did he do?"

"Nothing. He did nothing to me."

Instead of continuing the conversation, I stormed away and to my car. I couldn't tell him what had happened. They already had an idea of what was going on between me and Mr. Avery. But still, I couldn't. It was so embarrassing—too embarrassing.

After sliding into the car, I turned it on and hit the gas.

And the most fucked up part about this all? I still wanted to see him.

So, that was what I was going to do. I steered the car in the direction of his home. When he was done fucking whoever he was fucking, he'd get me. I'd show him what he was missing. I'd show him that he should have chosen me.

54

callan

AFTER MY WHOLE ordeal with Principal Vaughn, I drove to Sakura's house. And when I didn't spot her car in the driveway, I raced all around Redwood to find her. I really needed to talk to her. What she had heard … it wasn't the truth. I didn't want to fuck another girl.

I wanted her, and I needed to protect her from this sex ring.

She had heard it all wrong. But I didn't blame her.

If I had heard her say what I had said, I would have thought the same exact fucking thing. I would have thought that she wanted to fuck somebody else, that I wasn't good enough. And I needed to find a way to make it up to her.

But after driving for an hour and not spotting her car anywhere, I drove to the hospital to check on Gunther. I knew it was stupid, especially if I couldn't make it up to Sakura and explain myself. But I needed to make sure that he was okay and kept his mouth quiet.

If he woke up and told the nurse what had happened, I'd be fucking screwed.

Once I slammed my car door, I walked to the hospital and smiled sweetly at the front desk ladies to get inside. I didn't have time to sit and chat. I needed to get in and out of here as quickly as possible.

"Third floor," she said, smiling at me.

As soon as I walked away, I dropped the fucking act and headed up the stairs to Gunther's room. I stood outside his door and gazed in through the small window. He lay in the bed with tubes and needles sticking into his body.

"Mr. Avery," a nurse called.

Fuck.

I plastered another fake smile on my face and peered over at her. "Yes?"

An older lady with deep crow's-feet and white hair walked over. She looked familiar.

"Do you know any of Gunther Zurn's relatives?" she asked, looking down at her clipboard. "We haven't been able to get ahold of anyone. We've looked into him a bit more, and both his parents are dead. If you know any of his family members who might be of help to him ..."

"He doesn't have any family. Both his parents were only children," I said.

I had done my research on him as soon as he started showing interest in Sakura. I hadn't trusted him one fucking bit from the start. Sure, he might've had good intentions all this time, but he didn't come from a good family.

"He doesn't have insurance," she said. "So, even if he survives and comes out of his coma, he will be drowning in hospital bills. We can try to offset the initial cost, but health care is terrible in America, especially right now." Her lips pulled into a frown. "Even worse than it was when your mom—"

"I know," I said, cutting her off. "I remember how bad it was then."

"That was almost two decades ago," she said.

When she glanced up at me nervously, I finally recognized her as the nurse who had taken care of my mother after her accident when

I was still in high school. She had known me before all this shit happened with Georgina.

I stared at her for a couple of moments, eyes widening and guilt rushing through me. If she found out that I had done this to Gunther, I would feel even worse, as I should. The Callan she knew was still a boy, a sweet and innocent boy who'd bring her lemonade every Saturday night while visiting Mom.

"I'll take care of it," I whispered.

"But ..." She gulped. "Mr. Avery, if he does come out of it, his bills will be upward of hundreds of thousands. All I was asking for is if you know anyone of his family members who I can talk to about this. A grandparent, maybe a guard—"

"I'll take care of it," I repeated clearly.

This was the least I could do.

After Sakura had overheard my conversation in the hallway with Principal Vaughn, I doubted she would want anything to do with me ever again. I thought that following her into her next classroom and asking her teacher if I could talk to her would get Sakura to finally talk to me. But instead, she talked back, she told me no, she scolded me in front of everybody. The good girl, the valedictorian, had surprised everyone today.

And I didn't want to hurt her even more. She didn't deserve that. I had been such a dick to her.

The nurse gently grasped my wrist. "You're a good man, Callan."

But I wasn't.

I grimaced at her and walked away because I couldn't stand here and lie to the woman who had taken care of my mother. I couldn't do it anymore. I couldn't do any of this anymore—be in this fucking mob, take people's lives, live without Sakura.

As I walked away from the nurse, my phone buzzed in my pocket. I whipped it out and hoped that it was her. I'd been texting and calling her for the past forty-five minutes after leaving the principal's office. I needed to make sure that she was at least okay.

Vaughn had been talking so much about her lately, making

comments about her body. I feared that she'd be next to be added to this catalog of girls who were being pimped out to all of Redwood Academy. I needed to fucking stop it before it happened.

When I read the screen, Jett's name popped up. I cursed under my breath, realizing that I had to take care of him too. He was still sitting in his beach house, scared out of his fucking mind. I didn't have time for all this shit.

55

sakura

TAPPING MY FOOT, I clutched on to the steering wheel and stared at Callan's closed garage door. I chewed on the inside of my cheek and cursed underneath my breath.

Where the hell is he? Still fucking Vera?

I glanced into the rearview mirror and spotted him driving up his driveway. When he saw me, he slammed on the brakes and parked his car without driving it into the garage, like he usually did when I was with him.

Unable to stop myself, I threw my car door open. He hurried out of his car and over to my side, brows drawn together.

"Sakura, what are you doing here? I've been looking for you all over Redwood. We need to talk."

"Yes, we do." I shoved him back because he was too close. I had come here to show him what he was missing, what he had lost, but I couldn't get anything out, except, "Was it all a lie? Was it all a fucking lie?" Every word that came out of my mouth was spoken louder and louder. I couldn't stop myself. I was almost screaming in the middle of this driveway with all his neighbors around.

But I couldn't keep fucking doing this. I wanted answers.

So, I shoved him again. "Hmm? Answer me!"

"Sakura, please, calm down," he said, his voice a whisper.

He took my arm and pulled me inside the garage, where it was more private.

Because God forbid his neighbors find out he's been cheating on his wife.

"I just want to talk."

When we reached his front door, I yanked my arm out of his and stormed into the foyer. Fury raced through me. Hot tears welled up in my eyes, but I pushed them back. I'd come here for one thing. For revenge. To show him what he had lost.

I wouldn't be the weak Sakura he knew.

Today, he wouldn't take advantage of me. It was my turn.

"What you heard," Callan started, shutting the door behind himself, "it wasn't—"

"Shut up," I said quietly, narrowing my heated gaze at him.

Callan stared at me through wide eyes. "You're misunderstanding. I didn't mean what I—"

"Stop!" I shouted, tears building again because I couldn't control myself. "Stop lying to me."

"I'm not lying to you, Sakura," he whispered, tucking some hair behind my ear.

I smacked his hand away. "You told the principal that you wanted to fuck somebody else, another girl. Do you know how that fucking sounds? Did you think you could just screw me over like that? Do you think I'm that naive? That I don't understand what you're doing?"

"I'm not doing anything, except trying to protect you," he said.

"From what?" I shouted.

I felt like I was going fucking crazy.

"You literally killed somebody in front of me and then wanted to fuck somebody else behind my back." I shoved him back again. "I hope that you had a good fucking time with Vera this afternoon because I officially hate you." I shoved him again. "I hate you so much."

One last shove, and he fell back onto the couch.

"What do you mean, did I have a good time with Vera? Vera Rodriguez?" he asked, as if I was that fucking stupid. He knew exactly what I had meant. Even João had said something about them together. "What does she have to do with any of thi—"

I climbed on top of him and grabbed his chin in my hand, squeezing my fingers against his cheeks. "I don't want to hear it. I'm going to show you what you lost, Callan Avery. And when I'm done, you're going to be sorry."

56

callan

"SAKURA," I whispered as she lowered herself down onto me, "you don't have to do this."

She gripped on to my shoulders and glared down at me through teary eyes. Without saying a word, she dug her small fingernails into my back and nestled her pussy all the way down against me.

Pleasure rushed through my body, my balls heavy. But I didn't want to take her like this, while she was upset and on the verge of tears. I hated the way she was looking—glaring—at me like I was a monster, like she needed to *prove* something to me.

"Everything I've done was to protect you," I whispered. "I didn't—"

"Stop talking," she ordered, voice sharp. Yet I didn't miss the way it cracked at the end.

Moving her body against me, she lifted her hips and dropped them back down on my dick. I placed my hands on her hips and lightly dug my fingers into her ass. God, I fucking hated this so much, but I didn't want to upset her.

I didn't want her to think that I didn't want to fuck her because I was fucking Vera Rodriguez, apparently. I didn't know where the hell she had gotten that idea, but maybe it was when I had stopped Vera from embarrassing herself during lunch the other day.

"I hate you," she said, sinking her nails into me. "I hate you so much."

"I don't hate you," I murmured. "I could never."

"Stop," she growled. "Stop lying."

"I'm not lying."

She tore her gaze away from me and pressed her body against mine so she didn't have to look at me at all, her head buried in the crook of my neck and wet tears beginning to soak into my shirt.

"Sakura," I whispered. "Why don't you stop and talk to me?"

"No," she whimpered. "Y-you're going to lie to me again. You're going to hurt me."

After sniffling, she gripped on to me tighter and continued to ride me. I closed my eyes and tried fucking hard not to get soft because it'd just tear her to pieces even more. But how the hell did she expect me to stay hard while she was crying against me, while she was only doing this because she thought she had to prove something to me?

"I don't want you to cry," I said, wrapping my arms around her waist and pulling her closer to me.

But while her body began to tremble violently in my arms, she refused to stop bucking her hips against me.

"Please, I hate seeing you sad."

"Liar," she cried into my shoulder. "You're a liar."

"I swear, Sakura, I'm not lying to you."

She lowered her hips deep on my cock and stopped, body stiffening. "Y-you're not hard anymore," she whimpered, clutching on to me even tighter. "Am I not good enough for you? I can't even keep you hard? Is that why you want to fuck other girls?"

"No," I said, chest tightening.

I hated that she thought this way, that *I had made her* think this way. I wanted her to feel special, for her to love me the way that I loved her, for her to let me protect her, no matter the cost. So, I gently grasped a fistful of her hair and pulled back so she looked me in the eyes.

"I fucking love you, Sakura," I said. "I wouldn't choose anyone over you."

Heavy tears trembled in her eyes. She opened and closed her mouth about five times while shaking her head. Tears slid down her cheeks. "Y-you're lying. You d-don't l-love me. If you did … if you did, you wouldn't want anyone else."

Once again, she buried her face into the crook of my neck. But this time, she cried hard and loud, clutching on to me like she never wanted to let go. "Why do you want to fuck someone else? Why am I not good enough for you? I-I'm sorry if I did something wrong. I-I'll try harder. I'll be better, sexier for you, if that's what you want."

Fuck.

I blinked my stinging eyes a couple of times, scrunched my face, and desperately tried to keep myself together, but I hadn't felt like this for anyone before. And while I didn't want Sakura to change a damn thing about herself, nobody had ever wanted me that badly before that they'd do anything for me.

She hiccuped through the cries, body quivering in my arms. "I have to hate you."

"I'm sorry that I made you feel that way," I whispered, though I didn't think she could hear me over her sobs. I held her tighter and tighter with every word, desperate for her to love me, not hate me. I couldn't lose her. "I need to explain myself. Please, let me."

When her cries softened, I thought that she was finally giving me the chance to admit to her everything that had happened and what I planned to do about it, but her cries turned into whimpers, and her whimpers turned into soft snores.

I let out a shaky breath and picked her up off me, walking with her to the bedroom. Once I rested her on the bed, I lay down beside her and brushed the hair out of her face. Moonlight flooded in through the window, bouncing off her pale skin and highlighting the tear streaks on her cheeks.

"There is so much I need to tell you," I whispered, knowing that she couldn't hear me, but wishing that she could. "There are girls, Sakura, girls that Redwood is abusing. A sex trafficking ring that Principal Vaughn wants *you* to be part of. I can't let that happen. I can't fucking let that happen. I can't lose you. I fucking brought Gunther to the damn hospital for you. *For you.* And I'd do it again if it meant protecting you."

Even if she never forgave me for what I had done, I'd give my fucking life for her.

57

sakura

LYING IN CALLAN'S BED, I stared up at the ceiling sometime in the middle of the night.

I wished I hadn't fallen asleep so I could've left immediately. But with all the pain, I had found myself dozing off in his arms and listening to him mumble something into my ear about what had happened.

But now, in the middle of the night, he stood outside on the patio with the phone pressed to his ear, talking to his wife's father. The fun, caring, lighthearted Callan had done it once again—had fooled me into believing that he really cared, that he wasn't using me for sex.

Tears welled in my eyes, but I refused to let them fall. Instead, I sat up in the bed and stared straight ahead at the wall, where there looked to be a picture frame that had been taken down recently.

Like a zombie, I slipped out of bed, then out of the room. I snatched my keys from the coffee table. I needed a drink, and I *never* drank.

Without so much as a good-bye or a note that said I had left, I walked out of the front door and to my car. Callan's voice faintly traveled from the backyard patio to the garage as he spoke with Jett. I gritted my teeth and pushed back more tears.

Fuck, what was wrong with me?

I shouldn't be crying over him. I was the one who had come to his house in a fit of rage this afternoon and basically climbed on top of the man. I had so desperately wanted him to fucking hurt, to feel guilty.

But it was no use. No fucking use.

After slipping into my car, I swallowed and shut my eyes. A single tear rolled down my cheek. I had barely slept all night, had been tossing and turning in his arms since I had heard him mumble horrid things to me. I might've been half asleep, but I remembered some of his words.

"There are girls, Sakura, girls that Redwood is abusing."

Has he even been telling the truth? Is he really trying to stop whatever this sex trafficking thing is? Or has he been in it all along? Is he trying to get me into this ring, too, so he can pimp me out?

And Vera … maybe she was in it too. Maybe I had gotten this all wrong. Maybe I … maybe I still wasn't getting it right. I didn't know what the hell was going on in Redwood, and honestly, I wished that I wouldn't ever know.

When I reopened my eyes, I glanced at the car clock that read three a.m. in glowing white numbers. I started the car and backed out of the driveway before he could stop me. I should've stayed and heard him out more, but I didn't have it in me.

My heart had been shattered, the pieces stomped on by the man I loved.

The man I love?

Heart racing, I shook my head and continued down the streets. I couldn't think that way. How could I begin thinking that I loved that man? He had hurt me purposefully one time after another after another.

Gunther … *He was protecting me.*

Vera … *He was protecting me.*

Jett … *He was protecting me.*

I curled my hand around the steering wheel and shook my head. When I stopped at the Stop sign to exit his street, I glanced back into the rearview mirror, hoping his crazy ass had realized that I was gone and was following after me the way he had done to the Overlook.

But I'd expected too much.

He had been outside in deep conversation when I left. Even if he had gone back inside by now and noticed I wasn't in bed, he would have to search for me through that entire mansion before seeing my car wasn't in the driveway any longer.

When I started driving, his words from earlier rang through my head again.

"I fucking brought Gunther to the damn hospital for you. For you."

Shaking my head, I desperately tried to shove the thought away. I didn't want to believe him. I wanted to hate him so much for hurting me, but my mind wasn't in the right space right now. I was making rash decisions and couldn't stop myself.

Dad must've been looking for me, calling me, texting me all night.

I should go home.

But instead, I found myself taking street after street away from my home and to Redwood Hospital. If what he had said about Gunther was true, then maybe … maybe it all was. Maybe I was being a hormonal kid right now.

Visiting hours didn't start until nine a.m.—six hours from now.

Yet all I needed was confirmation that Gunther Zurn was here.

Once I braced myself for the worst, I stepped out of my car and walked to the front entrance. If Gunther wasn't here, then I couldn't believe anything that Callan had told me tonight. If Gunther wasn't here, then I would … I would have to stop this craziness.

My chest tightened as I stepped into the hospital, the air-conditioning making me shiver. I walked up to the front desk and patiently waited for a nurse to spot me. Heart pounding, I bounced on my toes.

A couple of moments later, a nurse appeared from the back. "How can I help you?"

"I'm looking for a patient," I said.

"Visiting hours are over for the night," she said. "Come back in a few hours."

"I just … I need to know if he's here," I said.

"Are you a family member?" she asked.

"N-no, but … please," I whispered. "His name is Gunther Zurn."

"I'm sorry, ma'am. That's private information."

"Please," I pleaded, heart dropping. "It's important."

"I'm sorry." She glanced at the security guard. "I'm going to have to ask you to leave."

Not wanting to get into any trouble tonight, I lowered my head and walked out of the front doors. As I turned the corner, I bumped into a tall woman dressed in a white jacket with her curly brown hair pulled back into a bun. Her name tag read Dr. Abara.

Abara? Is she Imani Abara's mother?

"Excuse me, dear," she said, walking by me.

"Are you Imani's mother?" I asked, knowing that this would be my last hope.

She paused and turned around, giving me a huge smile. "I am. Do you know her?"

"Yeah," I said, smiling softly. "I go to school with her. Um …" I intertwined my fingers. "One of my friends from Redwood is actually in the hospital. I just found out about it tonight and wanted to know if you knew his room number so I could come back tomorrow during visiting hours. His name is Gunther Zurn."

"Gunther Zurn," she hummed, brow furrowing for a moment. "Ah, yes. Mr. Avery brought him in the other night."

My eyes widened. *Oh my gosh.*

He had been telling me the truth this entire time. If he had really brought Gunther to the hospital after I begged him to save him, then he had done it for me and for me only.

"I believe he's on the third floor," Dr. Abara continued, glancing into the sliding glass front doors. "I would need to double-check, but if I'm still here tomorrow when you return, I'll show you to his room."

"Great," I whispered. "That's great."

58

sakura

BECAUSE MY PHONE had died hours ago, I drove back home instead of to Callan's place. Mom might've been high off prescription drugs somewhere, but Dad was most likely at home, worried sick about my whereabouts. I had been staying out late more than usual recently.

When I pulled up to my house, the living room light glimmered through the front window. I parked in the driveway and gathered my belongings from school, then walked to the front door, where Dad stood nervously.

"Thank God," he said, opening the door for me. "I thought you were dead."

"Sorry," I said, walking into the house and replacing my shoes with slippers at the door. "My phone died."

"Where were you?" he asked.

"At Ichika's," I said, avoiding eye contact.

"I called her hours ago," he said. "You hadn't gone over."

I walked into the living room and froze when I spotted Mom passed out on the couch with drool dripping from her lip. If she hadn't made it to the bed, that meant she had been high, like I'd expected. Between her and me staying out late … it wasn't fair to Dad.

"Please, don't tell me that you're hanging around with bad kids," he whispered from behind me. "I … I don't want you ending up like your mother, Sakura. Please, talk to me. Have I done something wrong?"

Tears welling in my eyes, I dropped my head. "I would never take medication like her, Dad," I whispered, turning around and staring at the anguish in his eyes. "You haven't done anything wrong."

"Where were you?" he asked, pushing up his glasses. "You're never home anymore. I don't want to push you away because you're my only daughter … the only person I have left in this family. But I … I'm worried about you."

"You don't have to worry about me," I said, brows drawn together. "I'll always be here."

"Where were you?" he repeated again.

I pressed my lips together, knowing that I would disappoint him if I told him the truth, that I was at my Literature professor's house, fucking him for some kind of sick revenge. That, the other night, I had watched him shoot another student. That, just yesterday, I had learned there was a damn sex trafficking ring in Redwood.

"Dad," I whispered, "I'm tired."

"I'm looking out for you," he said. "You're going to be valedictorian, Sakura. You've worked so hard, and I don't want you to blow it on … on whatever it is that you're doing, *whoever* it is …"

Freezing, I swallowed hard. *Whoever? Does he know about Callan?*

"Okay," I whispered. "I was out with a guy that I've been seeing for a couple of weeks now."

"A boy?" Dad said.

A boy? Callan is not a boy.

"Yeah," I lied. "Someone from Redwood."

An awkward silence fell over us, and I dreaded the day that I would have to tell my dad about Callan. Maybe that day would never come. Maybe his wife would come back, and he'd stay with her. Maybe we would never be able to be together.

I wasn't sure.

"Are you being safe?"

My cheeks warmed, and I looked away. "Dad!"

"What? I don't want anything to happen."

"Yes, I'm being safe." *Sorta.* At least, I was being safe in the way that he was implying. I had gotten an IUD placed inside me a while ago, when this entire thing had started. I walked toward the stairs. "Now, I'd really like to sleep."

When I reached the stairs, Dad hummed, "I would like to meet him."

Pausing on the steps, I widened my eyes. *Fuck, this is awkward.* I didn't even know what we were right now, was still getting over everything that had happened these past few days, and trying to comprehend that Callan had really taken Gunther to the hospital for me.

I didn't think I would be ready for something like *that* for a long, long, long, long, long time. Not until I was out of high school and Callan wasn't a teacher anymore. Because how on earth could I tell Dad that I was fucking someone almost *his* age?!

"Maybe sometime," I said, hurrying up the stairs. "Good night."

"Good night, sweetheart."

Once I successfully made it up to my room without any more questions, I dumped my backpack onto the ground and collapsed on the bed. I plugged my phone into the charger and stared up at my bland ceiling.

Part of me wished that I had stayed at Callan's, but I needed a break. I needed to get away from him so I could finally think straight. I had been such a bitch to him lately because I was insecure and on edge after I found out what had happened to Skylar.

I just hoped that I wasn't falling into a lie, that I wasn't falling for a man who would really hurt me one of these days. I had blindly believed what I'd heard—for good reason—but still, Callan was in the mob. I didn't know what he was capable of.

I feared Callan Avery would ruin my life, from the inside out, because I was far too gone for that man, far too deep in whatever these goddamn feelings were inside me. I was madly in love with my Literature professor.

59

callan

"THE FUCK DO YOU WANT?" João asked, stepping out of his Mercedes with tinted windows the next morning at five a.m.

Sakura had left me last night while I was talking to Jett—who wouldn't stop fucking calling me—and I feared that I had screwed up beyond repair with her.

I should've blocked his fucking number, like I had with Georgina, when I had the chance, but I answered it so he wouldn't wake her up. I really wanted to talk to her this morning, but I had blown that one.

After glancing around to ensure no other students had driven into the student parking lot, I pulled two black duffel bags, stuffed full with stacks of hundred-dollar bills, from my trunk and tossed them to his feet. João and Poison wouldn't pass up this kind of money.

"Vaughn is part of a sex trafficking ring at Redwood. He has a list of girls he's helping the mob pimp out to the billionaires who run this town." I pulled out the recording I had transferred from my phone to a flash drive this morning of my conversation with Vaughn yesterday afternoon. "Take care of him."

João knelt and unzipped one of the bags, gazing into it. "Vaughn's the ugliest motherfucker I've ever seen. Don't know why any girl would trust him with anything even if he's the principal."

"Two million dollars total now and then another two once the job is done," I said.

"Why don't you do it yourself?" he asked, standing.

"Because I'm too fucking close to it all," I said. "I have other shit to deal with right now."

João leaned back against his car, pulled out a pack of cigarettes and a lighter, and stuffed one into his mouth. After taking a long drag of it, he pulled the cigarette from his mouth and blew out a puff of smoke.

"Make it six," he said. "These are our lives, Avery. We'd be tried as adults if caught."

"Cut the bullshit. I know you have killed people before and haven't been caught."

"Six million or no deal."

This was Jett's dirty money, so I really didn't give a fuck what happened to it. But still, João wasn't about to take advantage of me like he probably did all the other rich kids who asked him for favors, who'd pay two million just for information.

"Imani is on Vaughn's *wish* list," I said, briefly remembering that I had spotted a couple of members of Poison in the halls with Imani Abara recently. "Poison isn't the only men who've been intrigued by her looks lately."

João stiffened, but then turned away and stuck the cigarette into his mouth, inhaling the smoke into his lungs. "You're fucking bluffing, Avery. Imani is on no list, and if she were, why would I care?"

"Four million," I said.

Instead of answering me, he grabbed the flash drive from me and tossed the bags of money into his trunk. "If you're fucking lying about Imani being on the fucking list, I will kill you myself for free. Don't ask me for shit ever again."

Once he shut the trunk, he turned back to me and pulled the cigarette from his mouth. He stepped closer to me, until we stood toe to toe, and blew out a puff of smoke into my face. And I had to resist the urge to hurl my fist into his ugly face right then and there.

"Sakura asked Kai for a gun," he said, smirking. "Because of you."

"She what?" I asked, startled.

No way in hell would Sakura ask someone for a gun. João had to be lying to get underneath my fucking skin. And because of me? When had this happened? Yesterday? Today? A week ago?

"Stop fucking lying to me," I said between gritted teeth. "Leave and do the fucking job."

"You can ask her yourself," he said, pulling out a pack of cigarettes. "Why would I lie about that? I thought it was funny as hell. The valedictorian of Redwood Academy, asking Poison for a gun to off her boyfriend."

He's lying. He's lying. He's lying.

He has to be fucking lying.

Does Sakura want to kill me? Have I driven her that crazy? All I did was protect her, and she wants to kill me? She had barely let me explain myself last night, and the little explanation I had given … I doubted she even believed. I doubted she had even *heard.*

"Kai told her no," João said, turning around. "But it really makes you think …"

With fury rushing through me, I wrapped my hand around his throat and shoved him against his car door. "What the fuck do you think you're doing?" I asked through gritted teeth. "Did she pay you to tell me that? To fucking scare me?"

"Sakura didn't pay me shit," he growled, shoving me back and straightening himself out. "But she did watch you murder Gunther Zurn in front of her the other night"—he glanced down at the parking lot—"right fucking here."

"How the fuck do you know about that?" I asked. "You disabled all the cameras here."

"Avery. Avery. Avery. You think we're that stupid to disable one of the school cameras and *not* set up one of our own? We know everything that goes on in this section of Redwood Academy. Watch yourself next time."

And with that, he walked around his car to the driver's side and slipped into the hunk of metal. I balled my hands into tight fists, watching him drive off before any other students or teachers turned up for school today.

That fucker had to be lying.

Sakura had waited for me at my house last night, marched right into my living room, and fucked me as she cried her pretty brown eyes out. She didn't have a hurtful bone in her body. She wouldn't ask for a gun.

But what if I had driven her insane, thrust her past her breaking point?

Between Gunther and Vaughn, letting her believe that I really wanted to fuck someone else, and Skylar's death ... any innocent woman who didn't know how corrupt Redwood really was would fear for her life.

60

THE NEXT MORNING, I woke up ten minutes before I usually left for school and scrambled through my bedroom, running a brush through my hair and skipping a shower altogether. I really wished that I could've skipped today, too, because I didn't know what I would say to Callan.

After checking my phone to see no messages from him, I hurried downstairs, grabbed a couple of pieces of toast, and slipped into my car.

He had really brought Gunther to the hospital for me. After everything.

Once I made it to school, I spotted Callan's car parked in its usual spot and trudged into Redwood Academy. I didn't have his class until a couple of periods from now, so I had between now and then to really figure this all out.

What could I say to him? Should I apologize? Ask him if he really meant the other parts of his confession about the sex trafficking ring? Possibly see if the mob had anything to do with it? Because if they did, then that meant Callan did too.

When I stepped into Redwood, the entire student body chatted loudly and laughed at their phones. I glanced around nervously, hoping that they weren't gossiping about me, and walked to my locker.

I took out my books for the first few periods and checked my phone for any messages from Callan, only to find my messages dry. A couple of notifications popped up from Instagram and Redwood's social media. When I tapped on one—because I needed a distraction right now—an image of someone's Google Docs popped up.

My eyes glanced down at the story on the page, heat warming my cheeks.

God, this is raunchy.

When I finally read it all, I glanced at the caption to see Vera's name and a trending hashtag in the comments section. I swallowed hard, a terrible feeling in the pit of my stomach, and closed my locker.

As much as I'd hated Vera yesterday—for potentially sleeping with my ... my *fling*—I pitied her now, especially if what Callan had said was true and he had no interest in her. This story was so intimate, and I highly doubted that she had released this herself.

Just as I slipped my phone into my pocket, Vera and Blaise Harleen walked into the school through the main entrance. Vera glanced around nervously, cheeks flushed from the cold and brows drawn together.

They walked by me toward Vera's locker down the hall, where her two best friends stood.

"What's going on?" she said softly, voice traveling, even beyond Redwood's loudmouthed students.

I frowned and clutched my backpack straps, eyeing them. I didn't want her to feel bad. I wasn't staring because I liked this drama, like the rest of Redwood did, but I didn't know how to go talk to her. I was terrible with people—*cough, cough*—especially with Callan.

After gazing down at the phone, she widened her eyes and stepped back into Blaise, her hand trembling. Blaise glanced over her shoulder and froze too.

She shook her head. "My writing ..." she whispered. "Someone found my writing and released it to all of Redwood Academy."

Blaise seized the phone from her and scrolled through it.

Vera took another step back against his chest and wrapped her arms around her body, shaking her head and mumbling, "What am I going to do? What am I going to do? I've tried so hard to keep this a secret."

"It's okay," her friend said, gently rubbing Vera's shoulder.

"Don't worry about it," Maddie, her best friend, reassured. "We'll take care of it."

"How are you guys going to take care of it?" Vera asked, tensing. "The entire school—even the teachers—has already seen it. They've been snickering at me all morning since I stepped out of Blaise's car."

"We'll get someone to take it down," Maddie said. "Hopefully."

"That won't do anything," Vera whispered, glancing up at Blaise with fearful eyes. "Are you—"

"I didn't do it, Vera," Blaise said. "I fucking promise, I didn't do this."

"I know you didn't. I just ..." She glanced down at her feet and shrugged, a single tear falling down her cheek. "I don't even know what I was going to ask you. I don't know what I can do. I hate it here."

So do I, girl. So do freaking I.

"They're going to make fun of me," she whispered, resting her forehead against his chest. "I don't want them to make fun of me, Blaise. All I wanted was to be invisible this year. Redwood Academy is so cruel—so fucking cruel."

"They're not going to tease you, Vera," Maddie reassured.

But Vera was right. Redwood would taunt her over this.

"It's not Vera's," Blaise suddenly declared to the students in the hallway, capturing everyone's attention. "The writing is mine. Vera is writing an amazing romance story in her free time, and she asked me to write a sex scene for her because she couldn't write it herself."

The murmurs slowly faded to complete quietness.

"Come on," Blaise continued. "You guys think Vera could write something that fucking filthy?"

"*You* wrote that?" someone—who obviously wanted his ass kicked—said through the silence. "I'd believe the good girl wrote that before *you*. You can barely pass English class without your parents' money."

Blaise gritted his teeth and glared at the student.

"Blaise," Vera whispered, tugging on his shirt, "it's okay. Don't do this."

"So fucking what if I can pass English or not? I wanted something to jerk off to," Blaise said, rolling his eyes and picking up his skateboard. "The fuck do you guys care? Half of you think that I murdered one of our own classmates already anyway."

"Blaise," Vera whispered again, her voice even quieter.

"Isn't that right, Sunshine?" Blaise asked. "You needed some help."

Vera softened her eyes, her entire persona suddenly shifting. She parted her lips and stared up at Blaise.

He watched her for a moment, then asked, "Isn't that right, Vera?"

"Vera …" Maddie nudged her.

"No." Vera grabbed Blaise's wrist and stepped forward. "Blaise didn't write that scene."

They began bickering back and forth quietly, and I glanced around at all the curious students. And in the crowd, I spotted Callan Avery staring at me with sadness in his eyes, like I had done something that he never thought I would do.

I sucked in a sharp breath, my stomach twisting into knots, and glanced down at my phone to see if he had messaged me. But still, I had no texts from him. And when I looked back up at him, he was gone.

61

callan

"TURN to chapter eighteen in your books," I announced, standing in front of class.

Sakura flipped the pages of her book and stared up at me, her eyes wide, as if she wanted to talk. I pulled my gaze away from her and walked to the other side of the classroom, gazing aimlessly at the students who didn't care for Literature.

Looking over her shoulder, Sakura followed my gaze and pressed her lips together, spotting some cheerleaders in the back that she must've thought I had been staring at. She flared her nostrils and glared down at her book.

Possessive.

My girl was possessive over me.

I needed to talk to her, but—I glanced at the window that had been bugged, probably this morning by Vaughn or someone who worked for the mob—it wasn't safe to talk to anyone at school about anything anymore. I had noticed the bug last class and didn't want to remove it or else they'd know that I was onto them, that I had something to hide.

We would need to find another way. Maybe tonight.

Fifteen minutes later, someone knocked at the door, and Vaughn walked into the class.

"Good morning, Sakura," Principal Vaughn said, addressing her and nobody else.

Maddie—someone who I'd seen Sakura talk to briefly every now and then—gave her a funny look. Sakura forced a smile and looked back down at her textbook, knee bouncing underneath the table.

I balled my hands behind my back and clenched my jaw. *What the fuck is that?*

"Can I talk to you privately, Mr. Avery?" he asked.

I sighed and followed him to the door. "Begin reading the next chapter."

We walked out of the class, and I shut the door behind us.

"Sakura sits up front," he said. "How … great that must be for you."

"That has been her assigned seat since the beginning of the year."

He nodded. "Have you seen the Redwood social media lately?"

"Vaughn, I'm teaching a class."

"Vera Rodriguez is a phenomenal writer. Her words …" He rocked back on his heels and whistled lowly, stuffing his hands into his pockets. "Have you given it any thought? I think she'd be perfect for you, if you're against Sakura."

"I haven't had time," I said, running a hand through my hair. "I need to get back to class."

"Make a decision by the end of this week," he said. "Your boss has been itching for more clients and more girls. These young pretty cheerleaders go for a lot of money, but those nerdy, shy ones sell for even more."

My fist twitched. And I almost hit him square in the jaw.

"Sure," I gritted out. "Will do."

After talking to that fucking idiot, I walked back into the classroom and sat at my desk. I couldn't even think straight anymore, couldn't even begin to teach class again. If he planned on taking

Sakura next, I swore I'd kill him my fucking self after Jett was handled.

Ignoring Sakura wouldn't get either of us anywhere.

I wanted to talk to her so badly, to tell her to stay safe, but my fucking room had been bugged. But if anyone found out about us, they would use her against me.

And if I didn't get my act together and stop showing interest in Sakura, Vaughn might snatch her into this sex trafficking ring himself because she was another of Redwood Academy's good girls, who he suddenly had a thing for. I needed to keep my distance.

João had better have taken me seriously and had plans to kill him because I couldn't get my hands bloodier. Not right now. Not with people connected to the mob, as I was desperately trying to get out of this fucking life for Sakura.

"Mr. Avery," Sakura said, walking up to me at the end of class. "Can I talk to you?"

I fucking forced myself to keep my gaze glued to the stack of exams in front of me, aimlessly marking them up with red pen. "I'm busy now, Sakura," I said, flipping the page and ignoring her. And I fucking hated it.

She shifted from foot to foot, her skirt scrunching between her thighs. I clenched my jaw and drew my tongue across the back of my teeth, pants tightening around the crouch. Part of me wanted to lock the door behind all the other students, bend her over my desk, and fuck the truth out of her.

Had she really asked Poison for a gun? Did she want to kill me because of what I had done?

I gritted my teeth and dug my red pen into an exam. How could she do such a thing? João had to be lying, loved stirring up drama in Redwood Academy so his gang could fly under the radar. She didn't have a harmful bone in her body.

"Please, Mr. Avery. It's important," she said. "It's about Gunther."

Fuck, if she opens her mouth and says something about him here … I'll be screwed.

"I don't know why Gunther hasn't been here, Miss Sato," I said, voice hard. I straightened out my shoulders and looked up at her, gaze stiff. "You're going to miss class if you don't leave, and I'm not going to write you a late pass."

Her brown eyes widened. "B-but …"

"Leave, Sakura. Now."

She swallowed and turned on her heel, hands looped around her backpack straps as she dragged her feet to the door. "I'm sorry," she whispered, pausing in the doorway without looking back. "I'm so sorry."

62

sakura

I LINGERED outside of Mr. Avery's classroom, even after he told me to leave. Part of me hoped that he'd have a change of heart and ask me to come back into the room to talk. But he was utterly pissed at me today.

Was it because I hadn't believed him? Because of how I had reacted last night with him? Stormed off even after he asked me to let him speak, explain himself? Guilt washed through me, and I wrapped my arms around myself and walked down the hall.

These damn hormones …

He had every right to be pissed at me. I had been nothing but rude to him these past couple of days, but I'd … thought that *I* had every reason to be angry. How would *he* have reacted if I had shot someone he told me not to, then proceeded to watch me tell Ichika that I needed another older man to fuck because he was boring me.

Nobody wanted to feel like absolute garbage. He wouldn't have enjoyed that.

After glancing over my shoulder one last time, I frowned and turned the corner. I walked down another hallway to the staircase.

My next class was in the science wing, and I couldn't seem to care to get there on time anymore.

What did grades even matter if a Redwood Academy student was in the hospital and apparently a sex trafficking ring had been going on right in these halls? Grades almost seemed insignificant. I wanted to help out, too, but Callan was the only person with the information.

When the bell rang through the empty halls, I found myself dragging my feet. I didn't want to go to class. Even though AP chemistry was sorta, kinda hard, I had already reviewed all this material during my free time in the summer. I didn't need anyone forcing it down my throat for a second time.

Hopefully, I would be able to talk to Callan tomor—

"Miss Sato," Principal Vaughn hummed from behind me. "Late for class?"

I snapped my books to my chest and froze, throat drying. After sucking in a shaky breath, I turned around to face him and smiled softly. "Y-yes, sorry about that. I'm heading there now. I was just … taking care of female problems."

"No need, Miss Sato. I'll write you a pass," Principal Vaughn said. "I'd like to talk to you."

"I really need to learn this new material," I whispered, stepping back.

"I'll make sure your next teacher gets all the information to you by the end of the day. And besides, you pick up material very quickly. A very studious learner. One of the best in Redwood," he said, turning around to head back down the hall. "Follow me."

Fuck.

Deciding that I didn't want detention—especially with *him*—I followed Principal Vaughn to his office and hesitantly walked into the room. He followed me in, shutting and locking the door behind us.

Double fuck.

"Take a seat," he said from behind, pulling out a chair.

Nervously, I sat and clutched my books to my chest.

"How's Mr. Avery's class?" he asked, placing a hand on my shoulder.

I stiffened, feeling his fingers curl around me. "I-it's okay."

"Mr. Avery has been giving you special attention, hasn't he?"

"N-no," I whispered. "He hasn't."

"No time after school?" he asked. "No extra work?"

"Only if I ask for it. I-I really like Literature," I said, not wanting to get Callan in trouble.

We might not have been talking to each other, but I still cared about him. When I had told him I hated him, that was all a lie. A big, fat lie. If I'd hated that man, I wouldn't have cared what he did with other women, wouldn't have gotten jealous and stormed over, wouldn't have climbed into his lap and felt … safe.

"I'm sure you do," he hummed. "Mr. Avery makes Literature exciting."

"It's not about Mr. Avery," I said, heart pounding.

Principal Vaughn placed his second hand on my other shoulder and squeezed, digging his thumbs into my back. I stiffened even harder and pressed my eyes closed.

Why is he touching me like this?

"Are you sure about that?" he asked.

"Yes, I'm sure. I-I've always l-loved Literature."

"Miss Sato, you're stuttering," he hummed. "There's no reason to be nervous."

But he had his damn hands on me, he stood between me and the locked door, and his office was the last door in this entire hallway, far away from anyone else. There were plenty of reasons to be nervous.

"You won't get in trouble for telling the truth," he murmured, mouth suddenly near my ear. He inched his fingers down my arms and dangerously close to my breasts. "I won't tell anyone your secrets."

I gulped and bit back a whimper.

Please don't move any lower.

Please don't move any lower.

Please don't move any lower.

"Your silence makes you seem guilty," he said.

"I-I am telling the t-truth," I whispered, tears pricking the corners of my eyes.

I should've listened to Callan and headed directly to my next class after Literature. I shouldn't have been lingering around, hoping that he'd talk to me. Why was I so stupid? I literally fucked everything up.

When he brushed his fingers across my breasts, I snapped my books to my chest tighter and leaped up from my seat. "I need to g—"

He shoved me back down so hard that I landed on the seat. "We're not done."

"P-please," I stuttered. "I need to go to class. I am missing—"

Instead of groping me like I'd thought he would, he released me and walked around his desk to his large chair. He sat down and straightened himself out, not even bothering to hide the boner he now had.

"Has Callan Avery ever touched you?" he asked.

"No."

"Are you sure?"

"Yes, I'm sure."

"He's never been inside you?"

My cheeks flushed. "No, of course not."

"Never stared at you for longer than you were comfortable with?"

"No."

"Why not?"

"Wh-what?" I whispered.

"Why hasn't he tried to come on to you?" Principal Vaughn asked. "You're beautiful."

My throat dried. "I—"

Suddenly, the door flew open, and João strutted into the room. "The fuck do you want, Vaughn?" he asked, taking a hit of his cigarette. "Lisa at the front desk said that your annoying ass has been looking for me." He paused when he spotted me in his chair. "The hell is she doing here?"

"Just leaving," Vaughn said.

I scrambled to my feet and rushed to the door. I needed to get out of here. Now. "Y-yes, just leaving."

63

callan

BRIGHT AND EARLY, I walked through Redwood's halls and rolled my eyes at the flyers posted of Jace Harbor and Allie Hall together in the locker room. They were littered around school, and I wished that I never worked here.

God, this place is fucking terrible.

I grumbled to myself and headed to my classroom, which was still bugged. Last night, I had wanted to talk to Sakura, but I had other shit to take care of with the mob.

"Who the fuck did this?" Jace Harbor shouted in a hallway somewhere.

After dropping my bag at my desk, I walked back downstairs to see if I could find Blaise.

In the midst of students rushing around to get to class and chuckling at the naked pictures of Jace and his stepsister, Blaise stood in the hallway and watched Vera and Maddie run around, tearing pictures off the lockers.

When Blaise glanced at me, I nodded toward the stairwell for him to follow.

Once I reached the classroom, I lingered inside and waited a couple of minutes for him to show up.

"What do you have for me?" he asked.

I stood behind my desk and shuffled through some papers. "How's your father?" I asked him, scribbling words down on a blank sheet of paper.

"Don't know," Blaise said. "Don't give a fuck."

"He's home," I said, folding the paper and looking up. "You haven't seen him?"

"I left that shithole my parents call a home."

"How's he feeling about that?" I asked, sliding the paper across my desk that read, *Don't say a word out loud. One of my students who works for the mob has bugged the room, thinking I wouldn't notice.* It hadn't been Vaughn, to my surprise, as I caught the student staring over at it like a dumbass during class, making sure it was still there.

Blaise stepped closer to me and glanced down at my messy handwriting. "Like I said," Blaise started, his eyes widening slightly, "I don't care how that fucker feels. I hate them both."

I took the sheet back from him, turned it over, and scribbled another couple of words down on it. "You should go see him. Your father doesn't stay in Redwood for a long time. Wasn't he supposed to be on vacation?"

"In Bali or Greece or some shit," Blaise said, rolling his eyes. "I don't know."

When I slid the note back to him, he glanced down at it and gritted his teeth. Between getting him out of trouble and keeping Sakura safe, I had been so fucking busy lately.

I'm meeting with someone in The Family later this week to find information on who killed Skylar, the note read. The Family, meaning the Redwood mob who forced me to act like their family so they could use and use and use me for whatever they wanted.

After snatching a pen out of his backpack, he took the sheet and wrote, *And to get me out of trouble,* on it.

Instead of writing a response, I nodded. We couldn't really say much more. If he stayed here for too long, someone might get suspicious. He slung his backpack over his shoulder and walked out of my classroom without speaking another word.

64

callan

AFTER SCHOOL, *Jett* flashed across my phone screen while I walked into CVS.

I had wanted to find Sakura, follow her home, talk to her, but he hadn't stopped calling me throughout the entire day. He knew that I had work, but that fucker continued to pester me about when I would sort out his problems.

Only I didn't have plans to do shit for him anymore.

And he had pissed me off enough. Tonight, I'd get rid of him.

Depositing my phone into my pocket, I walked into CVS. This probably wasn't the best place to find a gift box for Sakura, but I didn't have much time tonight, especially if I wanted to get rid of Jett. I planned to visit her tonight at her home, sneak into her bedroom so we could finally talk.

"Do you have a box?" I asked the young woman at the front desk.

"Just a box? A gift box? Box of condoms?" She giggled.

Condoms? Who the fuck uses condoms? Who does she think I am?

If Sakura were here, I wondered how she'd react to another woman flirting with me. While she had been a mess the other night, her possessiveness had been sexy as fuck. I was hard, thinking about her climbing on top of me and showing me why her pussy was the only thing I'd ever be inside of.

What if she snatched my hand in her small one and told the woman that we didn't use condoms, that she loved being filled to the brim with my cum, that she loved the thought of me getting her preg—

Fuck, I really need to stop.

"A gift box," I repeated to the woman. "To hold a present for my ... girl."

What was Sakura to me? She wanted to talk, but was it because she wanted to officially break it off? Were we boyfriend, girlfriend? I scrunched my nose. That didn't sound right in the fucking slightest.

"Oh," she said, almost disappointed.

Once she led me to the card and gift aisle, I spent fifteen minutes trying to choose the perfect gift box and finally settled on a soft pink box and a blank card for Sakura. I really hoped she didn't want to break it off.

Because I didn't think I'd let her.

Fuck that. She was mine. She wasn't leaving me.

"Is this it?" the woman asked, suddenly distant.

"Yes," I said, pulling out my wallet.

"Did you find everything you were looking for?"

"Yep."

"Do you have a CVS card?"

"Scan my damn items," I growled. "I don't have time to play the question game."

She snapped her mouth closed and finished checking me out. I paid her in cash and walked back to the car, depositing the gift box into the trunk, next to *tools* for my time with the lovely Jett Harleen tonight.

I drove to his beach house and parked in the back so my car was hidden. I walked to the front door with my schoolbag and knocked twice.

Jett answered moments after the second knock. "It's about fucking time you showed up."

"Hey, Jett," I said, smiling. "Can I come in?"

He opened the door enough for me to walk into the house. "Where the hell have you been? I've been calling you all day. I think the mob has found this place. I've seen them walking up and down the beach all week. Did you—"

Before he could finish his sentence, I pulled a hammer out of my bag and swung it at the back of his head. He fell to the ground, blood seeping everywhere.

All those years of fucking torture … he'd pay for them tonight.

65

sakura

"STILL INTERESTED IN THAT GUY?" I asked Ichika while sitting in Escape.

Callan had ignored me again today during school, and I really needed to talk to him, really needed to apologize. If he had plans with the mob, then he had to be here, right? This was where they hung out.

"Sorta," she started, sipping on some water. "We fucked a couple of times, and ..."

Yet while Ichika talked, I couldn't focus.

I scanned the bar again, then stared out the window at the parking lot, looking for his car. But all the cars here were sleek with tinted windows. And it was dark outside, so they all looked the same to me.

"I'm going to use the restroom," she said at some point.

Unable to focus, I nodded. When Ichika searched for the restroom, I pulled out my phone and opened our messages to each other. My knee bounced uncontrollably, and I ground my teeth together.

Had I really been that much of a bitch?

I'd screwed up so badly. So freaking badly.

So, I texted him, needing some kind of response. Anything honestly. A red-faced angry emoji, a thumbs down, even a *no* would suffice. But not a *Delivered* message that I would stare at constantly until he read it.

Me: Can we talk this weekend?

Me: Please.

I waited for a few moments, and then *Delivered* changed to *Read*.

Three bubbles appeared on the left side of the screen, and I swallowed in an attempt to wet my dry throat.

Please answer. Please answer. Please answer. I refused to go the entire weekend without talking to him.

"Did you make up with Professor Big Dick?" Ichika asked, sliding back into the booth.

My cheeks flamed, and I clenched my jaw. "Don't call him that."

"Oh no," Ichika joked. "Is he small—"

"Ichika," I growled.

I loathed the thought of *anyone* talking about him like that. I didn't want him to be with anyone else, to flirt with anyone else, to have people flirt with him. The mere thought made my blood boil. He was mine.

But I had stupidly told him I hated him over and over again. I had fucking ruined it all.

What if he was with another girl right now? What if he was sleeping in her bed with his cock buried inside her, whispering dirty little words into her ear and telling her that he would do anything for her, just as he'd told me?

"Are you jealous?" Ichika beamed, leaning forward.

"No," I snapped.

Though if he were with another woman, I would be.

But I was working myself up for no reason at all. He was still typing back. I glanced down at the screen and chewed on the inside of my cheek, heart pounding. The three little dots continued bouncing, and then suddenly, they stopped.

Fuck.

No response.

I finished my food, and when we decided to leave, I dragged my feet back to my car.

After slipping into my car, I locked the doors and started the engine. My phone buzzed.

An image from Callan popped up in our messages of a ribbon-wrapped present lying in the center of my bed, next to the stuffed bunny that Mom had given me for Easter the year before she became a druggie.

My heart lurched. Callan had been in my house! I glanced at the time and widened my eyes. *While Dad was home?!*

Me: What is this?

Instead of giving me an answer, all he responded with was, **Your room is cute.**

And for some fucked up reason, I expected him to follow up with ... *Next time I see you, I'm ripping that IUD out of your pussy and will give you a reason to keep all those stuffed animals in your room for our baby.*

God, I am fucked.

Fucked. Fucked. Fucked. Fucked. Fucked. Fucked. Fucked.

Stepping on the accelerator, I sped home while making sure that nobody followed. I shouldn't have been at Escape, but I had wanted to find Callan and maybe figure out how to stop this sex trafficking ring.

Once I parked in my driveway, I shot out of the car and gazed around like a maniac for Callan's car parked on the street somewhere. But there weren't any cars parked on the road as far as I could see, and Dad was home.

I slipped inside the house through the back door so I wouldn't have to talk to him, took off my shoes, and then ran up the stairs to my bedroom. I shut the door behind me and stared at the present that lay in the center of my bed.

My heart pounded.

After dropping my purse, I jumped onto the mattress and sat

crisscross by the pillows. I took the small card with my name written across the white envelope and pulled it out.

> *Sakura,*
> *Only for you.*
> *Love,*

66

I PLACED THE CARD DOWN, grabbed the box, and set it in my lap. My heart raced in excitement, nerves pricking at my insides. Slowly, I tugged at one of the strands of ribbon, unraveling the bow.

No guy—besides Dad—had bought me a present before tonight.

But why? What had I done to deserve this?

Shaking my head, I forced all those little questions away. It didn't matter right now. All that mattered was that, despite him ignoring me these past couple of days, we were getting back to where we used to be.

Somewhere good.

While humming softly to myself, I grabbed the present's lid and smiled. Whatever this was … I promised myself I'd go find him and thank him, apologize for not hearing him out, for being so hormonal lately.

Excitement rushing through me, I pulled the cap off the box and stared down into it, eyes widening in horror when I saw Jett's head.

67

sakura

I SCREAMED and tossed the box away from me, the head rolling out and onto my carpet. A streak of sanguine blood stained the rug, dripping out from the gaping hole where his head had been attached to his neck.

"Holy shit! Holy shit! Holy shit!" I shouted, scrambling back until my back hit the headboard.

My hands trembled uncontrollably. I reached for my phone in the center of the bed to text Callan.

Me: Callan?! What the hell is this???

Me: What the fuck is wrong with you???

"Sakura," Dad called from downstairs. "Is everything okay?"

"Y-yes!" I shouted, heart pounding.

"What's going on up there?" he asked.

"It's, um … just a spider!" I yelled, shuffling to my feet, picking up the head with my bare hands, and hurling it into a black duffel bag that I hadn't used since the seventh grade. With my hands soaked in blood, I tore the blankets off my bed and laid it over the stain to cover it. "Just a goddamn spider."

"Want me to come kill it for you?"

"N-no! I'm pretty sure it's already dead." I dropped to my knees and zippered up the bag, bile rising in my throat as I caught a glimpse of my bloodied hands. "What the fuck? What the fuck? What the fuck is wrong with him?!"

Dad ascended the stairs, his footsteps loud and quick.

I sprinted to the door and locked it, my chest rising and falling quickly and sweat forming at the base of my neck. If he fucking saw me with a head in my bedroom, he would have a heart attack. A straight-up fucking heart attack.

"Are you okay, Sakura?" he asked, knocking.

"I'm having really bad girl problems right now, Dad!" I shouted, back plastered against the door. "Can you, um, get me a pad from the bathroom and slide it underneath the door? I, um …"

Quick, Sakura, think of something a guy would find gross.

"I leaked through my pants! There are huge globs of blood everywhere. Please!"

"Okay, okay," he said, footsteps hurrying away from my bedroom door.

After I took a couple of deep breaths, he returned and slid three different-sized pads underneath the door.

"I left a towel outside your bedroom too. Do you want me to make you tea?"

Fuck, I hate lying to him like this.

"No," I said quickly, pushing away a tear. "I just want to be left alone for tonight."

"Okay, sweetheart. I'll be downstairs if you need me."

Once he finally left, I blew out a deep breath and stood. *That was close.* I pulled out my phone to see if Callan had answered my texts and found my messages completely empty. For a moment, I thought about texting Ichika to help me.

But she'd think Callan was nuts. Absolutely crazy.

And he was.

Me: Callan, please answer me.

Me: I don't know what to do.

Me: Please.

When he didn't answer me in a tenth of a second, I called him. Voice mail.

I called him again. Voice mail.

And again. Voice mail.

Callan wasn't answering his damn phone, but I needed to get rid of this head as soon as possible. Kai had to know how to make people disappear, right? He was part of Poison and did those kinds of things on the daily. If I found him, maybe I could convince him to help me.

He has been hanging out with Imani Abara lately, I thought.

I glanced down at my phone and gnawed on the inside of my cheek. Maybe I could ask her if she had his number, but if they were a thing, I didn't want her thinking I was hitting on him or something.

Hell, I shouldn't care about that right now. I had a damn head sitting in my bedroom!

So, I wiped my bloody hands on an old tshirt, grabbed the duffel bag, pulled on a black sweatshirt, and hurried to the door. After opening it, I tiptoed out of my room and walked down the stairs to the back door, careful not to alert Dad that I was leaving.

Once I made it to my car, I threw the duffel bag into the trunk and slipped into the driver's seat. I sped out of the driveway, then the neighborhood, heading straight for Callan's house.

What the hell was that asshole doing that he couldn't answer my calls or texts?

When I reached his house, no lights were on. No cars were in the driveway.

Everything was dark, desolate.

My stomach twisted into knots as I walked up to the front door anyway and banged on it. Nothing. I walked around the back to the pool, nervously glancing at the water. Still … nobody. I stared into the windows, hoping to find any sign of life. But there wasn't any.

"Callan," I whisper-yelled so his neighbors wouldn't hear me. "Please, come out!"

Suddenly, a light turned on in the bathroom connected to his bedroom, and his wife appeared near the window.

"Oh shit!" I whispered, pressing my back against the house and ducking. "She's home?!"

Fuck this. I need to get out of here.

I waited until she stripped her clothes and stepped into the shower, and then I ran back to my car and sped out of the driveway as fast as I fucking could without her knowing that I was ever here. Callan had security cameras around his house, but I sure hoped he had turned them off.

Or at least, he hadn't given her access to them.

Otherwise, she would know—would see—everything that had happened between Callan and me. She would know that Callan had been sleeping with one of his own students. And she would be out to get me.

I shook the thought away. I couldn't think like that right now.

I needed to find Kai to get rid of this damn head.

68

callan

AFTER I LEFT Sakura's present on her bed, I had sped to Escape because Vaughn had sent me a picture of Sakura at the bar with her friend again. *After I fucking told her to stay away.* I didn't know why she insisted on putting herself in danger.

But what pissed me off even more ... Vaughn was now antagonizing me.

He didn't believe the barefaced lies I'd fed him, that I didn't care about her. He fucking knew that I did, that I wanted her more than I'd wanted anyone in my entire life. I didn't know why the fuck I had thought he'd be so foolish.

Skirting up to the back, I leaped out of my car and walked to the entrance, desperately trying not to seem suspicious. I wanted to keep a low profile here so nobody noticed me, so nobody talked to me.

I needed information for Blaise at some point, but first, I needed to get Sakura to safety.

Once I opened the door, I readjusted my jacket and stepped into the room. And while I expected at least someone to come up to me, everyone seemed to stay away tonight, which made me uneasy.

Since I had left school earlier, Redwood had felt off. Mobsters were becoming antsy, the way they did right before something huge went down. And when I walked into Escape, even The Family seemed off tonight.

"Where the fuck is she?" I whispered, scanning the room.

After looping around the restaurant and bar twice, I grabbed a shot from the bar to seem inconspicuous and leaned against it, crossing my arms and shaking my head.

According to Vaughn's text, she had been here thirty minutes ago.

I pulled out my phone.

Sakura: Callan?! What the hell is this???

Sakura: What the fuck is wrong with you???

Sakura: Callan, please answer me.

Sakura: I don't know what to do.

Sakura: Please.

I glanced further down at my notifications.

Missed call from Sakura.

Missed call from Sakura.

Missed call from Sakura.

Notifications for my security camera were posted underneath that. I opened one up to see Sakura squealing out of my driveway in a rush, then scrolled further in the past to see—

Fuck! What the hell is Georgina doing home already?!

When I tapped on Sakura's contact to call her back, to make sure that nobody had caught her, the bright white screen turned black, and my phone turned off, the empty battery popping up on the screen for a brief moment. I cursed to myself and stormed out of the exit, swinging around the corner and bumping into Vaughn.

"Ah, you're here," he hummed. "Finally."

"Where is she?" I asked through gritted teeth.

He smirked and rocked back on his heels. "What are you talking about?"

"Where is Sakura?"

"I thought you didn't care about her."

Tired of his bullshit, I grabbed him by the collar and slammed him up against the building. "Where the fuck is she, Vaughn? I'm not fucking playing with you anymore. You're lucky I don't kill your ass right here."

But if I pulled out a gun here, every single mobster would point theirs at me.

"Sakura left a while ago," he said. "You're a little too late."

"Where'd she go?"

"Back home."

I gritted my teeth. *How the fuck does he know that? Has he been following her?* Maybe he was the cause of all her quick, terrified messages and all those missed calls. She had been addressing me in the text, but all I had done was give her a present. If he had done something—

I tightened my hands around his collar.

Fuck it. I don't care anymore.

When I released him and he began straightening himself out, I slammed my fist into his face. Once. Then twice. Then, two Family members grabbed both my arms and pulled me off that sick son of a bitch.

"Let me go," I growled. "I'm going to kill him."

"Enough," Yui said, walking out of the building and toward us. "Vaughn, your job here is done for tonight. Bye."

"But—" Vaughn started.

"Bye," Yui said, sticking a gun to his head. "Leave. Don't come back until tomorrow."

Once Vaughn hauled his ass out of here, the guards released me. Yui nodded toward a back entrance that led to her office and shut the door behind all of us.

"Sit, Callan," she said, nodding to one of her chairs. "We have much to talk about ... like why you lied to me about Jett Harleen."

69

sakura

AFTER CIRCLING Redwood like a maniac three times, I pulled over at the Overlook and paced back and forth on the rocks. My car was locked, the head buried underneath a pile of my clothes in the trunk.

What the hell was I going to do?! I had a damn head in my trunk! Should I throw it into the ocean and hope he didn't pop up anywhere? I mean, that was why I had come here. If I could almost drown in the water, I could surely dump a head here and watch it sink too, right?!

Maybe I should toss it into a shredder instead?! Hurl an axe at it to get out all my hate?

I yanked out my phone to contact Callan *again*.

Me: We need to talk!!!

Me: NOW!

I didn't know how the hell to get through to him. He had been ignoring me for the past two days, then randomly sent me a picture of a gift he had left me in my bedroom that had a freaking *head* in it! Who the hell did that?!

If he was watching me from afar and snickering because I was losing it over here, I would kill that man. I paced on the rocks some more. The tide was higher than usual tonight, so I couldn't hike down that far.

Having friends at Redwood would really help with this situation.

But, no, I had to be shy Sakura, who couldn't socialize with normal people, and now, I was stuck with a damn head in the trunk of my car! If anyone found it, I would fucking go to jail for years and never be able to go off to college, start a new life.

After mustering up the courage, I messaged Maddie Weber.

Me: Hi! This is Sakura from Redwood. Do you happen to have Kai's number?

Maddie: Hey! Sorry, I don't have his number.

Me: Or Imani Abara's number? Sorry to bother you! I'm sorta in a jam right now.

Fuck, I really shouldn't have told her that. What if she asks what's happening?

I sat on a rock and ran a hand through my hair, impatiently waiting for a response.

Part of me didn't even think that Callan would have done this.

Sure, he might've killed Jett, but sent me the head?! Why would he do that? Just to show me that he loved me and would do anything for me? A book—literally any kind—and a sweet note would've done the trick.

But I had pushed him to do this. I had been a complete hormonal mess, screaming at him for wanting to fuck another woman, feeling like he didn't care about me at all, telling him that he didn't care, even after he said he did.

I'd caused this.

Callan Avery was teaching me a lesson. The hard way.

A couple of moments later, Maddie sent me a number along with a smiley face. I blew out a low breath and slumped my shoulders forward, thanking the Redwood gods who were on my side tonight.

Sorta.

Me: Thanks! I really appreciate it!

Maddie: Ofc!

My knee bounced as I opened up a new message and typed in Imani Abara's number. Besides projects at school, I hadn't talked to her much. She hung out with Allie—who was stepsiblings with Jace Harbor, high school football star—as well as Poison who, well, participated in a bunch of illegal activity.

And I hoped some of that activity included disposing of bodies or … body parts.

Me: Hi, Imani. This is Sakura Sato. I wanted to know if you had Kai's number.

Almost immediately, she read the message. Three bubbles appeared by her name.

While I waited for her response, a white Mercedes-Benz pulled up behind my car with a tinted windshield so I couldn't see who the hell it was. I stiffened and gazed at the car.

Don't seem suspicious, Sakura. It's just someone here to enjoy the view. Not to see you.

But they didn't exit their car.

Not that many people did here, especially in the chilly fall. More people than not sat in their cars and gazed out at the ocean with their significant other. And all the kids from Redwood came here to fuck.

I turned back to the water but still stayed highly aware of the car, watching from my peripheral. Still, I couldn't shake the feeling they were watching me. Maybe I just felt guilty.

Since we had started this little affair, I had wanted Jett and Georgina out of Callan's life. He was mine, and I had made sure that he knew that the other night. But I … I foolishly hadn't thought he would *kill* Jett for me. What would he do to Georgina? He hated her even more.

As far as I knew.

When he found out that she was back … I could only imagine how he'd react. He was so stressed out at the moment, most of the stress coming from me because I had been a hormonal bitch lately.

When I glanced back down at my phone, a message from Imani popped up.

Imani: Hi, Sakura! I'm actually not sure where Kai is tonight, but he doesn't like anyone giving his number out. People usually go through João to get to Poison, if that's what you want. Is there a specific reason?

Shit.

Me: Sorry for bothering you, but I just needed his help with something.

Imani: Something bad?

Me: Ha-ha, um, no?

Me: Maybe.

Me: Actually, never mind, it's fine!

I didn't want her asking questions, especially over text, because I wouldn't be able to answer them. I didn't want anyone finding out later down the line about this damn head either. I would be forever haunted by the possibility that I'd go to jail for this.

Suddenly, the bright lights behind me turned dark, the Mercedes's headlights shutting off. Nerves bubbled up inside me, and I hopped up from my place on the rock. I needed to get out of here. Not only to get rid of this head, but also because of this car behind mine.

I hurried toward the driver's door, just about to slip into the car, when someone cleared their throat behind me.

"Miss Sato," Principal Vaughn said. "Funny seeing you here."

70

sakura

NO.

This can't be happening. Not after yesterday in his office.

"I need to be getting home," I said, stepping back toward my door.

"Girls like you shouldn't be out so late," Vaughn hummed. "It's almost midnight. There are bad men who lurk around these streets at night. God forbid, someone might take advantage of a pretty schoolgirl like you."

Fuck. Fuck. Fuck. Fuck. Fuck. Fuck. Fuck.

"My dad is waiting for me," I whispered, fucking terrified.

Where the hell is Callan when I need him?! Like yesterday, when Vaughn had touched my breasts in his office. And now, after Vaughn had apparently followed me to the Overlook to do God only knew what to me.

Tears welled up in my eyes. *Why did Callan give me that damn head?!* To prove to me that he'd do anything for me? Well, I goddamn believed him now. I would never ever, ever question that again.

I just hoped I'd *get* a chance to question it again and that Vaughn didn't fucking kill me here.

"Sakura!" someone called from behind.

And for a split moment, I thought Callan had come to rescue me. Or Kai had magically somehow learned out that I needed to dispose of a head and found me down by the beach. Hell, even Akio would do at this point. I needed someone because Vaughn was creeping me the fuck out.

When I gazed behind me, Gunther jogged up to us. My eyes nearly bulged out of my head. *Isn't he supposed to be in the hospital, recovering from a damn gunshot wound?! Why did they let him leave so soon?*

"Gunther," I whispered.

As much as I didn't *love* the guy, he was saving me from this creep.

Still dressed in a hospital gown, he hobbled up to us while clutching his stomach and grimaced at Vaughn. "What the fuck are you doing here with him?" he asked me, lips curled in utter disgust.

I cowered behind Gunther's tall and scrawny figure, heart pounding. I didn't know how the hell *he* would protect me from Vaughn, especially after he had just left the hospital, but I needed to put space between me and the principal.

"You haven't been in school," Vaughn said. "You shouldn't be here."

"*You* shouldn't be here with an eighteen-year-old girl," Gunther said, eyeing him. "Someone might get the wrong idea and think you were trying to *take advantage* of the senior class's valedictorian. Wouldn't want that, would we?"

Vaughn clenched his jaw, teeth gritted. "Gunther," he warned.

"Get the fuck out of here," Gunther growled. "You pedophile piece of shit."

"Mr. Zurn," Principal Vaughn said sternly, "I could have you expelled for that."

Gunther slammed his fist into Vaughn's face and pushed me back. "Leave."

Vaughn grabbed his jaw, then straightened himself out and walked back to his car. In a moment, he started the ignition and drove off into the late night, away from the Overlook and back toward the heart of Redwood.

"What-what are you doing here?" I asked, eyes wide.

"I've been looking for you."

"B-but you were in the hospital, unconscious. They let you leave?"

"They didn't let me do anything," he said. "But I had shit to do."

"Gunther?! You could be hurt!"

"That piece of shit paid for my medical bills," he snapped suddenly, grinding his teeth together.

"Who paid for your medical bills?" I asked, glancing at Vaughn's taillights in the distance.

"Avery."

My eyes widened. "Callan paid for your medical bills?"

"Yeah, and I'm going to fucking kill him for it," he growled. "Where is he?"

I highly doubted that Gunther had insurance, so that meant that Callan had offered to pay hundreds of thousands of dollars for Gunther's bills. Sure, it was most likely dead Jett's money—definitely not from a teacher's salary—but ... damn.

Damn, he fucking cared about me. He loved me. He'd really do anything for me.

I need to find him. Now.

"He should've fucking left me dead," Gunther said, stumbling—probably from the loss of blood. He should've stayed in the damn hospital until he healed completely. "I hate this fucking town, my life."

I caught him and sat him down in my car. "You don't mean that," I whispered. My chest tightened. "Please, tell me that you don't mean that. Redwood is shit, but you can always leave once we graduate. Hell, you can leave now if you want."

"I have fucking nobody here. I was trying to protect you from the damn sex ring going on in Redwood, and my teacher fucking shot me," he said. "I would rather be fucking dead than live another day in this damn place."

"I told him to save you," I whispered. "Callan was protecting me."

Gunther's lower lip twitched. "I don't get it. What do you see in him?"

"He cares about me," I said softly, leaning against my car and staring out into the sea.

"He cares about you or getting in a young girl's pants?"

"He cares about me," I said with certainty.

While, on the outside, Gunther might've thought Callan wanted me because he was some sick pervert, I knew that it wasn't that. I had felt it, experienced it. I wasn't just falling into some trap, like immature girls my age did with older men.

Callan ... cared about me.

If he didn't care, he wouldn't have killed Jett–and he had to have killed Jett, if he gave it to me for a freaking present. If he didn't care, he would've used up my pussy the other night and not begged me to let him talk. If he didn't care, he wouldn't have lain in the back of his car with me while it poured outside, reading literature to me.

Smutty literature, but still beautiful words that had made me feel things.

"You have to believe me," I whispered. "It's not weird."

"You're fucking a teacher at our high school," Gunther said. "How is it not weird?"

I chewed on the inside of my cheek. I didn't have time to fight with him about this. I needed to figure out a way to get rid of this damn head and find Callan. Why the hell hadn't he returned my calls yet?! It had been almost two hours.

"I'll explain it later," I whispered. "Right now, I have ... someone's head in the back of my car that I need to get rid of! Can you help me dispose of it?"

71

sakura

"YOU HAVE FUCKING WHAT?" Gunther asked.

"A head," I squeaked, glancing around to make sure nobody else was lurking near the Overlook and watching us. After Vaughn had made his appearance, I didn't quite trust him or anyone else to *not* watch us. "Please, don't tell anyone."

Gunther lowered his voice. "What do you mean, you have a head?"

I popped my trunk, retrieved the black duffel bag that now leaked blood, and set it on his lap. Gunther unzipped it and glanced inside the bag, eyes widening.

I paced in front of the car, running a hand through my hair. "What am I going to do?"

"Sakura," Gunther said, "this is Jett Harleen's head!"

"I know!" I whisper-yelled. "Help me get rid of it!"

"Did you do this?"

I threw my hands into the air. "Do you *think* I did this?"

After gazing back into the bag, Gunther pulled the head out and stood. He walked over to the sandy-grass and hobbled down a couple of rocks until he was knee deep in the raging water. Then, he chucked the head as far as he could.

"It's not your problem now," he said.

"What if it washes back up on shore?"

"It's still not your problem," he said. "You didn't do this."

"But I have his blood stained on my rug!" I whispered, moving closer. "I need help."

He stumbled back over to the passenger side and slid onto the seat, leaning back and grasping his stomach where Callan had shot him. "Fuck, it hurts," he grunted. "I need to pick up some pain meds."

"I have some at my place," I said.

"The strong shit, Sakura. Not Tylenol."

Swallowing hard, I nodded. "I have some at my house. My mom … is an addict."

Gunther glanced over at me, his features softening. "Oh."

"Yeah," I whispered, shaking my head. Not many people knew about it, but I couldn't care less right now. "But it doesn't matter. If I get you some, will you help me … I don't know … rip up my carpet and dispose of everything?"

He paused for a moment. "I'm not as good as Poison, but I can help you."

"Good," I said, jogging to the driver's seat and starting the car. "Thank you."

We sat in silence for ten minutes while I drove to my house. My fingers trembled around the steering wheel, the adrenaline slowly wearing off as realization settled in. I had just committed a crime.

Jett's head had been in my fucking car! His head!

"Where did you get the head?" Gunther said, cutting through my thoughts.

"Callan," I said, gripping the steering wheel tighter and pulling out my phone to check for messages from him. Still nothing. "He left a present in my bedroom earlier tonight, a pretty pink box with ribbon and everything, filled with his wife's father's head."

"If he really loved you the way you say he does, he wouldn't have given you a head."

"He's crazy," I whispered. "He might have."

"He might be crazy, but he's not stupid."

"He literally sent me a picture of the box on my bed," I said. "He had to have."

"Why would he put you in danger like that?"

"To teach me a lesson," I said, turning onto my street. "After he shot you, we got into this huge fight. He mentioned something to Vaughn, wanting to sleep with other girls, and I lost it."

Gunther hummed, "And you think he loves you?"

"It was a misunderstanding."

"Let's say that it really was a misunderstanding and that he was trying to teach you a lesson," Gunther reasoned. "He wouldn't do this. And if he did, he wouldn't be ignoring you right now. He'd answer your messages, or he'd have been there when you opened it."

I parked. "So, who do you think did it if it wasn't him?!"

"Vaughn," he said without hesitation. "He found a way to get you alone and vulnerable."

My entire body stiffened, fear shooting through me again. What if he was right? What if … what if Callan had given me a real present, but somehow, someway, Vaughn had switched it out with something else? I wouldn't put it past him after he touched me in his office.

"Do you think something has happened to Callan?" I whispered, throat drying.

Gunther shrugged. "I don't know, and frankly, I don't give a shit what happens to him." He glanced out the windshield at my house. "Didn't think you lived in the nicer part of town, Sakura. Usually, druggies are in the slums."

"My mom works at a pharmacy," I said. "Come on. I'll get you medicine."

When we reached the front door, I took a deep breath. I didn't know how I would explain this to Dad, but I had to come up with something fast. When I'd left him, he'd thought I just had the most explosive period ever. Now, I was home with a kid dressed in a hospital gown with blood all over his hands and a gunshot wound in his stomach.

Fuck.

Before I could even open the door, Dad pulled it open. I stepped forward.

"Dad, I can explain later, but I really need to get him medication. Some of Mom's strong stuff," I said, hurrying into the house and heading for Mom's stash of drugs that she'd stolen from the pharmacy. "He just got out of the hospital, and they didn't prescribe him medication."

Dad arched a brow and followed us, crossing his arms and grimacing. "Sakura, stop lying to me," he said sternly. "You've been lying to me for weeks now. You didn't have your period earlier, did you? I saw you sneaking out of the house."

My eyes widened. "Y-you did?"

Dad looked at Gunther. "Is this the boy you've been seeing?"

Gunther snorted. "I fucking wish."

He fucking wishes?! What does that mean? That he likes me?!

"Then, who is he?" Dad asked me. "Because you can't keep fucking doing this."

I sucked in a sharp breath. Dad never swore.

"Dad…" I whispered, handing Gunther the medication. "Gunther is one of my classmates. Someone shot him the other night. There is a sex ring going on in my school. And I'm fucking terrified."

72

callan

FACE BRUISED AND ACHING, stab wounds in my side, and my hands scarred from the mob torturing me last night, I gripped the steering wheel in pain and drove like a madman to the skatepark, where I knew Blaise would be.

I hadn't told the mob shit last night and stayed true to the lie I'd fabricated for them about Jett. And those assholes had told me to prove that I still had allegiance to them, that if I was really telling the truth, I would show up at the auction tonight for Vera Rodriguez.

Blaise's girl.

How the hell had they gotten her? I didn't know. What did they plan to do with her? Probably have a creepy, old man like Vaughn fuck her in front of the entire town. The reason why? I couldn't fucking tell you.

Once the mob had released me this morning, I'd texted Sakura and told her to meet me at the library today. I didn't know when I would get there, but I needed to see her and bring her somewhere safe.

After speeding into the parking lot, still bleeding, I slammed on my brakes and leaped out of my car. "Harleen!" I shouted, spotting him riding down into the bowl and coming up on the other side, headphones covering his ears.

He glanced at me, kicked up the board, and walked over to me as slowly as he fucking could with a smug smirk on his face. "Last time I saw Callan Avery at the skatepark, he was threatening a kid with a gun."

"Where's your girl?" I asked, no time for bullshitting around with him.

"Vera?" he asked. "Why do you want to know about her?"

I snatched his arm and dragged him to the parking lot. "I'm not here to play games and talk shit to you, Blaise. This is fucking serious. I talked to someone who had more insight on Skylar Walker's murder."

"What'd they say?"

If he couldn't tell by the bruises and blood on my body, they didn't have anything *good* to say about her death or about the girls they were constantly trafficking to the Redwood rich, even Blaise's damn father. I was glad I'd fucking murdered Jett. That entire family, besides Blaise, was too fucked up.

"Get in the car," I growled, shoving him into the passenger seat of my car. After slamming his door, I slipped into the driver's seat and locked the car. We needed to get to Vera now, before the mob did. "Skylar was fucking your father."

Blaise widened his eyes. "What?!"

"Don't fucking scream," I scolded, backing out of the parking spot.

"You can't drop a fucking bomb on me like that and expect me to whisper-yell it to you," he said more quietly. "Dad was barely ever in Redwood, never home. How the hell was she fucking him?"

"He was never in Redwood to see you," I said. "Apparently, he met up with her a few times these past few months before her death. They'd been seeing each other for nearly a year in secret at an upscale hotel."

Blaise ran a hand through his hair. "What the fuck? So, are you saying my dad killed her?"

"That's not even close to everything," I continued, gripping the steering wheel to ease the pain shooting through me. I didn't know how much blood I'd lost last night, but it was enough to make me see stars every so often. "There's a sex trafficking ring happening within the high school. Cheerleaders and many of the popular senior girls have been roped into it for a few years now. I've been trying to stop it, but—"

"What the fuck?!"

"Blaise, listen—"

He stared at me in shock with his mouth hanging the fuck open. "Was Skylar in it? How didn't Principal Vaughn find out?"

I tightened my grip on the wheel and growled, "Oh, he fucking knows."

"He's taking part in it, isn't he?" Blaise asked through gritted teeth and glared through the windshield. "I can't fucking believe this. I should've known because he's such a fucking pervert, but ..." He ran his hand through his hair again. "Fuck. Skylar was really in the ring?"

"That's how she met your father, I believe."

"Bro," Blaise said. "I'm about to fucking puke. The fuck is wrong with him?"

When I pulled up to the end of the road, I stopped for a moment at the Stop sign and rubbed the lines on my forehead. "As soon as I found out that the mob was involved, I tried to stop it because I knew that something like this was bound to happen to one of my students."

"Can't we go to the police?"

"No."

He shook his head. "I know that you can't because of your relations to the mob, but I can."

"You don't get it," I snapped. "The police chief is in on it too. This town has gone to shit."

The police chief was pimping out his own daughter. The principal was asking teachers to get in on this sick shit. And I was caught in the middle of it, trying to protect my students and most importantly trying to keep Sakura out of this completely.

"What can we do?" Blaise asked. "This isn't fair."

"It gets worse, Blaise," I said, staring emptily out of the car. I clenched my jaw and shook my head, the veins pressing against the backs of my hands from my harsh grip. "Where's Vera?"

"She's at work," Blaise said, brow furrowed in confusion. "How can this get any worse?"

"Because your mother found out that your father was cheating again." I let out a low breath. "And she hired the mob to kill Skylar."

"That fucking bitch knew the truth this entire fucking time?!" Blaise exclaimed.

Why his mother had tried to put the blame on her own son, I would never fucking know.

"It doesn't make sense," he whispered.

"Where does Vera work?" I asked.

"Why do you keep asking about her, like you haven't been telling me all of Redwood's secrets? Besides, why would the mob kill Skylar if they needed her to be part of their trafficking ri—"

"Because your mother promised them that Vera would take Skylar's place."

73

callan

WHEN I PULLED up to the library—after I finally got Vera's place of work out of Blaise—he leaped out and ran into the building before I could even stop the car. I parallel parked on the side of the road, between a bright yellow sports car and a large red van, then pulled out my phone.

Sakura: I won't be able to get there for another hour or so. I had a long night.

Fuck, I really wish she were here now.

I wanted to just fucking hug her, hold her in my arms. It had been too long without talking to her and way too much shit had happened. Besides, Vaughn was getting too close for comfort with her. If she was with me, she'd be safe.

After peering at the library doors to see if Blaise had found Vera yet, I gazed back down at her messages. She had sent it a half hour ago, at some point while I had been at the skatepark with Blaise, trying to calm his ass down.

I hopped out of the car to head toward the entrance and began typing her a message.

Me: I hope you liked your gift. I had—

Before I could finish and send the message, Blaise slammed into me in a rush. I slipped the phone into my pocket and followed him back toward my car. If he hadn't come out with Vera, that meant she wasn't here and that they could already have her.

"Where is she?" I asked.

"She's gone. She's fucking gone."

"Fuck," I cursed, running a hand through my hair and storming to my driver's seat. I started the car and sped down the road, heading toward the slums. "Where would she have gone? Home?"

Blaise slammed his fist against my dashboard, denting it. "Fuck!"

"Where's her house, Blaise?" I said.

"Fuck!" he growled. "She's fucking gone!"

While I wanted to slam my foot on the brakes, curl my hands around his collar, and shout at him to tell me where she lived, I kept my cool. If this were Sakura, I would be the exact same way right now.

"Where's her house?" I asked again.

"The slums," he said, peering out the window at every house.

"We'll find her."

"No, we fucking won't."

"She'll be at home."

"She wouldn't have made it home in a few fucking minutes," Blaise said. "She's gone."

It sounded like Blaise had found out that she had just gotten off work. And if she lived in the slums, she probably didn't have a car. A friend could've picked her up, or maybe it was something much, much worse.

He slammed his fist against the dashboard again. "No. No. No. No. No. No. No."

"Settle down, Blaise," I said, pulling into the slums. "Tell me where to go."

"Two streets down. One-story house. Across from João Rocha."

I followed his directions and pulled up to the side of the road in front of a rundown house. Blaise leaped out of the car and sprinted toward Vera's house. None of the lights were on, but he slammed the front door open and searched every last inch of that house for her.

"No," he cried, voice fucking trembling when I walked in. "Fucking no. You can't be gone. You can't."

I searched her house for a second time while Blaise tore her bedroom to shreds, screaming and shouting that he had lost her. And when I went to check on him, he had collapsed onto the bed, tears streaming down his face.

"Vera," he cried, head hanging low. "P-please, fight them."

"Blaise," I said from the door. Sitting here, crying, wasn't going to find her. We had to search for her. They couldn't have taken her *that* far if she had gotten off work only a few minutes ago. "She's not here. We must—"

"No fucking shit!" he growled, pushing the tears from his cheeks and standing. He shoved past me and marched across the street to João's house. He pounded his fist against the door. "Open the fuck up, João!"

A moment later, Landon—the muscle of Poison—opened the door. Kai, João, and a young girl who couldn't be older than six sat in the small living room, looking over at us. Blaise stormed into the house and glared at João.

"Tell me you know where she is," Blaise said.

"Where who is?"

Blaise snatched his collar and lifted him off the couch. "Vera, you fucking asshole. Tell me you know where she is."

"Get your hands off me," João said, shoving Blaise away. "She said she had to work until six. She's supposed to watch Ana in fifteen minutes. I don't know where the fuck she is. I'm not on her ass twenty-four/seven." João eyed me. "And the fuck is Avery doing here?"

I stepped forward and placed a hand on Blaise's shoulder in an attempt to calm him down. "The mob took Vera."

João's face dropped. "No, they fucking didn't."

"You need to help us find her," Blaise pleaded.

Blaise knew that I couldn't get that much more involved. One wrong move by me at this moment, and the mob would have no problem with killing me, especially if I tried to stop this. I had worked for them for years, but they wouldn't forgive this.

Poison took one long look at each other, and then João finally turned back to Blaise. "What do you need?"

74

sakura

"IF CALLAN SEES me here with you, he is going to really kill you this time," I said to Gunther, nervously chewing on my inner cheek and glancing around the library.

We had been here for about an hour, waiting for Callan to show up.

Gunther tilted his seat back and scrolled through social media. "I don't give a fuck. He already tried to kill me once. This time, I'm going to kill him for what he did to me," he said, cutting his gaze up at me. "And don't call him Callan."

"He's Callan to me, and you're not going to kill him."

When he narrowed his eyes, I narrowed mine back at him. I had never been the threatening kind, nor did I even know if I *looked* threatening right now. But nobody was going to lay a hand on Callan.

I didn't know where the hell he was or if he had really been the one to send me that head, but he must have killed Jett for me. Right? I had always hated him. And who the hell knew what he was doing or *would do* to his wife. Hearing what she had done to him all these years made *me* want to kill her.

Finally, Gunther turned back to his phone. "He's not coming."

My knee bounced underneath the table. "He'll be here."

"Well, he'd better fucking hurry up," he hummed. "The library closes in an hour."

I sat back on the chair and pulled my book onto my thighs, sighing. After taking another look at the doors, I gazed back at my textbook. Lately, I had been spending almost all of my time with Callan or worrying about him, so I was falling behind in my classes. Not by too much, but it was a lot for me. I still wanted to be valedictorian. I'd spent my whole entire life studying to be.

Still, where was he?

"Your dad is pretty cool," Gunther said.

Arching a brow, I raised my gaze to meet his. "My dad is cool?"

"He loves you a lot," he said. "It must be nice."

While I didn't ask much about his parents, I sorta, kinda knew he didn't have the best home life. Callan had mentioned his parents had committed a murder-suicide a year or so ago, so Gunther had mostly been on his own. I was surprised he hadn't dropped out of school yet.

"I'm glad he let you stay the night," I said truthfully.

Callan would probably kill Gunther for it, but he had a roof over his head after getting out of the hospital as well as warm meals for once. Gunther had mentioned over breakfast this morning that he hadn't had someone make him food in almost a decade.

So, I was content about that.

But I was still in disbelief that, somehow, I'd convinced Dad to let Gunther stay at our place for a little bit. While completely leaving Callan out of the whole story, I'd told Dad what had been happening at Redwood. He must've felt pity for Gunther, though ... I wasn't sure I still trusted him. Not that I'd *ever* trusted him.

The library door opened. I glanced over and impatiently waited for someone to walk into the room. And when a man I didn't recognize walked in, I slumped down in my chair and frowned. Maybe Gunther was right.

I shook my head. No. Callan was going to be here.

75

callan

I CIRCLED around every mob hangout in Redwood multiple times, finally spotting an empty van that I had never seen before in the back of one. After I checked it for Vera and found nothing, I blew an angry breath from my nose and texted Blaise, who had stayed back with Poison.

Me: I checked the van as well as the building where we thought Vera was. Nobody is there. Even the cellar has been cleared out.

Gripping my stomach, I winced as the pain from the stab wounds shot through me. I hadn't had a fucking minute to myself since they had released me this morning, and I just wanted to sleep for a few fucking days.

Maybe longer.

Blaise: What the fuck do you mean? Where the hell did they take her?

Me: Meet me at the state beach. That's the closest place they could've gone.

There was one place that I hadn't checked out yet. Last night, Yui had told me that they'd be at the beach for Vera's auction, and I faintly remembered her mentioning something about the state beach.

Hell, it had been such a long night. I might've hallucinated it all.

Blaise: How would they get her there without anyone noticing?

Me: Just meet me there.

So, I gritted my teeth and started my car once more, heading in the direction of the state beach. Problem was that half of Redwood *was* beach, and the state beach stretched on for a good mile or so with too many bars and restaurants to count.

But since it was fall, nobody should be down there now. All I had to do was find Yui's car.

When I pulled into the state beach parking lot, I spotted three cars parked at the base of a stilted building, where tourists hung around during the summer months. I parked my car about ten parking spaces away from the others and texted Blaise.

Me: The mob has a place here, but I need to figure out how to get in.

Hell, I didn't even know *where* they were in this building. Maybe the basement, if it had a basement. I highly doubted it because it was the fucking beach. It would be flooded if the water rose too high during hurricane season.

Me: Let me go in first. I'll unlock it. Wait five minutes, then come in.

Me: Understand?

Me: I can't be seen with you or else the mob will know that I've betrayed them.

João pulled into the parking lot and parked a ways away from my car.

Instead of waiting for his response, I got out of the car and walked up the stairs of the building to the platform up top, where I used to hang out when I had been a teenager years ago. I padded around the top for a few moments, scanning the area.

Chatter drifted out from a back stairwell that I had never noticed before, even in all my years of visiting this dirty place. I slipped inside a room and behind a door, watching a kid who I'd had in school a couple of years ago, named Jim, walk up the stairs and toward the parking lot.

Me: Jim's here.

I wasn't sure if Blaise knew who Jim was, but I didn't have time for that now.

Me: He's going toward the parking lot.

Me: I'm heading down to where he left now.

When I reached a door at the bottom of the stairs, I blew out a low breath and cursed at myself that I was even going to do this. It was to protect my students, but I felt so … so fucking wrong and disgusted that this was even happening in Redwood.

I opened the door and began descending another set of stairs until I spotted Vera Rodriguez blindfolded on the floor in the middle of a cell with Peter something on top of her while everyone fucking watched.

"I'll pay to take her first," I said. "Get the fuck off her, Peter."

"Callan Avery." Yui chuckled. "Ah, I didn't think you'd want a taste of her." She sauntered over to me and leaned closer. "I thought you'd really decided to betray me after"—she brushed her fingers against the side of my stomach, where she had stabbed me last night —"all the fun we had."

"You thought wrong," I growled, looking at Vera.

She scrambled back from the man between her legs and shoved herself back against the wall again, curling up into a ball. A sob escaped her lips. And while I couldn't see her face, my chest was tightening.

What if this were Sakura? What if they had taken her instead and auctioned her off to everyone and their brother in Redwood? What if she had been brutally raped by these men and women?

"How much?" Yui asked because she was a greedy bitch who had asked me to come and fuck a student tonight to prove my loyalty but still wanted me to pay for it.

"How much do you want?" I asked.

"You know what our price is for a student from Redwood."

After grumbling, I walked toward the cell. "Take it out of my cut for this month," I said, pushing the cell door open, the sound of metal scraping against the concrete. I grabbed Peter by the back of his neck. "Peter, I already said to get the fuck out of here. Vera Rodriguez is mine."

People shuffled around the room, and then I moved closer to Vera. I seized her upper arm and pulled her to a standing position, but her legs gave out, and she dropped to her knees in front of me.

Where the fuck is Blaise and Poison? I didn't want to touch her.

"Let me fuck her alone," I said, wrapping my hand around Vera's throat and lifting her.

"Only for double the price," Yui sneered.

"Fine," I growled.

"Please, make it quick," Vera whispered as the others began walking up the stairs. A couple of stray tears fell down Vera's cheeks when the last of The Family members walked out of the room and onto the patio section of the state beach building. "Please."

And then a gun went off outside.

Vera jerked in my arms and ducked, a horrid scream exiting her throat.

Finally, those fuckers had shown up.

76

callan

AS SOON AS gunfire blazed around outside, I pulled off Vera's blindfold and thanked the fucking Redwood gods that this wasn't Sakura. If she had been the one taken tonight, I would've gone on a fucking rampage, killing everyone here.

I'd have gone to prison for murder many times over.

Vera tilted her head to the ground, shielding her eyes from the bright light that hung overhead, her hair falling into her face. I crouched down in front of her and undid her restraints so she wasn't trapped here any longer.

Blaise sprinted down the stairs, nearly tripping over his own two feet. Just as I unraveled the ropes around Vera's ankles, Blaise collapsed onto the ground next to Vera, scooped her into his arms, and hugged her tightly.

"My fucking God," he said. "I thought … I thought we were too late."

She tucked her face into his chest and sobbed. "I wanna go home, Blaise. Please, I wanna go home. I'm cold and …" She shivered, goose bumps rising on her skin. "And I …" I could only imagine what she had heard, what they had tried doing to her. "I—"

"It's okay," Blaise reassured her, peeling off his jacket and pulling it around her shoulders. He tugged her to her feet, her legs wobbling. "You don't have to tell me. Not now anyway."

She grasped on to his shoulders to steady herself. "J-Jim ... he—"

"Don't worry about Jim," Blaise said.

"But he kidnapped—"

"He's dead," I said, glancing at Blaise.

While Blaise was a decent kid and didn't kill people like Poison did, I knew that he wouldn't let Jim live after what he did to Vera.

"And we have one last person to take care of, if you haven't already. Your mother."

After swallowing hard, Blaise nodded. "Can you take her home?" he asked me.

She huddled next to him, shoulders shaking, and buried her face into his chest. "No. Don't leave," she whimpered, shaking her head. "Please, don't go. I don't want to be alone with anyone, except you."

"I have to finish this, Vera," he said. "My mom ... she doesn't deserve to live."

Vera stared up at him through wide eyes. "Are you going to kill her?"

"If that's what it takes," he whispered.

While the room was empty, I couldn't fucking leave here with them. I didn't know what kind of people the mob had stationed around the beach. If they saw me bringing Vera home, I'd be in deeper shit.

"I can't take her home," I said. "Nobody can see me leaving here with you."

"They're going to know something is up if you walk out of here, unwounded, anyway," Blaise said.

I drew my tongue across my teeth, reached into my pocket, and pulled out a knife. Knowing that what he had said was true, I shoved the knife deep into my thigh and bit back a grunt. Blood soaked through my pants.

"What the fuck are you—"

"Leave," I growled, handing him the keys to my car and leaning against a wall, sliding down to the ground and clutching my thigh. *Fuck, that hurts.* "I can't be seen with you. If anyone asks, say you stole my car."

Once they ran up the stairs and out of the room, I closed my eyes and waited a long fifteen minutes. I needed to get to Sakura, but I didn't have a car right now, and my fucking leg was leaking blood.

It'd be a forty-five-minute walk home, but it was closer than Sakura's house. I'd clean myself up and then head to the library if it was still open tonight. Hopefully, I'd be able to avoid Georgina altogether because I didn't have the energy for her right now.

So, I hobbled to a standing position, stumbled up the stairs, and started home once enough cars skirted out of the parking lot and guns stopped blazing.

Forty-five minutes later, I clutched my thigh with my blood-soaked hand and walked up my driveway. João's car was parked up top, and he got out when he saw my pitiful ass trying to make it to my front door.

I bit back a curse and walked over to him, stars in my vision.

"When the fuck are you going to deal with the principal?" I asked through clenched teeth.

"Soon," João said, arms crossed over each other as he leaned against his car.

Kai stood next to him and shoved his hands into his cargo pants.

"We can't do all this shit at once. We were working on it before your nephew bothered us."

"You need to kill him," I started.

There was no question about it. If he wasn't gonna do it, then I would. Vaughn was a growing problem, but I was just thankful that he hadn't laid his hands on Sakura yet. Or else all hell would break fucking loose.

"Just get it done," I growled, heading to my front door.

João chuckled and lit his cigarette. "Have you checked on Gunther lately?"

"No."

"He's out of the hospital," Kai said.

"And he might've been at the Overlook with Sakura last night," João taunted. "He even went back to your girl's place, so she could nurse him back to health."

"João," Kai said, cutting his gaze to him, "that's not what—"

I gritted my teeth. "What?"

"He stayed at her place last night," he said like I was fucking deaf.

"What the fuck do you mean, he stayed at her place last night?" I growled, taking him by the collar of a shirt and slamming him against his car. "I'm not playing around with you any-fucking-more, João."

I hadn't seen Sakura and talked to her for days. I'd told her that I would be at the library today, so I could chat with her. It was already almost eight o'clock on a weekend. The library was probably closed now, and I'd missed my chance.

She probably thought I was ignoring her purposefully at this point. I hadn't had time to stay while she opened the present I had gotten her. And I had been fucking up over and over and over again. Worst part about all this was that I could do nothing about it.

I released him from my grip and walked to my front door. "Get off my property."

My life was fucked. I had the mob even more suspicious of me now. Sakura would never be safe. If I wanted to truly protect her, I would put as much distance between us as possible. I wouldn't head to the library or to her house ever again, wouldn't even look at her during class.

"Fuck that," I growled while they pulled out of my driveway.

Sakura was mine, and I wasn't going to let her go.

When I reached the front door, I slammed my hand into my pocket to pull out my key. I rummaged around for it in my front right pocket, then my left, then my back two and found nothing. I growled and knocked on the door.

Georgina was home.

No answer.

This fucking bitch …

Hobbling to the back doors near the pool and our bedroom, I ignored the stars in my vision and pounded on the door again. "Georgina! Unlock the door, you stupid fucking bitch!" I shouted, slamming my fist against the glass and glaring into the dark bedroom.

She was putting up the picture frames that I had taken down, ignoring me. In the fucking dark because this bitch was fucking psycho.

"Open up!"

The harder I banged, the more stars danced in my vision. I had lost too much blood on my way home and last night. If I didn't bandage up my wounds and go find Sakura, I would be in some serious shit with—

I went to bang on the door once more, but found myself stumbling backward against the concrete. My gaze went dark for a moment, then came back as I tripped backward, my foot slipping back into the pool.

And as I fell into the water, my vision blackened for good.

77

sakura

AFTER SQUEALING into Callan's driveway, I leaped out of my car. Something wasn't right.

Callan had told me that he'd meet me at the library, and while we hadn't been having the best time together, he wouldn't ditch me. I had even stayed out front on the library steps two hours after it closed.

Gunther had told me that Callan had purposefully not come, but that wasn't true. It couldn't be. His text messages had sounded so serious, and I so desperately wanted to make up with him. Plus, he hadn't responded to any of my messages or calls for basically the entire day.

I walked to his garage window and peered inside the room, only seeing his wife's car.

He's still not home? Where did he go today? Maybe his car broke down?

Fuck, I didn't know. At this point, I was just making shit up and hoping that he hadn't gotten into trouble with the mob for killing Jett. I wouldn't put it past Jett to have been participating in mob business.

Glancing down at my phone, I messaged him again. "Callan, please answer," I muttered.

Nothing. Not even *Delivered*.

Which meant his phone was off or dead.

My stomach twisted into tight knots. I paced in front of my car and ran a hand through my hair, tears welling up in my eyes.

Something isn't right. Something isn't right. Something isn't freaking right.

But I had no way of getting in touch with Callan without his phone. I had waited at the library for almost all day, like I'd promised. I was standing at his home and staring into an empty garage. And he was gone.

"You deserve this," a woman said from Callan's backyard.

Fuck.

I plastered myself against the siding and peered around the corner of the house to the backyard. Georgina Harleen-Avery stood at the pool, staring down into it with a glass of wine in her hand. She brought it to her lips.

"Should've come with me to Paris," she said, placing the glass down on a side table.

It sounded like she was talking to someone, but nobody was in the pool.

I really needed to find him, and this was my only hope.

"Excuse me," I said, stepping into the backyard.

She snapped her head in my direction. "Who are you?"

I walked toward her and swallowed hard, my heart racing. It might've been the stupidest thing I had ever done, but I needed to find Callan. I couldn't run around anymore and worry about him. Georgina didn't give a fuck about him. I did.

"Where is Cal—" I started, my gaze dropping to the tinted pink water.

Then, I saw his body, facedown, in the pool.

"Oh my God!" I screamed, rushing toward the edge and about to jump in to rescue him.

"Get off my property," Georgina shouted, grabbing my arm and yanking me back.

I twirled around and hurled my fist at her face as hard as I could, sending her to the ground. She scrambled back to her feet and lunged at me, but I grabbed the small glass side table that she had placed her wineglass on and slammed it into the side of her head.

On collision, the glass shattered everywhere. Still, that didn't stop her from leaping back up with shards of glass jutting out from her cheek, scattered in her hair, and hanging off her clothes. Blood dripped from her wounds.

Fury and pain rushed through me. I sprinted toward the outside bar and grill area that Callan hadn't closed up yet for the fall and slammed open one of the metal cabinet doors, adrenaline pumping through my system.

I shoved my hand into the cabinet and grabbed the first thing I could use as a weapon against her—a meat tenderizer mallet. She rushed toward me, lips turned down into a scowl, screaming something about how she was going to sue me.

But Callan was possibly lying dead in the fucking pool.

Clasping the mallet with both hands, I swung at her head. She dropped to the ground, body twitching, so I struck it into the same spot again and again until she had a huge gash in her head and she wasn't moving.

78

AFTER TEARING OFF MY SHOES, I ran on the concrete to the pool. Shards of glass slipped into my feet, sending shocks of pain through my body, but I continued forward and dived into the freezing cold water.

While they had a heated pool, Georgina hadn't put the heater on before she dumped his body into it. I hated that fucking bitch so much. She didn't care about him in the slightest and had decided to come back to Redwood just to kill him?!

Pumping my legs back and forth like Dad had tried to teach me multiple times, I opened my eyes underneath the water and raced to grab Callan's sinking body. After taking hold of him, I swam to the surface and gasped for air, spitting out mouthfuls of water.

With all my strength, I pulled him to the low end of the pool. When I reached the stairs, I flipped him over so I could see his face, wrapped my arms underneath his shoulders, and tugged him out of the water.

Every stair I climbed, he became heavier and heavier, his clothes completely soaked. Once his entire body lay on the concrete, I collapsed by his side and opened his mouth, beginning what I knew of CPR.

I pounded down on his chest in a steady rhythm for a few beats, then pressed my lips over his and pushed air into his body. My hands were shaking, my heart thumping.

He couldn't die on me. He couldn't fucking die on me.

"Callan, please," I sobbed, tears streaming down my cheeks. "Please, stay with me."

I continued for what felt like hours, trying to revive him, sweat dripping down my forehead. I needed to call an ambulance or someone, but I didn't have time to stop. After sucking in a sharp breath, I pushed more air into his lungs.

This time, he spit up some water, but didn't open his eyes.

I rested back on my heels, wiping the beads of sweat off my forehead with the back of my wrist and trying to find some hope that his body had reacted to the CPR. But still, he had lost blood—and a lot of it.

My gaze dropped from his mouth to his abdomen, where blood had completely stained his shirt. *What the hell did she do to him? Stab him?* His shirt was cut in multiple areas around his abdomen, which meant that he had multiple wounds.

Wind whipped around the trees in his backyard, giving us both goose bumps. If I kept him out here, he would get worse. I was already shivering, and his lips were turning blue. Did that mean he was dying? Dead already? He had a faint pulse.

So, I lifted as much of his upper body as I could and dragged him to the back door. More glass slipped into the bottom of my bare feet. I kicked the shards off our path, my blood staining the ground, and tugged him into his bedroom.

Once I closed the door and locked it, I laid Callan onto his bed. I pulled off his shoes and socks, then undid his belt and took off his wet pants too. And when I undid the buttons of his shirt that he had worn to school yesterday, I saw all the stab wounds in his abdomen and thigh.

Tears welled up in my eyes, threatening to spill over. *What the hell did she do to him? How can she be so cruel? What happened to Callan? Did she see me in the cameras last night and decide to kill him? Is this my fault?*

After gulping down the pain—because I didn't have time since Callan was dying—I continued to pull off his clothes. Once I finished, I grabbed a medical kit from the bathroom and did my best to patch up his wounds. Then, I wrapped him in blankets.

And I waited. And I waited. And I waited.

My stomach was in knots. Tears were racing down my cheeks. I couldn't stop bawling.

This isn't fair.

Sitting on the bed next to him, I wondered if I should bring him to the hospital or call someone. I didn't know if I would be able to drag his body all the way to the car. And what the hell would I say when I got there? Should I call Imani to talk to her mother? She was a doctor.

I slammed my hand into my pocket and pulled out my wet phone, my lips pulling into a frown. I pounded on the screen with my fingers, desperate for it to turn on so I could call someone, but the water had completely ruined it.

"No!" I sobbed, lying down next to him and wrapping my arm around his shoulders.

I needed to do something, so I leaped back up and immediately collapsed to the ground as the shards of glass slid deeper into my feet. A yelp of pain escaped my lips, and I found myself sitting on my ass and staring at my bloody feet.

I glanced down to see shards of glass sticking out of them. Wincing, I pinched the glass between my fingers and pulled out a huge chunk. Blood oozed out and onto his bed, but I continued tugging pieces out of my flesh.

There were so many little shards that I didn't even know if I had gotten them all, but I reached for the med kit and pulled out the last few pieces of gauze to wrap my feet. I twirled the material around the wounds over and over.

Tears fell from my eyes, and I leaned against the bed, shaking my head.

I didn't have a usable phone. Callan's phone was dead. I didn't know where the hell his wife's phone was. And nobody had a house phone anymore, especially not in Redwood. But I needed … God, I needed to do something.

"Please," I whispered, feeling so defeated. "Please stay alive, Callan."

79

sakura

AFTER I WRAPPED my feet in gauze and cleaned up the bloody mess in Callan's bedroom, I peered out the back door at Georgina, who lay in a puddle of her own blood near the bar. My throat dried. I hadn't meant to hurt anyone, but she had deserved it.

She ... she had hurt Callan. She'd stabbed him, then tossed him into the pool!

Probably thought that her daddy would take care of him and dispose of his body, but she didn't know that her father was dead. Part of me wished that I would've kept his head, so I could thrust it into her face and laugh at her horror.

I disappeared back into the house, hurried to the garage, and searched for rope or honestly anything I could use to tie her up. I didn't want her escaping or running away if I ended up bringing him to the hospital. She would blab to the mob or maybe her brother and get us both killed.

Once I finally found some rope—that wouldn't be enough to restrain her—I took an empty hose sitting on one of the shelves and a bundle of wire. Hell, I wasn't sure what I would do with this, but I needed to restrain her as soon as possible, especially before she woke up.

When I had all the materials, I dragged a dining room chair into Callan's bedroom and dropped the rope, hose, and wire at the foot of the bed. I walked out onto the back patio, my feet aching from the glass wounds, and stared down at Georgina's body. She was still breathing.

Unfortunately.

Blood seeped from the mallet wound in her head. I gulped at the damage I had done, then at the bloody meat mallet. My stomach twisted into knots. I curled my hands underneath her armpits and dragged her from the bar to the back door, then into their bedroom.

She was much lighter than Callan, so tiny, like Mom, and I wouldn't put it past this bitch to be on hard drugs or even popping pills.

After I lifted her body to sit in the chair, I circled the rope around her ankles and the chair legs. Then, I cut the rope with a kitchen knife, pulled her wrists behind the chair, and tied them together, using the remainder of the rope. I didn't have time to go buy more, and I didn't even know if this would keep her restrained.

Maybe I should ask Poison. They'd know, right?

I shook my head.

I grabbed the hose and bound her torso to the chair as many times as I could until the hose ran out, and then I tied the ends of it. And because I hated her, I took the wire and tied her neck to the chair too. She'd have a fun time, trying to escape this.

Bitch.

Once I finished, I collapsed back onto the bed and took a couple of deep breaths, sweat rolling down my forehead. I lifted my gaze to her and stared at the bloody woman, my heart racing. In pleasure and in fear.

Less than a damn hour ago, I had been searching for Callan. Now, I had rescued him from drowning, knocked his wife out, and tied her to a damn dining room chair in the middle of their room! If anyone found out ... I would be screwed.

Absolutely screwed!

The thought of calling Gunther for advice crossed my mind. His parents had been in the mob and probably shown him how to … restrain a body. Get rid of it. Maybe? He would have some knowledge of something, right?

But not having a phone was killing me.

I could try dragging Callan's body to my car, but I feared I would hurt him even more.

Screw it. I had to do something.

And just as I stood, Georgina's body twitched.

I narrowed my gaze and glared at her. How was she waking up already? I had hit her so hard. She didn't deserve to breathe another breath in this world after what she had done to Callan. I glanced over my shoulder at Callan, who was now bleeding through his gauze.

Tears welled up in my eyes. This wasn't fair.

She deserved to die. Not him.

The knife I'd used to cut the rope glimmered under the dim room light at Georgina's feet. I stared at it for a couple of moments, my brow furrowing in pain. I had never killed anyone ever. I had never thought about taking a life before tonight.

But Georgina … had nearly killed my Callan.

Who knows if he will wake up? My hands balled into fists. *What if he doesn't?*

I shouldn't. I shouldn't. I shouldn't.

I pushed myself off the bed, walked to her body, and grabbed the knife.

I had to.

80

callan

SAKURA SAT at the foot of my bed with a knife in her shaky hand. I blinked my eyes open a couple of times, adjusting to the light as pain shot through my body. I thought I was seeing things in a dream—or a nightmare.

What is she doing with a kitchen knife?

I squeezed my eyes closed, then reopened them.

She still sat there, gripping the knife even harder until her knuckles were white. "I have to do it. I have to do it. I have to do it," she muttered to herself.

I gazed past her to see Georgina bound to a chair across from us, her wrists, ankles, neck, and waist tied tightly to the chair with thick rope, hose, and wire. She bled from a huge gash in her head and was covered with glass.

What the fuck is happening?

Maybe I had lost too much blood and was hallucinating. The last thing I remembered was seeing stars and falling into the pool. And my torso hurt like a motherfucker from those damn stab wounds.

Sakura stood up and stepped toward Georgina.

"Get away from me!" Georgina screamed. "You're psychotic."

My head pounded in agony. If this were a dream, she'd be fucking mute. I used all my strength to push myself to a seated position, wincing. Sakura took another step toward my wife, the knife trembling in her small hand.

"Why do you have a knife?" I whispered, voice hoarse.

Sakura jumped up and snapped her gaze to me, eyes growing wide. "Callan ... y-you're alive!" She dropped the knife and ran over to my bedside, throwing her arms around my shoulders and pulling me closer. "You're alive!" she cried.

I stiffened as pain flooded through me.

Sakura immediately pulled away from me. "Sorry!"

"Of course I'm alive," I murmured, the pain slowly fading. I glanced down at the bandages covering my stab wounds to keep them closed. "Did you think you'd get rid of me that easily?" I chuckled, trying to lighten the mood.

"It's not funny. You almost died," she said, standing at my side and capturing my hand.

"I already told you, Sakura, I'm not going anywhere," I whispered. "You're mine."

Tears welled in Sakura's eyes, threatening to spill over. When she blinked, a stray tear rolled down her cheek.

"Callan!" Georgina screamed. "Are you serious? Get me out of here!"

I wiped it away with my thumb. "Don't cry for me."

"I-I love you," Sakura sobbed, sniffling. "I thought you were dead. It's so selfish, b-but it hurt so m-much." She sat at the edge of the bed and gently brushed her fingers against my palm, shaking her head. "I can't lose you."

"Callan!" Georgina shouted, like the bitch she was.

Sakura set her hand on my stomach and stood up yet again, glancing at the knife that had clattered onto the ground near Georgina. She walked over to it, her shoulders trembling back and forth while she continued to sob.

"She pushed you," Sakura cried, grabbing the knife from the floor.

"She didn't push me," I said softly, not defending Georgina, but not wanting Sakura to feel like she had to hurt anyone for me. It already looked like she had hit Georgina with something and then tied her up to one of my dining chairs. "I fell into the pool."

"She deserves to die," she whispered, pain in every word. "She deserves to die."

"She does"—I pushed myself up the bed even more—"but you don't have to do it."

"I need to," she said, back turned. "I need to do it for you."

"Come here."

Sakura stood in front of Georgina, not moving toward me or toward her. I couldn't see her face, but by the mere way she stood, she didn't want to hurt anyone else. She couldn't kill Georgina without feeling guilty for it.

Sakura Sato was a good girl. *My* good girl.

I didn't want her to think she had to kill anyone for me.

"Come here," I whispered again. "Please, Sakura."

Sakura glanced over her shoulder at me, her brows drawn together and her lips quivering. Yet she walked over to me with the knife.

I placed my hand over hers. "No, you don't."

"Yes, I do," she sobbed. "I love you, and she … she's hurt you."

"You're not a killer," I whispered, pulling the weapon from her hand.

"Sometimes, you have to be to prove that you love someone."

"I believe that you love me," I said.

She stared at me with tearful eyes. *I have to,* she mouthed.

"If you want to prove something to someone"—I wrapped my hand into her hair and pulled her closer to me—"come here."

And then I kissed the woman I loved in front of my wife.

81

sakura

AFTER CALLAN PLACED his lips onto mine, I gently brushed my fingers up the column of his neck, then across the stubble on his jaw. I didn't want to hurt him more than he already was. Those stab wounds were terrible.

"I want you on top of me," Callan murmured into my mouth, capturing my hips and using all his strength to pull me onto his lap.

I hovered over him, not wanting to put pressure on any sensitive areas. He traveled his hands up my bare thighs, then underneath my skirt and tugged my hips down as close to him as they would go, letting me feel every inch.

Stiffening, I deepened the kiss. We were in front of his wife. His wife! Was he really going to fuck me instead of letting me kill her? Part of me was … glad. I didn't think that I would be able to go through with it. I hated the thought of murdering anyone after witnessing what Callan had done to Gunther.

And then Jett's head.

"Get off my husband!" Georgina screamed.

"Pull your panties to the side," Callan murmured against my lips.

"Are you sure?" I whispered. "I don't want to hurt you."

"Pull them to the side," he repeated, his voice sterner.

Once I posted one hand on the headboard next to his head to steady myself, I arched my back slightly and pulled my thong to the side. Callan readjusted himself underneath me, lining the head of his cock up with my entrance.

"Now, sit on my cock and ride your professor."

Heat rushed through my body, but I lowered myself. The head of his cock pushed my pussy lips apart, disappearing inside me inch by inch. And when he was inside me, I sat down all the way and moaned out in pleasure.

It had been too long since he'd been inside me. My pussy had been craving him every night, waiting to swallow him and every last drop of his cum.

Callan rested his hands on my hips and grunted, "Fuck, Sakura."

I laid my hands on Callan's chest, careful not to touch the bandages in his side, and moved my hips slower against his, my pussy tightening every time I slammed my hips back onto his. Waves of pleasure rushed through me, the feel of his huge cock stretching me out in front of his wife, making me shiver in delight.

"Get off him, or I'll … I'll—"

"Or what, Georgina?" Callan hummed, curling his fingers into my thighs and staring past me at his wife. He slid his hands underneath my skirt once more and groped my ass. "What are you going to do? Call your father?"

"He will torture you for this!" she shouted.

Callan drifted his gaze back to me and helped me buck my hips faster against his, eyes rolling back in pleasure. "I killed your father last night," he said, grunting as he lifted his hips to meet mine. "And I loved every second of it."

"You what?!" she screamed.

I smiled softly at Callan, gently gripping his face in my hand. "He did it for me."

Callan smirked, stared up at me, and tucked some hair behind my ear. "All for you."

"Callan!" she screamed. "I swear to God, I will kill you myself!"

"Faster, baby," Callan said. "You're taking it so well."

Heat coursed through my body. I whimpered and bounced my hips faster and faster, the pressure growing inside my core. My legs began trembling slightly, but I continued to ride my Literature professor, getting myself to the edge.

"Come inside my pussy," I whispered.

"That's the only place my cum belongs." He pulled me closer to him so his lips brushed against my ear. "I should rip that IUD right out of you," he murmured against my lips.

My pussy tightened even more around him.

"Get you pregnant with my child in front of my wife."

I moaned. *Holy f-f-fuck.*

"Would you like that?" he murmured.

"Y-yes!" I cried out, pleasure exploding through my body as I came all over him.

"Get off my husband!" Georgina shouted again.

Callan grunted and slammed my hips down onto his, filling up my pussy with his warm cum. "One day, sweetheart," he mumbled into my ear. "One fucking day. Soon."

Soon? More warmth shot through my body, sending me over the edge again.

"You little bitch!" she screamed. "He's my husband!"

After lifting my hips off him, I knelt on the bed next to him with my juices covering his throbbing cock and wrapped my lips around it. Once I licked it clean, I collapsed onto the bed and curled up next to Callan, my hand slipping around his bicep. "He's mine now."

82

sakura

ONCE GEORGINA BEGAN SCREAMING at me, Callan gently took my chin in his hand and brought me back up to him. He kissed me right on the mouth after I sucked him off, and it sent heat coursing through my body.

When he pulled away, I cuddled up next to him. I had so many questions that I wanted answered—most of them about his gift of Jett's head—but I didn't want to bother him right now. Especially now that he was recovering from being stabbed multiple times and nearly drowning.

"Callan!" Georgina screamed. "Look at me! Get me out of here!"

Callan tucked some hair behind my ear, his lips curled into a small smile, then grasped my thigh. "There is tape in the garage—second cabinet, third drawer down. Can you get it for me, please?" he murmured against my lips.

Glancing from him to Georgina, I nodded and walked out of the room. As soon as I shut the door behind me, I sprinted to the garage. I didn't know what Callan was planning on doing to her, but I hoped that he would kick her out of our lives for good. I didn't want her bothering us anymore.

And if she lived ... we would never hear the end of all the *pain* we had caused her. Because she'd definitely flip it around and play victim. She had been abusing him for years. But this was the end of it. The complete and utter end of her wrath.

I would do anything I had to do to protect him.

Once I returned with the tape, Callan had pushed himself to a standing position and had tugged on some sweatpants. He took the roll of duct tape from me and stumbled over to Georgina, nearly falling over multiple times throughout his five-step trip.

He tore off a piece and smacked it across her mouth so her screams were muffled. Then, he handed it back to me and took my hand. I began leading him back to his bed, but he urged me toward the doorway.

"Callan," I whispered, "you really should be getting rest."

"I'm hungry," he said. "I haven't eaten in the past twenty-four hours."

After opening the bedroom door for him, I followed him out of the room and gently shut the door behind us because I didn't even want to hear a single *peep* from Georgina. She had ruined his life and nearly killed him.

Even if she hadn't pushed him, she hadn't attempted to save him.

"Sit," I said. "I'll make you something."

"*Us* something."

My lips curled into a smile as I opened his fridge, searching for food. But it seemed like Georgina had completely cleaned him out, or he hadn't been to the grocery store in a long, long time. So, I found some veggies and broth in the pantry for soup.

Callan sat back on an island stool while I cooked, watching me quietly with a small smile on his face. And when I finished and placed a bowl of soup in front of him, he took the spoon, scooped some veggies onto it, and placed it at my mouth.

I wrapped my lips around the utensil and swallowed the food.

"Thank you for making this for me," he said, leaning across the table and pushing hair off my forehead again. "Go grab some for yourself."

"I want to make sure you have enough," I said. "There's not much food in your fridge."

"Do you want to go shopping with me?"

Shopping with Callan in Redwood? Not only would everyone see us, but he also wasn't healthy enough to be walking around a grocery store for thirty-plus minutes. He should be lying down for the rest of the night.

"Maybe some other time, Callan," I said, grabbing an empty bowl anyway and filling it with soup. "I'll run to the store after you get back to bed and buy you some food for the week. You are in no shape to go out."

Instead of putting up a fight, like I'd expected, he scooped more soup in his spoon and ate.

"So, um," I started, pushing my spoon around my soup, "I got your gift."

He glanced up at me, his lips set in a small smile. "Did you like it?"

I chewed on the inside of my cheek and stared at him for a few moments. Gunther had told me that Callan wouldn't do something like that, but after the last forty-eight hours we'd both had, I wouldn't be surprised about anything in Redwood anymore.

And I wouldn't blame him.

"Did you really give me Jett's head?" I asked.

His spoon clattered against the glass bowl, the hot soup splashing everywhere. "Jett's head?" he repeated, staring at me in horror through wide eyes. He shook his head, dark bags underneath his eyes. "That's what you found in the box?"

"Yes," I whispered. "Gunther tossed it into the ocean. I-I didn't know what to do."

"I didn't give you anyone's damn head." He paused and dropped his gaze to the table, brow furrowing. "Who was in your room? Who has access to your house? Because I didn't give you a fucking head, Sakura, especially if I wasn't there with you to open it. I know how upset you would've been."

"I-it's fine, Callan. I just wanted to let you know."

"It's not fine," he said, jaw clenched. Then blew out a low breath. "I'll handle it."

Though I didn't think he was suited to do *anything* but rest right now. Maybe even for the next week or more. He should take all the vacation days he needed from Redwood Academy because he couldn't go back to school like this either.

"I think you should rest," I whispered.

"Did you get anything else with the head? A note? Card?"

"There was a note."

"Where is it?"

"I'll go get it," I said, standing. "It's in my car."

After retrieving it from the car, I slid it across the island to him. What was so wrong about this whole thing was that the hand-writing looked nearly identical to Callan's from what I remembered in class. Whoever had planted the head had been watching us.

Sakura,
Only for you.
Love,

83

CALLAN READ THE NOTE ALOUD, then crumpled it in his hand. "I'll kill whoever did this to you."

84

sakura

ON WEDNESDAY, Callan returned to school. I had really wished that he'd stayed home this entire week, but he'd said he had work to do. And secretly, I believed that *work* was to do me any possible chance he could find because he cornered me in his classroom during lunch.

"I'm ready for lunch," he said, placing me on his desk and moving between my legs.

When he ripped my thong off me, I giggled. "Someone's feeling better."

He slid his hands up my bare thighs, lifting them off the desk and holding them apart. He moved his chair closer to the desk and rested one of my thighs on his shoulder, his stubble tickling my inner thigh.

I wasn't sure if he had found the person who had sent me that head yet, but he'd asked me to let him handle it, so I was going to. No more fighting him to do something a certain way or not to do it at all because I'd learned the hard way that he did what he wanted.

"I've been thinking about this since Sunday," he grunted, then dipped his head and placed his hot mouth right onto my salivating cunt. He trailed his fingers down my legs to my pussy lips and gently pulled my folds apart to give himself better access.

He flicked his tongue against the sensitive skin and sent a wave of ecstacy throughout my entire body. Another grunt escaped his mouth, and I clenched. He started off slowly, licking and sucking on the sensitive bud.

But then his hunger seized control of him.

Burying his face deeper between my legs, he savagely sucked and licked and tormented my aching clit. My juices decorated his stubble as he closed his eyes to enjoy me. I wrapped my arm under the leg not resting on his shoulder and pulled myself apart for him.

"C-Callan," I moaned and thrust a hand into his hair and pulled his face closer to my pussy as he lapped at my juices, like it was his first taste. "P-please don't stop. It feels too gooood."

He pushed two thick fingers into my pussy and stretched out my hole, pumping them in and out of me while he flicked his tongue across my clit. I whimpered, my legs beginning to tremble uncontrollably.

"I want that IUD out of you now," he growled.

"R-right in the middle of the classroom?!" I exclaimed.

Maybe it was his dirty mouth getting to me, but I wanted him to do it so badly. I wanted—*needed*—him to fill me to the brim with his cum. Force me to get pregnant. To carry his child. To ruin my sweet and innocent facade.

He stood up and pulled down his pants, taking his hard cock in his hand.

"It's lunchtime, Sakura, and your pussy is hungry to swallow my cum."

Fuck. I tightened around him, breath hitched. "Pull it out of me then."

"No," he said, rubbing the head of his cock against my clit. "You do it."

"Me?" I squealed.

"Take those strings and pull," he ordered.

My eyes widened, heart pounding inside my chest. I couldn't …

I couldn't believe that this was happening right here and right now. We were in the middle of lunch period. Anyone could come in at any moment.

"Pull it out or not," he said, drawing a hand over my stomach, "I'm going to fill this belly with my cum one day."

"F-fill it up?" I whispered, pussy tightening around him.

"Make it round."

A moan escaped my lips, and I tightened even more around him. "P-please."

"Let me see how much of a desperate Redwood slut you are then," he ordered.

I plunged my fingers inside myself, snatched the IUD strings between my fingers, and watched him stroke his cock. Pleasure completely grabbed hold of me, and I pulled the strings until a slight pain spread throughout my lower back and the IUD slid out of me.

"Oh fuck," Callan grunted, immediately thrusting into me like a wild animal.

I didn't even have any time to react before he grabbed my body and slammed into me repeatedly. I threw my head back, the pain quickly subsiding and delight rushing through my body at the mere thought of Callan loving it so much that he couldn't control himself at all.

"Beg me to get you pregnant."

"Please, Mr. Avery," I whimpered. "C-come inside me."

He wrapped his hand around my throat. "I said, beg me to get you pregnant."

Heat coursed through my body. "Get me pregnant. God, please, get me pregnant!"

He grunted savagely. "Everyone's going to wonder who gave the quiet, shy valedictorian a baby. What're you going to say when people ask whose child you're carrying?" He reached down between my thighs and began rubbing my clit, pushing me closer to the edge. "Are you going to tell them that it's your teacher's? That you were such a pretty little slut for him that he gave you detention just so he could fill you?"

"C-Callan!" I cried, the pressure growing between my thighs.

"God, it's going to be so *fucking* satisfying, watching you walk around Redwood with my baby in your belly for the next nine months," he growled, slamming deeper into me. "You're going to have my child before you fucking graduate."

"God," I moaned, "it's so wrong."

"So fucking *dirty*, baby. You're so fucking dirty for me."

He continued to pump wildly into me, thrusting to my cervix every single time, his huge cock filling up every inch of my tight little hole. I grasped tightly around the edge of his desk, eyes rolling back into my head.

"Barely even a few weeks ago, you hadn't even sucked a cock before," he murmured into my ear, his stubble brushing against the soft skin of my neck. "And now, look at you. A pro at swallowing cum and getting stuffed full with it. Are you ready to come for me?"

When I nodded, he pinched both my nipples between his fingers and tugged harshly on them, pushing me hard over the edge. I cried out, pleasure crashing through my body.

He slammed his cock into me. "Get"—he thrust deeper—"you" —deeper—"fucking"—deeper—"pregnant." Even deeper.

He grunted and stilled, stacking me on his desk and letting his cum slide to my cervix. "Just like I promised."

85

callan

"KNOCK, KNOCK."

Gunther whipped open the door and leaned against the doorframe, head tilted and backpack thrown over his shoulder moments after I pulled out of Sakura. I stuffed myself into my pants and pulled down Sakura's skirt, wiping a bead of cum that had dripped out of her pussy and shoving that finger into her mouth.

She sucked hungrily on it, then looked over her shoulder at Gunther. He walked into the room, scrunched his nose at Sakura, and tossed his bag onto an empty desk.

"Look," he started, "I don't really want to be here, so what'd you want?"

Sakura glanced between us. "You asked him to meet you?"

"Yes," I said.

I had told one of his buddies to relay the information to him this morning when I got into Redwood. I hadn't had the time or energy to find his ass earlier. I was honestly surprised he had shown up. Sakura had said he hadn't been here all week either.

"Can you give us a moment?" I asked Sakura, my hands on her thighs.

Arching her brow, she suspiciously gazed between us.

"I'm not going to hurt him," I said.

"I'm not worried about you," she said, moving her gaze to Gunther. "Don't hurt him."

"He nearly tried to kill me, Sakura," Gunther said, clenching his jaw.

"He's not going to hurt me," I said.

"That's what you think," Gunther said under his breath.

After a couple of moments, Sakura hopped off my desk and grabbed her backpack from her seat. She twirled around, her skirt flowing through the air and her lips curled into a small smile. "I'll see you after school." She walked back over and pecked me on the lips. "Be good."

A small chuckle escaped my lips as she skipped out of the room, leaving us alone.

"You two are gross," Gunther said, nose scrunched. "I don't approve of it."

"Our relationship is none of your business," I said. "We don't need your approval."

He stared at me in disgust for a few moments, then slid up on a desk. "What'd you want?"

"I apologize," I said to Gunther, swallowing my pride and wanting to at least be civil for Sakura. "For what I did to you."

A smug smirk stretched across his face. "Gonna have to be more specific."

"For shooting you," I said through gritted teeth.

While I'd had every right to protect my girl, I wanted to get this over with already. I would never get along with the guy, especially after what I had heard him say about Sakura a few weeks ago—that he wanted to fuck her—but still, I didn't want Sakura to hold this over my head.

"And?"

"And what?" I asked.

"Why the fuck did you pay for my hospital bills?" he growled.

"Should've let me rot in that parking lot, Avery. I fucking hate it here."

"I wanted to let you die," I said honestly. "You pulled a gun out in front of Sakura."

We stared at each other for a few moments without saying a word, and then he jumped off the desk and grabbed his backpack.

"Great talk," he said. "Thanks for wasting my time. I'm skipping for the rest of the semester, and I expect at least a B-minus after what you did to me."

"Wait," I called.

"What'd you want this time?" he asked, pulling out his phone.

"Do you want to stay with me?" I asked before I could decide against it.

As far as I knew, the house his parents owned had been fore-closed a couple of months ago. I didn't know where the kid was staying, but it definitely wasn't with family around Redwood. Maybe he slept on the streets of the slums.

"The fuck did you just say?"

I clenched my jaw and stared at him. "Do you want to stay with me?"

"So you can act like my daddy? Make up for your wrongdoings? Relieve yourself of your guilt?" He laughed lifelessly and turned away from me. "Fuck no." He lit a cigarette. "I've already had enough of that in my life. I don't need more of it, especially from you."

"Where are you staying?"

"I'll find a place," he said, shrugging and turning away. "Besides, Sakura's family is letting me stay with them for a while."

What?! Why hasn't she told me about that?

I balled my hands into fists at my sides and took a deep breath. *Stay calm, Callan.*

"They're not going to let you stay there forever," I said.

"And you will?"

"You don't have to stay with me, but there is an empty house that belonged to Jett Harleen that won't be in use until his son realizes that his father isn't alive anymore," he said. "Which won't be for another six months or so. That bastard is too into himself to give a fuck about anyone, even his own father."

He paused. "What's the address?"

I scribbled it onto a sheet of paper, ripped it out of my notebook, and handed it to him. "I'm only doing this so you stay out of trouble and away from my girl."

"Stay away from your girl?" He laughed. "I protected her while your ass was rightfully getting stabbed by the mob."

"Protected her?" I asked, brow arching. "From who?"

Gunther walked to the door. "Vaughn."

Before he could slip into the hallway, I snatched his shoulder and slammed the door closed with my palm. "What the fuck do you mean, Vaughn?" I asked in a hushed whisper.

I had gotten rid of all those damn bugs placed in my classroom this morning—because I didn't give a shit anymore—but I still wanted to be discreet.

"After Sakura found Jett's head, she went to the Overlook to dispose of it," Gunther said. "And could you guess who showed up and tried to come on to her? I heard that, the other day, he brought her into his office and touched her too."

"You're lying," I growled through gritted teeth.

Gunther walked out of the room without saying another word. Though it was only lunchtime, I had business to take care of now. Vaughn hadn't been in school today, which meant he was either hiding out or with Poison.

If he'd touched a hair on Sakura's fucking head …

As I stepped onto the first floor, I caught Landon walking out of Redwood Academy with a lit cigarette between his lips and his hands stuffed in his jeans pockets. I stormed up to him, fury rushing through me in hot waves, and grabbed him by the shoulder.

"Where the fuck is Vaughn?" I asked him.

"The fuck, dude?" he said, shaking me off him. "You're lucky I didn't pop you in the mouth."

"Where *the fuck* is Vaughn?" I repeated.

"We have him," Landon said. "Don't worry about it."

"Is he dead yet?"

"Not yet."

"Good," I growled. "Take me to him."

"Why?"

I grabbed him by the collar. "I don't have time for the fucking questions. Bring me to him now."

After shoving me away again, Landon tossed his cigarette onto the asphalt and smashed it out with the heel of his shoe. "You got a car?" he asked.

Screw Poison taking care of Vaughn. I'd kill that motherfucker myself.

———

"Where is he?" I roared, storming out of my car and into a small, run-down house fifteen minutes later.

"Down here, Landon!" Kai shouted from the cellar.

I took two stairs at a time and thrust the bottom door open, sending João flying against the wall. He growled and took me by the back of the collar, but I shook him off me and barreled through the rooms to find Kai sitting with a tied-up Vaughn.

Before he could say two words, I slammed my fist into his face. "You touched Sakura?!"

Kai almost jumped into the scrap, but João pushed him back. "Let Avery have him."

With his arms tied behind his back, Vaughn grinned up at me through bloody teeth. "If you'd let me add her to the ring, we would have both been able to enjoy her." *Punch.* "You're lucky," Vaughn said, splattering blood everywhere. "I bet her pussy felt—"

"You fucker." Seizing him by his hair, I slammed his head onto the concrete floor.

After knocking his head into the concrete a couple more times, João finally grabbed my shoulder and yanked me back as Landon took one of my arms to hold me in place. Because if they hadn't, I swore I would've smashed Vaughn's head in until his brain splattered in pieces.

"Let me kill him," I growled.

My hands ached to wrap around his throat, to kill him for good. I'd bet that fucker had been the one to replace my gift with Jett's head and put it into Sakura's room. He had known that I had mob business to take care of, and he had known that Sakura would be freaking out.

He knew he would be able to get her alone.

"No," João said. "We have plans for him first."

Vaughn laughed menacingly at me. "I've seen every Redwood football player change, watched horny high school kids fuck in the locker rooms, slept with the head cheerleaders throughout the years, but nothing could ever compare to wanting Sakura. She's the definition of good girl—perfect grades, tight little body, and those schoolgirl outfits that she wears …"

I pushed back against João, Landon, *and* Kai now. "I'm going to fucking kill you!"

"Cool it," João said. "We're heading to the warehouse to finish him off."

"I'm going to finish him off," I snarled, ripping myself away from Landon.

"Calm your shit," João growled again, shoving me back. "You can come with us, but we get to fuck with him a bit before anyone kills him. Let us do this, and it'll keep the mob out of your business for a couple of weeks."

So, I reluctantly calmed myself and let them do their thing because I had to if it would keep the mob out of my hair. Yui hadn't been too happy that I'd lied about Jett, and this … this would be a perfect distraction. Especially if Poison killed the mob themselves.

"Make it good," I growled at João. "Torture the shit out of this fucker."

86

sakura

"CALLAN," I said, tugging on his jacket, "I don't know if this is a good idea."

We walked into the stadium for Redwood's Friday night football game five minutes before halftime. Students from school screamed and cheered at the players on the field, some females flashing their tits to the other team.

I sank down into my jacket and hoped nobody saw us together. I didn't know why he wanted to come to a Redwood football game tonight. Hell, I had never even been to a Redwood sports game, never mind football.

Wasn't this a bit obvious that I was out with my teacher? Granted, we had been flirting a lot more during class since Wednesday. But that didn't mean we had to go public. Maybe I should've mentioned that before agreeing to come with him tonight.

"Relax," he said. "Nobody will see us. And if they see us, they're not going to remember."

"What do you mean, they won't remember?" I asked, following him up the bleachers to an empty spot near the parents' section. "We stand out like sore thumbs together and will be the talk of

Redwood by tonight, Callan. You know how quickly people spread drama."

"Don't worry about it," he said again, so … calm.

Scratch that. *Suspiciously calm* was more like it.

He had been this way since Thursday morning, and I … wasn't sure what was happening. One moment, he had been fucking me on top of his desk and telling me that he would put a baby inside me, and then the next time I had seen him, he was like this.

So collected.

Gunther had told me that he mentioned he was living at my house for a little while, and I'd expected Callan to go insane, but Callan hadn't said a word to me about it yet.

"Go Redwood!" Allie Hall screamed from the student section.

My cheeks reddened, and I stared at the field. Maybe if I ignored everyone else, they would all poof away. Maybe they wouldn't notice me. I was a loner and wanted to desperately keep it that way at least until the end of the year.

Jace Harbor walked up and down the sidelines, chatting with his teammates.

After another play, the entire student section jumped up and cheered. "Touchdown!"

Heart leaping from the sudden screaming around me, I rested a hand on my chest and glanced over at Callan, who watched me. I wanted to ask him to leave, but we had just gotten here, and I had a feeling that he would say no. He wanted me to watch for some ungodly reason.

"Let's go, Redwood!" Nicole, the head cheerleader, shouted. "Woohoo!"

Someone from the opposite team grabbed the ball and ran about halfway across the field before a Redwood player slammed into him. Their helmets crashed together, the sound of hard plastic on hard plastic making me wince. *How do people like watching this?!*

A buzzer rang throughout the stadium, the bright white lights on the scoreboard reading 14 to 6. The teams retreated to their sides of the field, packing up to head to the locker room for halftime, when the lights in the stadium turned off.

Callan placed his hand on my thigh and leaned closer to me. "I found out that Principal Vaughn was the man responsible for switching out the present I'd bought you for Jett Harleen's head."

I peered over at him through wide eyes. "Really? How do you know?"

I was glad that he had found out who had done it, but why was he telling me this now? Here?

"Poison," he said, and nothing else. And honestly, I wasn't sure if I *wanted* to know.

My phone buzzed in my pocket—along with everyone else's—but Callan stopped me from retrieving it and captured my hands in his in front of everyone in the stadium.

"I made sure that he will never hurt you again."

"How did you do that?" I whispered, but was cut off by a loud voice over the intercom.

"Redwood Academy, your principal has been jerking off to hundreds of recordings of Redwood students, naked in the locker rooms," someone said, voice changed.

I furrowed my brow and glanced at the dark field.

"Is this who you think is fit to lead your school? Is this who we're giving thousands of dollars to every year? Is this someone you think deserves to live?"

I leaned closer to Callan and intertwined my fingers with his. "Wh-what is going on?"

"Whatever happens—whatever *happened*," Callan started, "I did it because I love you."

"What are you—"

"That's not the only punishment that the Redwood rich will receive for their sins," the man said over the speakers. "Over the course of the next few months, all the lies, all the secrets, all the scandals that have run this town will be exposed. Nobody is safe from the truth."

Callan pulled me onto his lap and rested his head on my

shoulder as the lights brightened the field. Someone hurled a ball onto the grass. It bounced once, then twice, and then people began screaming.

Principal Vaughn's head sat at the forty-yard line, his blood staining the white field lines.

People raced down the bleachers, nearly tripping over each other. Students hopped the fences and ran away from the field and right out onto the street. But I sat in Callan's arms and stared at Vaughn's pitiful head.

"Welcome to the end, Redwood," the man said over the intercom.

And while parents, students, and players spazzed out around us, I smiled and prayed to the Redwood gods that this would be the end. The end of the billionaires ruling our lives. The end of those in power using us. The end of Redwood Academy as we knew it.

87

LONG AFTER EVERYONE cleared out of the stadium, Callan and I still sat on the bleachers. The police had taped off the field so nobody could enter it and then removed our principal's head from the grass.

"Was it Poison on the intercom?" I asked.

"Yep."

I turned in his embrace and straddled his waist with my arms around his shoulders. "Did you know that they had decapitated him?" I whispered. "Is that why you brought me here to watch tonight? To show me that he got his payback?"

"Did I know?" He chuckled, large hands gripping my waist. "I did it."

My eyes widened. "You what?"

He peered over at me, his dark eyes glimmering underneath the bright lights. "I chopped off that motherfucker's head," he said with no ounce of remorse, no pity, and absolutely no guilt about any of it.

Callan had promised me that he was done with the needless criminal activity, especially associated with the mob, which meant that he would only do something like this if … he was doing it for me.

"Gunther told me that Vaughn asked you to come into his office during school one day last week. That he touched you." Callan tightened his grip on me even though I wasn't going anywhere. "That he followed you to the Overlook."

My mouth dried, and I didn't say anything.

So much shit had been going on lately that I'd completely pushed Vaughn to the back of my mind. Everything he had done to me felt like it had happened a century ago even though it was just last week.

"Is that true?" Callan asked.

"Yes, it is," I whispered, then gazed down at my thighs. "I'm sorry I didn't tell you sooner."

And while I would've flipped out on him if this had happened a month ago, I felt relieved that Vaughn was gone for good tonight. I hugged Callan tightly and buried my face into the crook of his neck, breathing in his cologne.

"I love you," I mumbled into his hair.

He wrapped his arms around my waist and hummed softly, "I love you too, Sakura."

After a few moments, I pulled away. "What's going to happen with your connections to the mob?"

"After the show Poison put on tonight," Callan said, "they'll have their hands tied." He dropped his hands to my thighs, picked me up, and stood. "Let's grab milkshakes. I have something for you."

When he set me down, I snatched his hand and followed him down the bleachers and back to his car. "Something for me?" I asked, butterflies fluttering inside my stomach. Maybe he had found his original present in Vaughn's possession.

Once we drove and ordered milkshakes from Redwood Milkshake Co. down by the beach, I leaned against the front of his car and stared out into the ocean. The view wasn't as beautiful as the

Overlook, but the water seemed to stretch to the ends of the earth, the waves endless.

He had set two gift bags on the hood of the car, but hadn't said anything about them yet.

So, after finishing, I placed the cup on the car and faced him. I wasn't sure how to say this to him, but I needed to come out with it already. It had been on my mind since Sunday night, when I claimed Callan as mine in front of his wife.

"Can we … stay a secret?" I whispered, intertwining my fingers with his and standing on my tiptoes. My lips were inches from his, his eyes glimmering underneath the moonlight. "At least from my father until I graduate."

With his hands on my hips, he brushed his thumbs across my belly and let out a low, defeated sigh. Since Wednesday, he had been more and more open around school with showing me a little … *favoritism.*

Like asking me to stay behind after class. Brushing his fingers across mine.

Other students would catch on soon, but with all the other shit going on in Redwood now, I doubted they would care until something major happened. Like the valedictorian showing up at graduation with a round pregnant belly.

Still, I didn't want Dad pressuring me throughout the year.

"I'll keep our dirty little secret until … we can't anymore."

I arched a brow, wondering what the heck he meant about that, and watched his gaze fall to my stomach.

"That's not going to happen," I teased.

Though … I wasn't too sure. We might've had sex without protection a couple more times since Wednesday. And every now and then, in passing conversation, he kept mentioning how he wanted me pregnant.

At first, I'd thought it was a sex kink, but it seemed like a bit more than that.

"Here," he said with a smirk painted on his lips. He handed me the larger gift bag. "This was my original gift for you. I found it in Vaughn's desk. It wasn't anything special." He glanced down, almost blushing. "But I thought you would enjoy it."

Once I reached into the bag, I felt around and found books. I whipped them out and grinned. It was the entire collection of Kayleigh Stone's spicy romance books! Heart racing, I flipped through one of them and snapped the book open to the title page.

They were all … signed.

"Callan," I whispered, unable to hold back a grin. I gazed up at him and wrapped my arms around his shoulders, excitement rushing through my veins. "Callan, you didn't have to do this. It's too much."

"You deserve it," he murmured into my ear. And when he finally let me go, he handed me the second bag. "And this is … something I found just lying around back home."

I reached into the bag and pulled out a small rectangular box. I opened it up.

A single severed finger with a wedding ring.

"You killed Georgina," I whispered breathlessly, eyes wide.

"She fell into the pool," he said, staring out at the Atlantic Ocean, finally at peace.

While I wasn't a fan of decapitation, severed fingers, or any sort of death, I wasn't complaining that she was out of our lives for good. From now on, it would just be us, together and happy.

"By the way, I almost forgot to give this to you," he said, pulling out a pink slip of paper from his pocket and handing it to me.

I unfolded it to see *DETENTION* written in large red capital letters across the top along with a list of reasons, including my not telling him about Vaughn or about Gunther staying with me and— my favorite—*because I can*. A giggle escaped my lips, and I playfully pushed him.

"You have detention after school on Monday," Callan hummed, wrapping his hand around my neck from behind and gently craning my head back so I stared up at him. He placed his mouth on mine. "Don't be late, Miss Sato, or I'll be forced to punish you."

Continue reading the Bad Boys of Redwood Academy with My Brother's Best Friend.

also by emilia rose

also by emilia rose

Scan the QR code with your phone to view all of Emilia's books!

about the author

Emilia Rose is a *USA Today* best-selling author of steamy romance. Highly inspired by her study abroad trip to Greece in 2019, Emilia loves to include Greek and Roman mythology in her writing.
She graduated from the University of Pittsburgh with a degree in psychology and a minor in creative writing in 2020 and now writes novels as her day job.
With over 18 million combined book views online and a growing presence on reading apps, she hopes to inspire other young novelists with her tales of growth and imagination, so they go on to write the stories that need to be told.
Join Emilia's newsletter for exclusive giveaways, early chapter releases, and more!